The Rainbow Talisman

By

George Acquah-Hayford

and

John Kitchen

ISBN: 978-1-291-68805-4

PublishNation. London
www.publishnation.co.uk

Prologue

Everett Tierfelder tapped his fingers impatiently on the steering wheel. It was another Washington snarl-up. Cars steamed in the late summer heat, inching lane by lane, getting nowhere.

Normally it didn't bother him, but today, getting to the airport was important.

He leaned forward and keyed a number into his phone.

"Carole," he said. "Could you look up for me? Is Jesse's plane on time?"

There was a pause, then "Sure, Mr Tierfelder. It's due fifteen minutes early."

He cursed under his breath. This was a good time to have gridlock on the freeway. "Just call through, will you? Tell them I'm in traffic. Get them to put the boy in the lounge or something, and make sure they keep him away from the press. Then call my wife. Tell her Jesse's plane's okay – going to be early – that'll set her mind at rest. Tell her he'll be back soon."

He fumed quietly. What would the press make of it? His kid missing for the best part of six months, and now, when he turned up, his father wasn't going to be there to meet him.

He gave a wry grin. Least ways he knew what Jesse would make of it. Although Jesse was only twelve, he knew his father – better almost than Everett knew himself. He had a man's head on a boy's shoulders, that kid. He'd figure his dad would be late. His dad was always late. Too much stuff on his plate. Jesse understood that.

*

The plane landed, easing itself towards the docking port. And, back on American soil after all this time, Jesse gathered his stuff. He made for the exit and headed towards immigration. There'd be a reception committee. He'd have to tread smartly to bypass that lot.

A porter was managing his luggage.

1

Jesse had been singled out and was being fast tracked, and there was a courier, a smart woman, trim, with dark, neat cut hair. "Your dad's stuck in traffic," she said. "When you've been through customs he wants you to go to the VIP lounge. He's anxious the press don't get hold of you till he's here."

"That's okay," Jesse said. "Only don't you think that's where the press will figure I'll be? Anyway, I'm hoping there's a mate meeting me. He won't be in VIP, and I've got to see him first, if he's here. Can we go to 'Arrivals' just to check?"

The courier nodded. "If that's how you want it, – only you've got to be in VIP when your dad gets here. It'll be more than my job's worth if he turns up and you're hanging around in the public area."

They passed quickly through customs. Then, milling with the crowds, he worked his way down the moving walkways, through to the foyer and the rows of anxious faces. And there, shoving beneath the arms holding notices announcing, 'Mr Spellman', 'Dorothy O'Hara', 'Miss Madeleine Barnes' he saw the brown tight curls of an African boy. He saw a face as smooth as chocolate, he saw wide eyes, laughing and sparkling, a squat nose, and a grin, broad, gleaming with the whitest of teeth. A body followed, pushing between the waiting throng and the boy shoved his way under the barrier, running for Jesse, a small bag in one hand, and, under his arm, what looked like an Imam's prayer mat.

The two practically collided half way between the gaping courier and the barrier. With the briefest of formalities they offered 'High Fives' and laughed.

"Kofi," Jesse said. "You made it. I saw you fly by on your mat. I saw you from the plane, but how did you get to the airport?"

The African boy laughed. "I landed in a field outside the city. Then I hitched a ride on a truck. The driver stopped by the field for a pee and I slipped in the back. He brought me straight here – not that he knew anything about it."

"I knew you'd do it," Jesse said. "I figured you were cunning enough." Then he looked at the package in Kofi's hand, and he lowered his voice. "Where's the talisman?"

Kofi touched his chest and grinned. "Around my neck, where my mother put it the day I was born."

"Great," said Jesse. "And don't worry about passports and stuff. My dad will sort that out. He can pull strings with anybody." He turned to the courier. "This is my pal, Kofi," he said. "The guy I said would be here to meet me. It's okay – we can go to the VIP lounge now. Make sure we don't get caught up with press people though. It wouldn't do for me to be seen with this kid, not till my dad turns up and we figure out what we're going to tell folk."

*

It seemed like an age before the jam cleared and Everett was free to give the car some gas.

It had been like a lifetime, this past six months with Jesse missing.

He'd gone to Africa on a mission.

Everett smiled – a twelve year old on a mission! He'd wanted to find out what could be done to solve the food famines in Africa – to follow in his mother's footsteps and work with the environment.

"I want to see everybody gets a fair chance, Dad," Jesse had said.

Honest to God, you'd have thought the boy was some high-ranking politician – a politician with altruism – and the kid was just twelve. He was after a cure for cancer too. He'd reckoned there was someone there – some kid with the power to cure cancer. Jesse's mother had cancer. That's why she wasn't here now. She was in regression. She wasn't too good.

The kid had disappeared in Africa though. There'd been no contact for months, and, for Everett, those months were the worst in his life. And what with Ursula ill, it was as if the drive for living had gone. He kept his businesses going. He carried on making the dollars. But his heart wasn't in it. He knew he'd been on automatic pilot.

Jesse had contacted him on line, a couple of months ago. He hadn't told him much about his disappearance; but he did say he'd met the kid he was looking for. He was a sort of African tribal leader, and they'd got something – a talisman or something. Jesse reckoned it was really special – with earth-changing properties. But, what the hell! A talisman. Earth-changing properties. Even with his wife ill, talismans and earth-changing properties weren't uppermost in

3

Everett's mind at the moment. He was getting his boy back, and that's what mattered.

He parked up and headed for the VIP lounge. There was a clutch of reporters hanging round, flashing with cameras, shoving microphones and recording devices under his nose.

"Is the kid all right, Mr Tierfelder?" "Who found him?" "Is someone claiming the bounty?" "Do you know what happened to him?" "Mr Tierfelder!" "Mr Tierfelder!"

Everett pushed through, waving a hand. "I'll give you a statement when I've seen the boy, okay?" he said.

Then he was through to the VIP lounge, and there, with a wiry young African, sitting by the window, was his son.

Jesse was slight, but muscular, with blonde hair, and loose curls hanging about his forehead. He had Mediterranean blue eyes, laughing, but gentle, limpid with a compassion that was way beyond his years. He wore glasses that tended to enlarge the eyes and he had the warmest, widest smile. His features, animated with intelligence, were bronzed with the African sun, and his face was touched with the faintest hint of freckles.

He looked up as his dad walked through the door, and he beamed.

"Dad?" he said.

Everett just stood there. Then he threw his arms wide and cried, "Jesse! Come and give your old dad a hug."

There was no teenage reserve about Jesse. He adored his father and made no secret of it. Arms outstretched, he made it across the room, and the two of them hugged with the warmth of a father and his prodigal son.

"We've been here ages," Jesse laughed. "Where've you been?"

"I left early enough," said Everett. "You blame the Washington traffic."

Gently he released his son and looked across at the other boy.

"Tell me about your friend."

"This is Kofi, Dad, the guy I told you about."

"The young African chief. The one with the talisman?" said Everett.

Kofi made his way across the room, his hand outstretched.

"Pleased to meet you sir," he said.

4

The boy had a firm handshake, and an assurance that would make him a good match for Jesse.

"You too, kid," Everett said. He led them to a seat by the window. "What about drinks? Coke okay?" He looked at Kofi. "There's one hell of a lot of questions I've got to ask."

"The talisman first though," Jesse said. "The rest can wait."

They sat down and Everett glanced at the courier. "One coffee. Black with no sugar and two cokes for the boys," he said. "Then we need to be on our own. Okay?"

The courier nodded.

"Yes, the talisman," Everett said. "The elixir of life, you said."

"It is, dad. Kofi's got it. Show him Kofi."

Kofi slid a thin leather thong over his head, and revealed a circular disc. Catching the rays from the window, it looked strange, as if it generated its own light. It broke the sunlight into a spectrum, but it seemed to be pulsing with some power stronger than any reflected light.

Everett looked at it closely. "Seems like a CD," he said. "Have you tried reading it on a computer?"

Jesse nodded. "It is a CD," he said. "But it's bigger and we couldn't put it on an ordinary drive."

Everett looked again, and frowned. "What makes you think it's so special? I mean, it's out of the ordinary, I can see that – like it's got its own power source or something – but – a device that'll save the world? How come?"

Jesse grinned. "You want to let Kofi tell you that, Dad," he said. "There's a story that goes with this disc that'll make your hair curl, and it's special like nothing you've ever seen. You should try analysing the stuff it's made from. You won't find it in any periodic table."

"And it's got the power of life, and health, and – a power of regeneration," Kofi said. His face was earnest, and there was a deep sincerity that made Everett catch his breath. "I really know that," he added. "And when you've heard my story you'll know it too."

"We've got to configure it," Jesse said. "We've got to break the code. We don't know how, but somehow the future depends on it – and so does mum. And you're the man to do it – the biggest

5

computer magnate in the world, the only guy with the know-how, and the only one with the resources. That's how it's meant to be. Kofi's got the talisman. He met me. I'm your son. It's fate."

Everett smiled and fingered his coffee cup.

"And, if you crack the code," Jesse added. "You'll get that Nobel Prize you've always wanted. That's for sure."

Everett sipped the coffee. "I don't know, son – not about the prize anyway – not any more. Losing your son and not knowing if you'll ever see him again – having your wife sick, that kind of stuff puts things into perspective. Recognition doesn't seem that important – not any more."

He looked at the anxious faces of the two boys. Then he said:

"I'll tell you what, though; Nobel Prize or no Nobel Prize, we'll crack this thing."

There was a sigh of relief from the Jesse and Kofi. "It'll be worth all the time it takes," Jesse said. "Because I know the power of this thing."

***

Chapter 1

In the Beginning...

The whole world shook. Nothing like it had been known since primeval days

In India jets of fire split rocks in the mountains. Coastal towns and villages were swamped with destruction as huge tsunamis drove the waves. Trees were felled, winds raged, lightning tore at the skies, birds flocked to mountain crags and animals fled to the rocks and caves.

On the foothills of the Himalayas, where the mountains touched the Indian plains, the great Gandhi stood, watching as rage and destruction tore the fabric of his country. Watching as holes gaped in the mountains, revealing the hell fires of the earth, watching billows of acrid smoke curl towards the skies.

"It is judgement day," he whispered. "Armageddon." And, as he watched, his heart ached for his people and for his country.

He made his way from the overhanging cliff, for fear that falling rocks would strike him, and, as he walked, for no reason, he turned to the east, and, in that moment, he saw, and in mid step, he stopped and stared, his eyes wide with wonder.

Because, across the valley, towards the heights of the opposite mountain was what could only be described as a pathway of light – a pathway that came from the stars, piercing the clouds, as bright as the sun, shining onto an outcrop of the mountain.

He watched fires dance on the outcrop, and then he saw a pinpoint on the pathway, high in the sky, glinting and gleaming, sliding towards earth, growing as it fell, changing colour, now violet, now green, now yellow and red, and then he saw it more clearly, a spinning disc with radii pulsing from its centre, every colour of the rainbow, and, as he watched, it tumbled, embedding itself in the fissures of the mountain ...and there was a great calm.

A peace spread across the plains of India, so still that Gandhi hardly dared breathe.

After a few moments he gathered his cloak and made his way down the hill to a village at its foot, to his people, cowering in their houses.

"My friends," he said. "Today I have seen, descending from heaven, something more amazing than I have ever seen. It fell among the crags of the mountains, and, tomorrow I will set out and I will not rest until I have found it; because I believe this thing will be the saving of the world."

*

Gandhi stood on the mountain's edge.

What he saw was unlike anything he'd seen before – something from the future; a disc of what looked like highly polished metal, yet it did not feel like metal. It was light, radiating a myriad concentric circles, and in the sunlight it gleamed.

"It is a talisman," he said, fingering it softly. "The source of all light, a talisman that harbours the rainbow."

He knelt down and removed a cord of leather from his sandal. Then he threaded it through the hollow centre of the disc and, carefully, he looped the cord, hanging it around his neck.

That night Gandhi dreamed, and, every night for the following month he had the same dream. He was in Africa, walking among the crowds, and there, in the cheering masses, edging to get near, was a young man, eager, sensitive, intelligent, a man he knew to be born for prison and for freedom. He saw himself passing the talisman to the man, and, when he woke, he knew that, one day, in a crowded street, he'd meet this man, and he knew he would be the one to take the talisman from him, but only as a keeper. In his dream, he saw the man in his prison, and there was a woman. He saw him pass the talisman to the woman, and he saw hardship and cruelty, and prejudice of the most evil kind, and he saw the woman dying. But there was a child, a boy child, in a reed basket, in the rushes of the river, and, around his neck was the talisman. The woman had gone now, but, in the child, he knew the talisman had reached its final keeper, because in that boy was the key to the healing of the world.

***

Chapter 2

The Prisoner

Mariam made her way down the long driveway. Her heart was in turmoil.

She ran the gauntlet of press reporters, photographers and television cameras, and it seemed the whole world was outside the prison. And everywhere there was a buzz of anticipation.

She showed her pass.

It was prisoner 466/64 she was heading for. She'd looked after him for the last year and he was a wonderful man – kind, gentle, patient. He'd taught her to read, he'd listened to stories about her village. He'd comforted her in her sorrows, and laughed with her in her moments of happiness.

They said he was a terrorist. That's why he was in jail, but there was no way he was a terrorist. If there was ever a man who was a saint, it was prisoner 466/64. He didn't even seem bitter that he'd been locked away for the best part of his life, and she knew he'd been subjected to vicious cruelties. He was like a father to her – not a real father. Her real father had beaten her, cursed her, shouted at her. This man was the father a girl would dream of, and today prisoner 466/64 was being released.

That's why she was in turmoil, because she knew she should be glad, but her heart was breaking.

She pushed the door of the cell and went in.

He was sitting on a bench below the window, and he was so much in shadow she could hardly make him out. But when he saw her he stood. He was a big man.

"Mr Mandela," she said.

"Glad to see you Mariam. And it's the last time, isn't it? Tomorrow you will have a new charge."

She couldn't help it. God knows she'd tried. She stifled a sob. She only hoped he wouldn't notice. "I'll miss you, sir," she said.

"Mariam," the prisoner said. He held her hands, looking into her eyes. "Mariam. Before I leave there's something I must give you. It's important, so listen to me."

He took a leather thong from his neck, and, hanging from it, she saw a disc, stunning, reflecting and refracting light in a way she'd never seen before.

"It's beautiful," she whispered.

"It's a talisman, Mariam. It was given to me by the great Gandhi, and now I am giving it to you. Believe me, it is very special, and one day, when you have your first son, I want you to give it to him. He will be its keeper just as I have been, and when he grows up he will know what to do with it."

"But it's such a great gift sir," Mariam whispered. "I don't know what to say. I can't accept it. Give it to someone else."

But prisoner 466/64 was holding her shoulders firmly, and she could see his eyes, serious, and full of resolve. "Mariam," he said. "You must keep it. When Gandhi gave it to me, he told me I would know who it must be passed to, and I've had dreams. I know you are its keeper. One day you will have a child. Then you must give it to him."

She slid the leather thong over her neck, and she felt the disc touching her. And, for the rest of the day she helped Mr Mandela collect his belongings. She helped him get ready for release. She said her goodbyes. She watched him walk the white road to freedom. She cried and she laughed, and, always, she could feel the touch of the talisman. And somehow she knew it was doing something to her, giving her a power and an understanding. She found she knew about it, and she knew what it could do. She knew about her son too, and she knew about the healing of the world.

*

That night the long ride back to the village in Sikaman country didn't seem so bad. Her mind was full of thoughts and, as she sat, gazing form the window of the bus, the hills, the woodlands and the patches of dry scrubland passed her by unnoticed.

When she reached the village she adjusted her dress, making sure the disc was covered. Until she'd fathomed its power, it was something she must hide.

She picked her way through the streets, past the newly built houses, the concrete churches, the chapels and the mosque. These more expansive buildings were not for the likes of her. For her it was the hut she'd grown up in.

But tonight she didn't feel envious. Whatever those other villagers possessed, nothing they had compared to the talisman hanging around her neck.

But by the morning things had changed.

When she woke, Mariam could sense the edges of her feelings jarring against each other. She felt ill. She had to drag herself back to the prison. She had no appetite for her work and her stomach was heavy with nausea.

The feeling was still there next day, and the day after. In fact, for weeks Mariam suffered, and, although she was worried, some instinct kept her away from the village doctor.

There was something indecent happening to her. Her breasts were swelling. Her nipples tingled. There was something wrong down below. She'd missed several periods, and she didn't want to discuss that sort of thing with the doctor.

She really didn't know who to talk to. Her only friend was Sisi, a near neighbour. Sisi had been like a big sister to her, but now she was married and had a small horde of children. It was difficult to get Sisi on her own.

But Sisi had seen what was going on, and one night, when the children were settled, she came to the door.

"You all right, girl?" she said.

"I've got something to tell you," said Mariam. "And I'm not easy, talking about it outside. It's a bit … well, there are things going on with me that I don't like. I don't know what's happening."

They went into the hut and Sisi looked hard into her face. "What things?" she said; but she knew. "You been sick in the morning, have you? You filling out down there?"

Mariam nodded. "And my breasts," she said. "Hurting, swelling."

"You've fallen for a baby," Sisi said, and Mariam stepped back.

"No. It can't be," she said. "I haven't been with anybody."

"You've fallen for a baby," Sisi said again. "I should know. I've had five."

But it was as if Sisi's words were a branding iron. "Neither man nor boy has come near me. You've got to believe me," she said.

"Don't tell me that, girl," Sisi said. "You got drunk or something. It's no good setting yourself up as no Virgin Mary with me. I've known you since you were a child remember, and you've fallen – some boy in the village when you were out of your head with drink, and, if you'll listen to me girl, you'll find him, because that child's going to need a father."

Mariam couldn't believe it. She sank onto a wooden bench in the corner of the room, and she wanted to hide. The queasiness in her belly was exacerbated by Sisi's hostility. Never had she imagined it was a child. It wasn't true. It couldn't be.

Her fingers grabbed at her neck – feeling for the thong holding the talisman. She pulled it into the open and Sisi stepped back.

"Do you think it's this?" Mariam said.

"Do I think it's what?" gasped Sisi.

"This talisman? Mr Mandela gave it me, the day he left prison. He said I've got to guard it until I have a son. Then it will be his."

Sisi edged further towards the door.

"Mr Mandela?" she whispered. "That thing came from Mr Mandela? No way, girl. That's a thing of sorcery. It's bewitched. Where's the light coming from? What makes it dance like it does? No way did that come from you're prisoner Mandela. I know about him. He's a good man. That thing is wicked. Get it out of my sight and tell me what you've been meddling with."

Sisi's eyes were burning, and, from the depth of Mariam's soul came a sudden stillness, because she knew the superstitions roused in her friend would be roused in every villager.

"What I've told you is true," she said. "Every word. It *was* Mr Mandela that gave me this talisman, and he told me to guard it with my life. It's for my son – and no man or boy has come near me. If you won't believe that, well … I don't know what I can do."

But it was too late. She saw the hate in Sisi's face, and she was frightened.

*

Not long after, Mariam stopped going to the prison. The sickness passed, but her belly swelled, and it was becoming clear to everyone she was pregnant.

And the villagers were suspicious about other things, too.

Since the day she'd come back with the talisman there'd been strange things happening – unexplained power cuts. People kept losing programmes on their radios and televisions, and, for a time, it was the only topic of conversation.

She also suspected Sisi of talking, because no one spoke to her, and it was clear many were blaming her and her rainbow disc for the unexplained phenomena. The looks and glances she got were hostile. People began spitting at her. Even if she sat in her doorway they spat, and, as time went on, their hostility grew.

She used her meagre savings to buy food, but she could only afford the minimum and when she went to the market, even when she bought from traders who came from outside the village, there was hostility.

The religious leaders passed her by.

Only the Imam smiled. Only he nodded in a sympathetic acknowledgement of her plight.

She didn't wear the talisman any more. She was afraid it was the disc that had brought about her condition. Instead she stood it on a wooden stool in the corner of the hut, letting it rest against the wall, and, at night, its light filled the room.

She knew the people could see it. It sent a path of light from her doorway, across the road. It was even more pronounced during the frequent power failures. She noticed people veering away, treading in the shadows and looking in the direction of her hut with fear and aggression.

As she grew, the light from the talisman grew too, and there were more power failures. The television and radio signals became so unstable, watching or listening to anything was impossible.

The villagers put it down to witchcraft.

There were gatherings.

They turned their heads away from her hut, and she could sense a growing tension.

"Witch," they called her. "Virgin whore," and "Harlot." And the meetings in the street became more frequent.

As time went on, she grew weaker, because, now she dare not go out at all, even to buy food.

She would have starved if it wasn't for one person.

At night, she would hear shuffling footsteps, and she would see the shadow of a man bending outside her door. Then, with a flurry, he would be gone, and when she went to look, there was a basket, with food – enough to keep her alive, and enough to keep the baby growing and active.

*

Then, one Thursday night, about nine months after the great Mandela had left prison, it happened.

All day the tension had been building. There'd been groups gathered outside her hut. People had been meeting in the churches and the other holy places. Religious leaders hurried by, averting their gaze.

By the time night came there was pandemonium, a constant clatter of feet, and she could sense even more people gathering outside. Occasionally someone would hurl a tin can or bottle against the wall and she heard stones rattling on the roof. She crouched, waiting, listening, not knowing what to do.

Then there were more organised assaults – bottles, cans, stones – and a terrifying chant. "Out! Witch out! Kill the blaspheming whore."

For a moment she backed into the corner of the hut, near the talisman, She was shaking. Then, her head in panic, she grabbed the rainbow disc and bolted, holding the talisman ahead of her to ward off attacks.

She weaved her way through the village making for the forest. Some instinct told her that this was the only place of safety. The forest was where the Nam-Nam tribe lived, and the villagers never went near the Nam-Nams. It was said they ate people.

But between her and safety was a plain of scrubland. She'd have to cross it and, as she ran, she could hear pounding feet behind her.

Some of the boys were within grasping distance. She could feel hands grabbing at her clothes, and then, with a scream, she let the clothes fall. The boys fell back, and, naked to the waist, she raced across the scrubland, with only her dashiki wrap to cover her. Blind with tears she stumbled, until she made it to the safety of the trees.

*

She fell to the floor gasping, listening to the shouts of the villagers. There seemed to be no easing of the venom, only subtle changes as the mob moved around the forest's edge. They were searching, hoping she might be within reach, but she knew she was safe. With the light of the talisman, she'd gone deep, well beyond any place they would dare venture.

After a while, she became conscious of running water nearby and she dragged herself towards it. She could make out clusters of rushes growing by a river and where the river parted the trees, she could see flashing torches, some electric, some tallow. And, further away, the serrated outline of the village.

Then she breathed sharply, because, mingling with the glow of streetlights, she could see, from the centre of the village, a more tremulous glow, – and she knew they'd torched her hut.

She pulled herself up to rest against a tree.

What was going on back there? Animosity, blind prejudice – she didn't understand. She'd done nothing wrong, and neither had the talisman.

This thing they hated was meant to save them – to give them life and prosperity. And they were trying to destroy it. They were like savages.

She would have given everything to guard the disc for the likes of Mr Mandela – but for this mob? … To think that this talisman was for the likes of them?

She began pulling reeds from the river's edge. Then, shuddering, she started to weave, fashioning the reeds into a shallow basket, and, as she worked, she felt the first pangs of labour.

***

Chapter 3

Kofi

The talisman was only giving off a dim light now. Its power seemed to be directed to the struggle inside her, helping her to bring the baby into the world. And while she waited, she wove, working through the night, binding the reeds with wefts and warps. It kept her mind off labour pains and thinking about what was going on out there on the plains.

There was constant movement, shadows – villagers dancing around fires. She could hear them baying for her blood. Someone had started beating a drum, and, much nearer, she could hear twigs crack as young men invaded the woods. They dare not come too far. Fear of magic, and the reputation of the Nam-Nams sent them scurrying back. But she was afraid.

She knew she could never go back to the village. Back there they saw the talisman as something dark with magic. The fact that she was pregnant made her a whore. Her claim never to have been with a man was blasphemy. Even the place she'd escaped to was proof she was possessed by the devil.

They would kill her, and they'd kill her baby.

But, if she was left here, she didn't know how she'd survive.

She wove vigorously, pulling the reeds tight, struggling to drive every thought out of her head, and every now and again she would touch the talisman, letting its strength filter into her.

And, when she did this, she knew.

She knew the greatness of the mission.

She knew nothing bad would happen to her son – nothing that would stop his destiny.

When she touched the talisman she knew that the hate of the villagers, her need to weave a basket, her proximity to the river, the very fact that she was in the forest – all were pre-ordained.

All night the villagers raged. Then, at the darkest hour, as the drumbeats grew more frenzied, she had her baby.

It was a boy.

She knew it would be. But she was too weak to feel any happiness and it seemed her weakened body made the talisman grow weaker. Its light was almost smothered by the glow of fires burning on the plain.

She could just make out the baby, streaked with birth fluids – and with blood. He was crying. She struggled to the river to clean him.

Then, she took her dashiki wrap and dried him with it. And she tore it, wrapping the driest part around him, and wrapping the remainder around herself.

His brown eyes looked up at her. They were deep and calm. "My little Kofi" she whispered. "My little child, born on a Friday. The great Mr Mandela, – he told me about you. He told me you were destined for great things my little appia."

*

It was four o'clock.

Dawn touched the sky and it was the time for morning mass. It was the time for the Imam to call his people to prayer and it was the time for Mariam to give Kofi the talisman.

She took it and placed it over his head, resting it against his chest, and, in that moment, as the village clock struck four, the world came alive. Bells cascaded, and the Imam called out from his minaret with a long wailing cry.

It happened every morning, and yet, today it seemed more significant, because, today it happened at the very moment Kofi and his talisman came together.

And immediately the rainbow colours became more intense. Suddenly it was sending light between the trees – first as bright as a star, then as bright as the moon, then as bright as a furnace, until it burned like the sun, its light filling the forest, flooding the plain and dazzling the village. It drowned out the embers of the fires, and, as its power swept across the plain, the villagers fled, shielding their eyes, and every one of them headed for the nearest church or mosque. And they cursed Mariam for her magic, they cursed her for her league with the devil, they cursed her for her blasphemy and they cursed her for the illegitimacy of her child.

Mariam didn't move for a while.

She stared at the talisman, and its light left shivering shadows on her eyes. She shielded some of it with her dashiki wrap, and then she looked at Kofi.

He was asleep and his face was beautiful. But it hurt her to look at him. She knew she wouldn't be doing that for much longer. She knew she was going to die.

How would he survive?

She thought about taking him to the Imam's house, but she didn't have the strength, and, besides, she knew if she went near the village she'd be killed. But now she had a mission. She had to move Kofi to the plain, and, even though he was barely the weight of a water pitcher, she could still hardly lift him. She dragged herself over the forest floor until the gaps between the trees widened and the light of dawn filtered through.

The plain looked like a battlefield with smouldering fires littering the scrubland; and the bitter smell of wood stinging her nostrils. There was a faint haze of blue where the smoke had dissipated and she looked around, in case some itinerant villager was still there. But there was no one. She was safe.

She picked up a half burned stick and blew it until it glowed. Then she took the talisman from Kofi's neck and slowly, with tiny dots, she began to burn a pattern of letters into its leather thong. Remembering the writing Mr Mandela had taught her, she formed the words: "His name is Kofi".

Whoever found him now, she thought, would know. And, even though she would never see it, for all his great life, he would be called by the name she'd chosen.

She carried him back to the forest, to the reed basket and laid him there, swaddling him tightly. Then she kissed him, and moved to the shallows of the river.

She pushed the basket and watched it gyrate, with the eddies carrying it out onto the river, away from the plain and away the village. And she watched it drift deeper into the forest, to where the wild animals were, and the Nam-Nam tribe.

Morning came and the sun wove its way between the branches.

For Kofi there was no food, no mother's comfort, no bodily warmth, just the water rocking him as he drifted farther into the forest.

He drifted on until darkness came again, and the reed-woven basket grew heavy.

Gradually it sank into the river with the water soaking into its fabric.

And the blackest night closed in.

Only on the water was there light and, on the water, it was the talisman that glowed, giving its strength to the baby, pulsing with his pulse, providing him with its own buoyancy – and Kofi lay there, a bobbing glow-worm in the darkness.

***

Chapter 4

A Troop of Apes

There was a crash as a troop of apes burst through the forest. They plunged towards the river, led by a female, her warm, weatherworn face fixed with a leathery grimace and her brown eyes darting, searching for danger. A horde of younger apes leaped beside her. Others followed, branching off, and behind them came the lumbering males.

They swarmed to the river, agitating for position and the noise of the dawn chorus vibrated around them.

As the mother scooped water, her eyes searched.

Then she stopped.

She could hear something.

Among the reeds she could sense a creature, alone, helpless, trapped – something hungry and frightened. And, although the steady wailing wasn't familiar to her, she knew it was the cry of something newborn.

She moved deeper into the water, searching, until she saw a tiny baby very much like her own, only hairless, black and shining where it was semi-submerged in water.

It was a boy child, and it had something flat hanging around its neck, something that seemed to shine like the sun, and for a moment she shied away.

But the thing on its chest – the thing that shone didn't appear to be harming him, and in a gesture beyond her control she scooped him up.

There was pandemonium around her. The cubs, the other females in the troop, all surrounded her, the cubs pushing and jostling, prizing their way to the front. Their hands grasped to touch the creature but the mother pushed them away.

Staccato screams registered their outrage, but they recognised something special about this black baby; and they knew, when the mother pushed them, she was right.

But not everyone shared their excitement. As they headed back towards the forest, the dominant male began to stir.

He'd seen from a distance, and the excited chattering had angered him. Something had come into his troop that wasn't his. He'd seen it plucked out of the river and one of his females was clutching it, suckling it like one of her own – and it wasn't one of her own.

He moved forward, pushing through the clamour, grabbing at the female's arm.

The black thing was not an ape. It was like an ape, but it had no hair on its body, and it was male. A male coming from outside the troop was a potential threat.

He pulled the female's arm again, gnashing with his teeth, but each movement to prize the thing away strengthened the maternal bond and she gripped more firmly.

As the tussle developed, other females began tugging at the male, while the cubs bounced and chattered, screaming their outrage.

There was a burning fury in the male's eyes now, and then, with both hands he grabbed the female's arms, and, with his teeth, he snatched at the glowing disc hanging around the creature's neck.

Then he let out a roar, because, where the disc came into the grip of his jaws there was a pain – and it shot to his brain, thrusting him back towards the rushes.

By now his fury was beyond reason. He screamed, his teeth bared back to his gums, his eyes on fire, and he lunged, grabbing the disc with his hands, and, as he grabbed, the hair on his body went rigid and his limbs convulsed. He could not hold on and the force felled him. The other apes fell back, screaming.

He tried again, but he could not touch the black creature, or the disc of sunlight that hung around his neck. Each time he was thrown to the ground and slowly, weighed down with shame, he shambled towards the forest. His troop had seen him thrashed. He could no longer make claim to be the dominant male.

The creature was crying again now, his eyes narrowed with fear and his limbs flailing, and, for a while the mother nestled him as the other females hovered, touching him gently when they could.

The cubs chattered, but the older males skulked away.

They'd seen the power of this creature, and, although they realised he would make them the most feared troop in the forest, they knew, too, that, as long as he was with them, none of them would be leader.

*

By the time they reached their territory though, the procession had livened up. The cubs were prancing around, weaving in and out of the older apes, chattering, and screaming, and there was common consent that the black thing would be leader of the troop – that he must be cherished and reared with all the care they could muster.

He was sleeping when they reached the outcrop, and the mother who'd rescued him rested against a rock, nursing him, while the others gathered grasses.

They made a soft bed and, with something near to tenderness, the female, the suckling mother, laid him down. The cubs processed, armed with fresh grass, and they covered the naked body and the glowing disc. Only the baby's sleeping head was visible, and, for the rest of the day, while the cubs played and the other apes foraged, one of the troop always sat, watching, guarding the precious thing whose disc had captured the rainbow and who would make them the greatest troop in the forest.

*

They looked after him like a king.

During daylight hours, when they foraged, there was always one ape with him. And always a male stood on guard on one of the higher outcrops.

There were occasions when it was necessary to take evasive action. News spread that the troop had a new cub, rescued from the river, a super-cub with smooth skin and the sun on his chest – one who, even new born, was more than match for the dominant male.

Other troops made a bid to see the creature, to test him. But the males fought them off. Surprise raids were useless, because the troop agreed to forage only where they could hear the guard's signal. A cry from him brought them back in force, the males beating off invading troops, the females forming a wall of protection around their

22

precious captive.

Then, one day, there was a lion. For hours he was slinking around in the undergrowth, hiding when the foraging apes came near.

He knew there was no chance for a kill among the trees. One move and the apes would be up a tree and beyond his reach; but, in the clearing, nestling on tufts of grass there was a young cub. He seemed special and it was clear that he'd been injured. He was lying on his back. Sometimes he fought to roll over, but he could only manage an ineffectual wave of his limbs. He was easy prey. If the lion could catch the female unaware, he could maim her and the injured creature would be his. With luck he could have the female too. There was a male on a high rock, but the lion knew the male's instinct would be to flee leaving the female and the injured creature defenceless.

It was just a matter of time. And then … the female moved, pulling more grass to soften the small thing's nest, and, with the silence of velvet paws, the lion pounced, streaking across the clearing.

What happened next left him reeling. There was a shriek from the high rock, a thumping beating of chests, and from all quarters a cacophony of wild fury unlike anything he'd ever experienced. He was barely halfway across the clearing when apes appeared from everywhere, not confused and fleeing, but converging, attacking, as if their own lives meant nothing. The female grabbed the creature, and she was across the clearing and up a tree before he could move, and the ferocity of the stampede was so great, he fled.

For the rest of the day the apes took positions in the trees, and, for several days, there were two or three guards on the rock, and the creature with the sun on his chest was nursed by several females at once. For a week, his suckling mother never left his side.

But this black thing was a puzzle.

In his eyes there was a growing perception. He recognised his suckling mother in a way she'd never been recognised before, and his eyes darted around, seeing and understanding things with a transparency that was beyond her.

He cried his own personal cry for food, but for the most part he was tranquil, with none of the wild uncomprehending instinct that drove the others.

And sometimes, in those moments of stillness, when he saw his suckling mum, there was a movement on his face. It would soften in a way that made her heart yearn, and his toothless mouth would move, widening and opening in a motion that was so beautiful, and his eyes would light up.

Sometimes, when he did this movement, he would kick his limbs, and make a sound in his throat, and when he did that, it was something very special.

But he was so slow.

While baby apes born some time after him were already cavorting and climbing rocks, this thing was barely able to move. He writhed, pushing with his arms, grabbing, holding and manipulating objects, but nothing else.

The other cubs grew impatient. They picked him up. They held him by his stomach so his limbs could move along the ground, but he always collapsed, sometimes into an outraged ball and at other times rolling over, doing that thing with his mouth, his eyes sparkling, his throat making the sound, and his limbs flailing with delight.

But it was clear he understood what they wanted and gradually, with the other cubs' help he began to move, first rolling, then dragging himself, pulling limbs too weak to support his belly, and then crawling, moving just as they did, and, at the same time, tiny teeth appeared in his mouth. He became weaned and began to stuff himself with soft fruit.

At first he could only crawl along the smooth ground. But he watched the others with an understanding and perception, and he seemed to think before he made a move.

Then he tried. He tried everything, grasping rocks, grabbing branches. His mates helped him, pulling him up trees, while his limbs were scraped, cut, and bleeding. But he still tried.

Soon he became strong, and could lope with the best of them, and then, one day, when the rest were foraging and he was alone with his suckling mother, he stood on his strengthened legs, without using his arms for support. He stepped forward in a way that no ape could ever do, using his arms to grab things, so he could maintain an upright position, and he staggered around the clearing, falling, picking himself up, tumbling, but always determined, walking, using just his hind limbs.

From then on he outstripped everyone. He ran faster, he used his arms and hands to greater purpose, he thought out strategies to outwit his mates, he began to use and understand their language, and he could manipulate their signs to indicate things that the troop had never imagined possible. He began to teach them and where they bared their teeth in aggression, he bared his in laughter. His eyes sparkled, he ran, he climbed, he hid, he played games, but above all, he began to think, to plan and to lead his troop. The supremacy that he had shown on that first day was now manifested in all he did.

*

In the meantime the apes' world was being invaded.

The people that lived around the forest feared both it, and the Nam-Nam tribe, but developers had no such fear.

Loggers, tree fellers, and lumberjacks from all over the world worked at the forest's edges. Even when Mariam had escaped to give birth, it was in bad shape.

Whole areas were being devastated – habitats destroyed, vegetation grubbed up – land was being laid waste and where it had been cleared, men began to quarry, prospecting for oil and sinking mines.

Around the perimeter, huge factories sprang up, chemical factories, paper manufacturing industries, oil refineries, power stations, many using wood harvested from the forest, and all pumping poisonous gases – and all pouring their waste into the river.

The forest was dying. There was no nourishment in the leaves. There weren't enough mangos, the banana harvest failed, berries were scarce, and what the apes did manage to forage was blighted.

Water from the river made them ill. The troop was in a bad way.

But they still remained loyal to their leader, and in return he scavenged. He plundered the stores of other troops, and because of the sun on his chest – no one dare retaliate.

He had been with the troop for five years now, and his manual skills and agility held all others at bay.

He knew how his tribe depended on him, even though he sometimes showed the weakness of a child, and ran, crying, to his suckling mother. In a way it was a mutual dependency. But he was different from the others, not only in appearance, but in his ways. He was restless, curious.

If something strange happened, when others fled for cover, he went to investigate. He was careful, using his forest skills to protect himself.

And he knew things were changing.

There were new sounds – distant metallic noises, roars and snarls that didn't sound like any animal he'd heard before, and there were sounds of earth avalanches and explosive bangs.

Sometimes he would wander away from the troop and try to locate the sounds, but the forest was a rambling maze, and he was still dependant. He was only five and he needed his mother. His forages were cautious and brief.

One day though he just had to follow the trail. There was a combination of sounds, all coming from the same area, and as he got nearer he could differentiate between them. He could hear metallic bangings and angry snarls. And there were screamings – not animal sounds. They were more like whining, ringing screams, lowering and rising. And he could hear noises that did belong to animals, but not to any animal he'd heard before. Short sharp sounds, strings of sound being answered by other strings, and noises that were like the sound he made when he was playing, or when his suckling mother tickled him, although these sounds were deeper.

He followed, listening until the ground fell away, and he was looking into a massive hole. And it was full of creatures – apes – but not apes, and his eyes widened, because these creatures were just like him, only bigger. They walked like him, they used their hands like him, and they laughed like him.

But they weren't like him. Some were brown and some were paler, and whereas he was hairless, from the neck down these creatures had a kind of fur – a sort of covering. Parts were in different colours and some had different patterns. Not only that but the animals could take the fur off! He distinctly saw some of them stop what they were doing, wipe their hands across the top of their faces and then peel off a whole layer of skin. He saw them fold it and lay it on a rock. One or two took the whole top half of their covering off, and underneath they were just like him.

But that was not all. There were other creatures, angular creatures that shone in the sunlight, crawling along on circular legs, legs the same shape as the sun hanging around his neck, and these creatures were gouging huge piles of earth and stone with their snouts, and building new hills with it. Some of the animals that were like him were riding the digging creatures, controlling them, showing them where to dig, pulling at bits of them, twisting bits of them. Others held circles in their hands, making them scream, cutting into rocks and sending showers of stars into the sky. He saw others with long pieces of wood that had shiny stone-like ends. They were swinging them, just like he swung pieces of wood to beat mangoes from the trees, and they were hitting rocks with them, breaking them into boulders and he was captivated.

He wanted to do what they were doing. He wanted to ride the big yellow creatures with the burrowing snouts, he wanted to peel off skin like they did, he wanted to run and laugh among them. But he couldn't. They weren't a part if his troop and he wasn't a part of theirs.

He drew back, uncertain.

They were bigger than him. They were stronger than him. They were a danger to him.

Then something else caught his senses – not from the pit, but from nearby, where the forest thinned, beyond the world, where no member of his troop would go.

He could smell something. It made his mouth water and his belly churn.

He slipped away from the pit and headed for the edge of the forest, and there, for the second time, his eyes widened.

He'd discovered a whole troop of these creatures, only this time there were small ones too, running and playing like the ape cubs did. Some were naked like him; others had the peel-off skins. There were bigger ones as well, and immediately he knew. The ones in the big pit had been the males; the ones here were the females, the suckling mothers.

They'd made strange mounds all over their territory, some of wood, some of stone, with holes where they went in and out – like

27

caves. – And the smell – the smell came in smoke from stones sitting on flames of sunlight.

There was one of these stones very near where he was hidden. He saw the female dip a long stick into it. The stick had a hand-like cup on its end. Then she took out some stuff in the hand like cup, and laid it on a slate beside the sun fire. There were other beautifully smelling things beside the slate too, and he waited.

As soon as the female disappeared into the cave mound, he darted forward, grabbing a handful of what lay on the slate and one of the delicious smelling things beside it.

From the safety of his hideout he devoured what he'd stolen. It was the most awesome thing he'd ever consumed. He'd never known anything like it, and unable to help himself, his stomach let rip with the most satisfied of belches.

He looked back at the territory. The female returned, and it seemed she didn't notice that stuff had gone missing – and everywhere there were females doing the same thing. There seemed to be so much stuff and he thought, for the first time, of his hungry troop back in the forest.

This was the most perfect place to raid. They could live on this forever. This evening, when the sun slept and the day was dead, he would bring his troop here. They would get this stuff and they would grow fat and strong again.

*

The Imam had heard rumblings, complaints that food was being taken. People's stores were being raided.

It was happening every night and no one could work out who was responsible. Traps had been set, vigilantes had been posted, but no one could catch the raiders.

The people were getting desperate and the Imam was worried.

They were beginning to contemplate actions that he could not condone, and, one night, he decided to climb the minaret at the Mosque and keep watch.

For a while he concentrated on the plains. But he saw nothing. Then, for no other reason than desperation, he looked towards the forest.

It was irrational. No animal had the cunning to do what these raiders did, but no one had come from the surrounding villages, and he waited for an hour. It was hard, but then ... he thought he must have gone to sleep, because, emerging from the forest, were rays of light, strong, yet so soft they barely disturbed his eyes – rays that would not rouse anyone in the sleeping village. And in the pool of light there were shapes, a procession of creatures crossing the plain – not human. They were loping on all fours and they had the bearing of apes. They *were* apes – all bar one. One walked upright, but he didn't have the stature of a man. He was a midget, and it was from him that the light was coming.

From the minaret the Imam watched as the troop infiltrated the village. The human, if it was a human, was clearly their leader. It sensed out traps. It directed them to avoid danger, and it searched out stores and food. It controlled them with silent signals and the raid was over in half an hour.

As they moved back, the Imam crept down from the minaret and followed, gradually closing in so he could see clearly ... and he stared in disbelief.

The leader was a child, about five, black, strong and naked, apart from a single medallion hanging around his neck. It was this ornament that seemed to be radiating the light and the Imam half closed his eyes so he could make it out more clearly.

Then his brain began to race, because he knew what the ornament was. It was the talisman that belonged to the girl Mariam. The boy must be her son, the one she'd been pregnant with when she'd fled.

Without thinking he stepped out, confronting the troop, searching to meet the child's eyes.

He didn't raise his hands. He was afraid the child would see it as a threat or a challenge.

The boy stopped and there was fear in his face. But the Imam smiled, hoping he would recognise the facial gesture, and while the apes jostled, the boy smiled back.

Then the Imam moved forward, still smiling and always he was watching the boy's eyes. He put out a hand, and the child's eyes never wavered.

Instead he lifted his own hand, holding it out, and, for a moment

29

the two touched. Then the Imam bowed and turned, walking quietly away.

*

It was Mariam's child. The talisman he'd seen hanging around his neck made the Imam certain.

At some stage he must have been abandoned and, somehow, with the power of the talisman to protect him, he'd come to the apes and they'd taken him in. Now he was their leader.

But it wasn't right – a human child with wild animals, especially this child. The Imam knew about this child. He'd had dreams. This child and his talisman were destined for great things, and something had to be done.

The next night he went out again, only this time he was prepared.

He hoped he hadn't frightened the troop away. The child hadn't been afraid of him – but the apes had been restive.

He waited, listening, watching, and then there was a slight disturbance among the trees, and he saw the light again.

He moved out into the plain, and stood in front of the procession, holding out his hand and smiling and, as he watched, the child smiled back, his face lighting up, his eyes sparkling, and two rows of tiny white milk teeth, sending beams of pure sunlight towards him.

The Imam knelt and beckoned.

The apes were still restive, but the child moved towards him and held out his hand. This time the Imam had brought chocolate, something he knew the child would like, and he watched as the boy took it. He watched him put it in his mouth, taste, and then devour it.

That night the Imam watched them at work, singling out houses that they'd not been to before. This child's cunning was beyond bounds. He was phenomenally precocious.

It bothered the Imam to see his people robbed, but he knew he must bide his time.

For days he waited, watching, meeting the troop, feeding the child chocolate, and each day the trust grew.

At first the child smiled and nodded, touching the Imam's hand, then he held it. He let the Imam lead him to a new area of the village,

30

to the mosque where he'd stacked food so the apes could eat without invading homes and, one day, when the Imam stood in front of the approaching troop, the boy came running, and in his hand was a mango. It was a gift.

This time the Imam led them, not to the village, but around the suburbs and out towards his own house. He'd placed small piles of food around to placate the troop, and immediately they swooped.

The child moved to join them, but the Imam leaned down, holding his hand, and quietly he said: "Come, little one. You are not one of these. You are in God's image. You must come with me."

He opened the door and led him through, and, immediately the apes stopped eating and began to follow, but the Imam closed the door.

He looked at the boy, turning him, holding him by the shoulders. He was certain it was Mariam's child.

But as the door closed fury erupted. The apes began shrieking. They were banging their chests, stamping, hammering at the door. They charged, slamming against the walls.

They clambered up to the windows. They scratched at the panes of glass. Some females set up a wailing noise, retreating to the corner of the garden, and the males assaulted the house again and again.

* * *

Chapter 5

The Prayer Mat

As the Imam stared at the apes rioting outside his house, he thought perhaps, this time, he might have made a mistake. Rescuing the child had been his focus. He hadn't thought about how the apes or the boy would react, and now he wondered what he'd done.

In time the apes would break down the door and that would be the end of it – and the memory of those faces peering through the window would haunt him for a long time – brown eyed, anxious, hurt, their leathery features full of pain. If possible he would have said they were crying, and the boy could see it. He could hear the cries, and this was his troop.

There was little time to observe what was going on outside though. The boy himself was inconsolable. The trust the Imam had built up had been shattered. He'd stolen the boy. He'd robbed him of his family, and the cries he could hear outside were piercing his heart.

He was running around the room, screaming, banging at doors and throwing anything he could, and the looks he gave the holy man revealed the betrayal. The Imam doubted he would ever build that trust again.

He tried soothing words. He tried holding the boy. He tried praying, but the cries from outside were dragging the child's heart away. He was beyond consolation.

Eventually he picked him up, wrestling him to a room at the back of the house, protected by a courtyard and further away from the noise. He held him there, firmly, consoling him.

But still the boy struggled and the Imam didn't know what to do.

He hoped he'd done the right thing bringing him here, but ... where was he to go next?

Outside the apes raged, but then there was another noise – a sudden cry of human voices and the intermingling shrieks and shouts of battle were more terrifying than ever.

*

There had been an explosion of fury, making the villagers leap out of their beds.

Some of them thought the village was under attack but as they staggered into the street, they realised the noise was coming from the Imam's house.

It was a savage, primitive fury and they set off, armed with clubs and machetes

They moved around to the back of the house, grouping themselves until a given signal, when they broke loose, waving their implements, yelling and plunging into the heaving mass of invading apes.

They beat them back, hitting them, driving and pushing them and the troop fled, shielding their bodies with their forearms, whimpering with fear, and with an animal grief for their leader.

The men followed, but only to the perimeter of the forest. Those who were native were afraid to go any further, and the incomers, those who worked in the quarries and mines, knew that any further pursuit was useless.

But whatever had made the apes attack, they were gone now, and the villagers knew they wouldn't be back.

*

The boy was exhausted. He crouched in the corner, whimpering – watching the Imam, and across to the east, dawn was breaking. It was the time for morning prayers, but the Imam couldn't leave the boy and go to his congregation. Instead he unrolled his prayer mat and prayed where he was, while, from his corner, the child watched. It was the first time he'd been completely still.

After he'd prayed, the Imam lifted the boy, sitting him on the table and slipping the talisman from his neck.

The boy didn't move.

He knew, when an enemy touched the rainbow disc, it would hit out, hurting him and it would drive him away – but this time nothing happened. If anything the disc gave off a brief shiver of brighter light. And the child became more still.

There were marks on the thong that held the talisman – small dots burnt into the surface. They formed letters.

"His name is Kofi," the Imam read.

And he smiled.

He knew that writing. It was Mariam's writing. It was all the confirmation he needed. This boy was the child he'd dreamed about – the one who Gandhi and Mandela had decreed would be keeper of the talisman and healer of the world.

In one sweep he gathered him up and whispered: "Kofi – little keeper of the talisman – Mariam's boy – my little Kofi Musa."

The boy was looking at the softened face, lined and creased. The old man's head was shorn and his beard was long and grey. Slowly Kofi reached out and touched it, grooming the hair in the beard.

The Imam lifted his hand and, with his own fingers, began to explore Kofi's unkempt mop of curls and they continued for some time, cementing a bond, and. in Kofi's case, removing an infestation. The boy's hair was alive with lice.

After a while the Imam moved him away. "I think, my little Kofi Musa, a bath and some clothes for you – but first, food. When I fed your family, I didn't give you a chance to eat. You must be starving."

He led him into the kitchen and got food together, figs, yams, mangoes, and while Kofi was waiting, he gave him a square of chocolate. The boy devoured everything … and then it was off to the bathroom.

For Kofi the bathroom was a place of fascination – a white, clean cave, a huge waterhole, with what looked like two waterfalls tumbling into it, one hot and steaming, the other cold, filling the hole with pure water. The Imam didn't make the water too hot. He guessed Kofi was used to the river. But the boy enjoyed his bath – until it came to the business of washing his hair.

Then it was all bubbles – stinging soap in his eyes and he fought so that, by the end, the Imam, the bathroom floor, the walls, everything was as soaked as Kofi. But the holy man just chuckled.

Now it was time to introduce him to clothes.

He thought there would be a fight when the boy saw shirts, trousers and underpants, but, for some reason, he laughed as he examined the garments and he chuckled with delight as the Imam dressed him.

34

He pulled the clothes away from his body and let them spring back. They were strange against his flesh, but they were the skins he'd seen at the quarry – the ones with bright patterns, and, for the rest of the day he amused himself, putting on and stripping off his newly acquired skins.

*

There were problems though.

The Imam had no knowledge of raising children, and Kofi was not a normal child. He was five. He'd been weaned already, in a community whose ways were foreign to the human race. He had no language. He was in no way house trained.

The first shock came when the Imam found him in the darkest corner of a room, squatting and defecating. He'd already urinated, and was paddling happily in rivers of his own waste.

The holy man wasn't sure what to do. He couldn't beat him. The boy had done what he thought was right. He'd found a most discreet and private place.

There was only one thing for it. He would have to show him the toilet and mime the correct procedure. That amused Kofi, but, having gone through the tortuous simulation, the Imam rewarded himself with a large piece of chocolate, and Kofi understood that.

Immediately he proceeded to imitate the holy man – but without passing one drop of water or the smallest piece of solid waste. The Imam gave him chocolate and hoped that, next time, there would be a more positive result.

Eating proved equally problematical.

Kofi insisted on sitting cross-legged, devouring fruit, spitting out stones and chucking skins and rinds to all quarters of the room, but with appropriate rewards he was soon performing activities at both ends of his body in a reasonably civilised manner.

On the first night the Imam prepared a bed – a soft mattress, pillows, a soft cover – he even took the precaution of lining the bed with a polythene sheet, but Kofi ejected the pillows, thrust the cover to the floor, and then he tossed and turned, finally leaping from the bed and running to hide in a corner.

The Imam tried miming to show him what to do, imitating sleep, re-making the bed, and climbing into it himself. He cajoled and pleaded, but all Kofi did was utter inarticulate screams, beating on his chest and shaking his head.

Eventually he pointed to the prayer mat.

By this time the Imam was beginning to read his signals and straight away he fetched it, opening it out and laying it on the floor.

Immediately Kofi ran to it. He curled into the foetal position, put his thumb in his mouth and fell asleep.

From then on it was no longer the Imam's prayer mat.

But there were still problems, and they were not just of Kofi's making.

There were the village people.

They'd rescued the Imam from the apes, but they didn't understand how the invasion had come about. They were puzzled as to why apes would assault the Imam's house and, in their gossip, they started to speculate.

For all his life the Imam had told the truth, but how could he tell them about Kofi – the lost child of Mariam? If he didn't though, it was a deception – something utterly abhorrent to him.

In the end he compromised. He told them he'd found the apes raiding their larders, and he'd tried to deflect them by putting out food himself. When they'd eaten the food, he said, they'd attacked the house in an attempt to get more.

For a time that story made him a hero, but he didn't like that either. He was basking in the merits of a half-truth.

Kofi became a problem with the villagers too. When the Imam went to the mosque for prayers, he had to take Kofi, but how could he explain away a five-year-old boy?

He told them he was a novice. He did teach him the rituals of his faith. He did teach him to pray and he did train him in the ways of the mosque … but it was still only a half-truth.

For a while Kofi's tendency to communicate in 'ape' was also a danger. When people spoke to him he had no language to reply, so the Imam taught him to be silent when he was out – but for a five-year-old novice to be mute was something the villagers couldn't understand.

But Kofi learned quickly.

At first he saw the Imam, through the culture of the apes, as his leader. The Imam had proved himself by capturing him. He'd been able to touch the rainbow disc. He was accorded reverence by his followers at the mosque, and so Kofi was obedient, and, when the Imam gestured for him to be still, to walk upright and not to thump on his chest in the streets, he obeyed ... because the Imam was his troop leader.

Later, though, he began to see the gentle kindness and the patience, and his blind obedience turned to trust, and gradually trust became love and adoration.

It was not a saintly adoration. Sometimes he lost his temper and reverted to screams and ape fury – but ... Kofi was a five-year-old boy. Five-year-old boys did that kind of thing.

Over time, communication grew easier. The Imam tried to learn the signs and sound of Kofi's language. Kofi'd been used to teaching apes, so he found teaching the Imam easy.

In return the Imam taught Kofi. He taught him English and Pidgin English. He taught him to read and to write, starting with the simple message burnt onto the leather thong – 'His name is Kofi'. He taught him to count, and later, more advanced operations in number.

But, as Kofi began to speak, his vow of silence became harder to maintain, and his stumbling words made the villagers even more suspicious.

People began to fit parts of the jigsaw together. The most perceptive noticed that the boy had never been seen before the incident with the apes. He was mute, too ... and now he was beginning to speak – stumbling in both English and Pidgin English. Had the boy come from the forest? Had he been with the apes?

The Imam knew about these speculations, but he didn't address them, and eventually speculation provided its own explanation. Some villagers did believe Kofi had come from the forest ... but not many, because, to most, the idea of a boy being reared by apes was impossible. They concluded he'd come from another part of the world – and if he had spoken they wouldn't have understood him – that's why he was always silent. Now he was learning their language.

There were still questions about his name though. Kofi was a local name … but the majority explained that away too. The Imam had given him that name because his own name would have been unpronounceable.

All the same, as Kofi grew up, there were suspicions. The villagers kept a close watch, and the Imam had to warn him.

"Kofi Musa," he said one day. "Be careful when you are with the village boys. They mustn't know about the forest and the apes. You mustn't say anything about your suckling mother – not even to your closest friends."

Kofi was clever and he cared with a devotion for his baba Imam. If the Imam said 'be careful', then he must be careful; but he didn't understand.

"Was it bad, Baba, to be with the apes? Did I do wrong to grow up in the forest?"

The Imam shook his head. "No my little man, you did nothing wrong. In fact it was a miracle of Allah. All the time you were with the apes, Allah was protecting you, because he knew you were a chosen child. He sent the talisman and he made you its keeper. I know. I've had dreams. When you are older and wiser, Allah will show you how to use the talisman – how to direct its power to do great things. But not yet. For now you must wait."

… But it was hard waiting. He could already do things with the talisman. If there was danger when he walked across the plain – from a stray leopard – or a lion – bearing his chest and revealing the talisman's light sent the danger away. And he could do tricks. If he thought hard when he held the disc, he could lift things. Sometimes, for fun, when food needed to be put on the table, he would look at the plates and they would glide across the room and land exactly where he wanted them to.

He never did tricks when the Imam was watching. It was playing with the power of the talisman, and that was wrong. Even now he knew he was only its keeper.

But he could do other things – fill glasses with water, burn weeds out of the garden, make fruit drop from trees. Sometimes he would sit on his prayer mat and, when he held the talisman and concentrated, the prayer mat would rise into the air. He'd take it to the plains where no one could see, and he'd lift himself high above the forest, sailing across the trees and he would ride with the clouds.

He never told any one. He never did tricks in front of his friends. The Imam had told him to keep the talisman a secret, and the Imam's word was holy.

But he didn't stay true to the Imam in everything.

By the time he was eight he knew about the Imam's beliefs. He went to the mosque for daily prayers, and the Imam explained that, as a novice, he would grow up to be a Muslim holy man – and, to Kofi, that was wrong.

"Didn't you say the talisman was for the whole world?" he said.

"Yes, for the whole world, my little Kofi Musa," said the Imam.

"Not just for Muslims, then?"

"No. For the people of the world."

"Then shouldn't I understand the whole world's ways? Shouldn't I learn about all its religions?"

It was a big question. "Is that what you think you should do, Kofi Musa?" the Imam said.

Kofi nodded, "If I'm to heal the world," he said.

"Then you must learn about all faiths, all peoples. You should go to the churches and synagogues, and to the Hindu temples and Juju shrines. You should learn as much as you can."

After that Kofi went with his friends to their churches, to learn about their beliefs. He didn't abandon the mosque, but he spent enough time in other religious places to put himself in danger. It revived the villager's doubts. How could the Imam's novice share in other religions, and with the Imam's blessing?

They began to watch Kofi even more closely.

*

In spite of his devotion to the faiths and beliefs of the world, Kofi was still a boy. He went around with his mates, doing the things they did. They played, they kicked balls, they climbed trees, set up races and games, they slung ropes over branches to make swings, they laughed and teased, they got into mischief.

And, when Kofi was ten, it happened.

One hot day the boys decided to go for a swim.

They'd been swinging and climbing in the shade of the trees and several of them were already stripped to the waist. By late morning, the heat was so fierce the branches scorched their hands.

A boy shinned down from the trees and shouted. "To the river." Then, like ants, they followed to a place where the poor people washed their clothes. Here the grass absorbed some of the heat, and it didn't burn their feet so much.

They were shedding clothes as they ran, and they plunged into the water, screaming and laughing. Most were strong swimmers, and the riverbed was shallow, so even the weaker ones could duck and dive.

Kofi watched from the shelter of the trees because there was an unwritten understanding that Kofi, novice to the Imam, wouldn't strip naked like the rest.

But it was so hot, and they were having such fun. At last one of them shouted, "Come on, Kofi Musa. Come and swim."

Then they were all calling. "Kofi Musa. The water's lovely. It'll be all right, Kofi. There's no-one around." ... And the water did look tempting. Even in the shade of the trees, the heat was stifling.

One of the boys clambered back up the bank and ran towards him. "Come on," he said. "It's fun in there. You can come in. You'll love it." – and suddenly he'd slipped off his clothes and was standing by the river, naked and ready ... and there, hanging from his neck was the talisman.

The boys stopped.

In the excitement, Kofi had forgotten, but he was quick. Fending off the stares, he plunged into the water, hiding the disc from view.

"It's something I've got to wear," he said. "Something to show I'm the Imam's novice. It's a sort of pendant. All novices have them."

The boys could see it setting the murky water alight.

"What makes it burn like that?" they said.

"There's a tiny battery," said Kofi. "It's so I can see in the dark."

"Why haven't you shown us before? If I had one of those, I'd show everybody," said the boy on the bank. "It's amazing. Can I get one like it?"

"If you become the Imam's novice," Kofi said, and he swam

strongly, plunging and diving.

As they got dressed, they carried on interrogating him. Could they buy them at the market? Was there a factory where they could order one? But Kofi kept to his story. It was a pendant and they were made in India just for novices. Become a novice and the Imam would get one for them. He knew none of them would – not even for the chance to own a talisman and he thought, as he made his way back home, he'd defused the situation well. He thought he might go swimming again. He might even strip off when he was playing in the trees. After all, he was the Imam's only novice, so no one could disprove his story.

But Kofi hadn't defused anything.

When the boys got back to their homes they told their parents about the amazing pendant … and there were long memories in the village.

The disc of rainbow colours – they'd seen it, ten years earlier. It belonged to the whoring witch, Mariam, and she'd fled to the forest to have a baby. Five years later, after the riot of the apes, a mysterious child had appeared, the Imam's so-called novice.

The child had come with the apes, and he had Mariam's talisman,

It was Mariam's son, the son of a witch, bearing the witch's token. He was born out of witchcraft and he had the powers of a witch.

Villagers met in groups. Churches became the locations for meetings. Even the Muslims met.

Did the Imam know, or was he the victim of the boy's sorcery? The congregation at the mosque melted away. When Kofi approached, his friends ran off.

The Imam understood why. He had never told Kofi about his mother. But he had to tell him now, and Kofi listened, spellbound.

He had never known a human mother, but now … there was a woman who had carried him from a tiny seed and he'd grown inside her to a fully formed baby. In the loneliness of the forest she had brought him into the world. Now he understood about the name burnt onto the leather thong.

His mother had been a good woman, chosen by the great African leader Mandela. She had been brave, and he was filled with pride and love for her. He couldn't understand why the villagers hated her, or why they hated the talisman.

"The boys saw it, Baba," he said. "When we were swimming. I stripped, and they saw it. I've done wrong."

But the Imam laid a hand on his shoulder. "You did nothing wrong, my child. You weren't to know. And Kofi, it isn't your friends that you must blame. They weren't to know either. It's the older ones."

"I don't blame them either, Baba," Kofi said. "They don't understand, that's all."

It moved the Imam to hear him say that. The compassion of a prophet in a ten year old – and the people of the village were branding him a devil.

That night they made their move. There were torches flickering, lighting the path and the Imam knew they were heading for his house. Some were singing hymns and religious songs, trying to give a cloak of righteousness to their mendacity. Others shouted.

"Are they coming for me, Baba?" Kofi said.

"Don't be frightened my Kofi Musa. I'll speak to them," the Imam said. "They won't harm you."

He stepped out and challenged the approaching mob.

The boy had been with them for five years, he said. In all that time he had not brought any misfortune. He had mingled with them. They had loved him, and their children had loved him. He'd been a force for good.

But the more he reasoned, the more they shouted and barracked … and gradually their tune changed. Now they didn't just want him banished, they wanted his blood.

They charged the house, throwing stones and the Imam had to retreat, locking the doors and barring the windows.

"We've got to get away, Baba," Kofi said.

"If there was a way, my son, we would, but they've got the house surrounded."

But Kofi just said: "Come with me." And he led the Imam into the room opening onto the courtyard. Then he unrolled the prayer mat and laid it on the floor, sitting cross-legged and fingering the talisman. "Now, open the window, Baba, and sit here with me," he said.

The window overlooked the courtyard and the Imam opened it.

"You think we should pray, do you my son?" he said but Kofi didn't reply.

He just pointed to the mat and said, "Sit there, Baba." And, if the boy said 'sit', then that was what he must do.

He lowered himself onto the prayer mat, and sat, facing Kofi … while outside the mob raged, hurling stones and firebrands.

**

Chapter 6

The Rainbow in the Night

Even in the back room the noise was terrifying. The Imam knew it was only a matter of time before the doors would be broken down. There was shouting and jeering, and the incongruous sounds of hymns and chants. Then he heard a window shatter.

He was sitting on the prayer mat – and he was praying, raising his pleas aloud, defying the bedlam and he was doing it not just for his own protection; but for Kofi.

Kofi had sanctioned the prayer. He'd directed him to sit, and, since Kofi had taken him by the hand and had led him to this room, the boy had been in control. He was so calm and focused, the Imam felt impelled to do what he told him. Kofi was special, and, besides, at a time like this, what greater protection was there than the power of Allah. He was right. Prayer was the only way.

But it did nothing to diminish the anarchy outside.

He could hear the stones shattering the windows. And there were chants and shouts. And it was as if the missiles were less heavy now. There was something being thrown that sliced the air.

Then there was the smell of burning.

They'd set the house alight with firebrands and there was nothing he could do.

Prayer. More fervent prayer. It was the only answer.

He could hear the flames crackling in the next room and the exploding sparks as furniture took light, and a rancid smell crept under the door.

Then a faint wind from the open window touched his face … and he felt the strangest movement. It was as if the prayer mat was lifting. It still supported his weight, but it was lifting – unbelievably rising into the air.

Instinct made him grab the sides and he opened his eyes. And, what he saw wasn't the seated figure of a novice. It was a boy standing, stretched to his full height, his eyes blazing.

Kofi was holding the talisman, and it was alive, sending spectrum rays towards the window.

Then, from outside he heard the resounding clash of thunder – and there was rain – torrents of it, pummelling the roof, driven by winds through the broken windows. Flames hissed and spat as the rain quenched the fires, and, in the courtyard, he saw something that just couldn't be. Even though it was night, there was a rainbow, and, where the rainbow pulsated, the rays from the talisman melted into it.

Kofi stood, legs apart, eyes transfixed, and, with the power of the talisman blazing, the Imam felt the prayer mat move through the window and on into the night.

*

It wasn't long before the clouds cleared, but the rainbow stayed, suspended across the plain, while the prayer mat rode its outer edge.

The Imam crouched, gazing into Kofi's face. The boy's features were carved like a god's, and, below, the creatures of the plain were like ants. Trees stood in pools, shadows cast by the moon, and the prayer mat flew on, touching the top of the sky and drifting above the forest. Then it descended, but, as it did so, the Imam saw something that made his blood freeze.

The mat was taking them towards the settlement of the Nam-Nam tribe.

*

Across the forest there'd been a storm – clouds crazed with lightning – peals of thunder – and the men of the tribe stared. There was a rainbow – in the blackness of the night, stretching out across the sky towards the plains.

It frightened them, not only because it was unheard of to see a rainbow in the night sky, but because its base plunged directly to the foot of the great Baobab tree – the ceremonial centre of their community.

Women and children came creeping out of the caves and the

mineshafts where they lived, and they grouped, staying close to the entrances.

Then the storm passed and the sky was full of stars. There was a moon, but still the rainbow stayed. It was a harbinger – holding time suspended, and the tribe's people held their breath.

A small girl was first to see the speck, high on the rainbow's summit.

She could see a kind of carpet, riding the spectrum. Then they all saw it, and they could see figures – a holy man crouched in prayer – and a boy, standing, holding what looked like a pendant.

They could see power coming from the pendant – a rainbow of pulsing light.

No one said anything, but the warriors slipped back to their caves and re-emerged with spears and swords.

Then they watched the carpet level itself against the descending rays, dropping horizontally, the boy straddling, and the white-bearded old man prostrate.

As the mat touched the ground, the tribesmen raised their spears.

But there was a rustle in the hollow of the Baobab tree, and a witch doctor emerged, dressed in full ceremonial regalia – grass skirt – headdress of peacock's feathers, and a multi-layered necklace.

He stepped out and the cowry shells and beads around his neck clattered, and he looked first at the old man, then at the boy with the rainbow talisman.

The boy let the talisman to fall to his chest. He stepped off the mat and held out his hand, and immediately the rainbow faded.

The men raised their spears again, but the witch doctor stopped them. He led the boy away from the prayer mat and said something to the people.

He didn't speak in a language that Kofi or the Imam could understand. It was more an ancient dialect known only to the Nan-Nams, but Kofi directed the talisman towards him, and the words reverberated in English. "People," he said. "I want you to welcome our king. The king of the Nan-Nams has come amongst us."

The Imam looked startled; and Kofi could see the spears quivering all around him. He had to say something. He spoke through the talisman. "I am Kofi Musa," he said. "We have come in peace, my baba and I." And the Imam could hardly believe it. It was as if his child, his Kofi Musa, understood. It was as if he knew this would happen.

Somehow, something had changed in the boy since he'd led him into the back room of the house. From that moment it seemed he understood his destiny – the words of the witch doctor hadn't fazed him. He'd known where the rainbow path was leading. He'd known how to use the talisman. He'd known how to defuse the fear of the people. He'd known about this greeting from the tribe's wise man.

He'd come of age, and now there was no doubt. Kofi Musa was keeper of the talisman. He knew its power. He knew how it should be used – and he had the wisdom to use it. He'd become all that Gandhi and Mandela had said he would.

The witch doctor was addressing the crowd in the dialect again and the Imam couldn't understand it, but he had Kofi standing by him, and Kofi looked up, smiling and he lifted the talisman, aiming its surface towards the Imam's face, bouncing the reflected voice of the witch doctor in English.

"My people," the witch doctor said. "It has been known in our legends from times way back that one day the Nam-Nams would have a king.

"It was known that the king would come from heaven, born on the path of a rainbow. This story has been told you from man to child, from generation to generation, from before time began. And tonight, my people, it has happened. The king has come, with power in his shining disc, to lead the Nam-Nams.

"Tonight you have seen it. You, who your forefathers would have envied, have seen the arrival of the king, and the birth of the era of the Nam-Nams, and tonight, I Okomfo Kalabulay will crown him."

There was a palpable change in the mood as the witch doctor spoke. First the spears were lowered, then the swords were dropped. Slowly the people's suspicions were transformed. The murmurs turned to adulation, and one by one, they fell to their knees. And all the time, Kofi – the Imam's dear Kofi Musa – looked up at his baba, smiling, his dark eyes sparkling, and he was holding the talisman so he could hear and understand every word.

They were clearing the area around the Baobab tree now, and

bringing a chair from one of the huts scattered around the clearing. The chair was intricately carved. It was some kind of ceremonial throne.

Okomfo Kalabulay led Kofi towards it and waved at the villagers, and it was as if they'd practised it – as if they'd rehearsed. The men formed two parallel lines, one on either side of the chair, and they raised their spears to make an arch. Two boys went back to the hut. One returned with a palm wreath, and the other with an ornately decorated spear.

They carried them through the archway, and first Kalabulay took the wreath, placing it on Kofi's head, then he took the spear, and put it in his right hand.

After that he stepped back and bowed. And, all the people threw themselves to the floor, shouting, "Akwaaba, Akwaaba, Akwaaba!"

Kofi looked at the Imam. His eyes were alive with excitement. He took the old man's hand, pulling him towards the chair. Then he lifted the talisman, aiming it at his face ... and the Imam heard the words of the people in his own language.

"Hail, great leader. Hail Kofi Musa, king of the Nam-Nams. Hail, great King."

***

Chapter 7

King of the Nam-Nams

There was a lot to learn.

The Nam-Nams had always struck terror into the people living around the forest. No one had ever come near them, and they had no dealings with anyone beyond their own borders. Neither Kofi nor the Imam knew anything about them.

The talisman translated the words of the ceremony, and Kofi kept it trained, so the chants and rituals were clear.

Then, as the crowning came to an end, the warriors stepped back and Kalabulay took Kofi through the bridge of spears and out into the clearing.

The older people were still prostrating themselves, while the children stood back, watching, awestruck.

The Imam followed and they crossed towards the cliffs and caves. They were heading to one cave in particular. It had a wider entrance than the rest. There were palm trees growing around it. It was almost like a cultivated grove.

"This will be your home, Kofi Musa," the witch doctor said. "It is the most sacred of our caves. It is the doorway to the treasure, and you will be the treasure's protector."

Kofi nodded.

He didn't understand, but he knew asking questions would suggest he was ignorant. He would have to learn through subterfuge and deduction.

"I will see my home, wise one," he said. "I will examine it, to see it meets the needs of my baba and me. Then we will rest. Tell my people to return to their caves and sleep. Tomorrow I will see the treasure."

Kalabulay nodded. He was carrying a lighted torch, but it wasn't needed. The talisman gave off enough light and, as Kofi and the Imam looked inside the cave, they gasped.

The floor had been strewn with animal skins, and, on a ledge carved in the wall, there was a leopard skin draped over what seemed to be a royal bed. At one end a fleece had been stuffed to make a bolster, and, at the head of the bed, there were two ceremonial spears, bound so they crossed at the tip.

All around the cave walls were torches, with tallow wicks, and, in their light, and in the light of the talisman, Kofi could see seams of gold, and white flashes of diamonds. There were hints of emeralds and rubies. He'd never seen anything like it.

Around the top of the cave, mounted on the walls were the heads of wild animals. It was like a king's palace.

"Is this the treasure you said about?" he said, nodding towards the jewel-encrusted walls.

"It is just a hint, great leader," Kalabulay said. "The main treasure is buried deep in the hill. This cave is merely its entrance. Tomorrow, when you have slept, we will go into the caverns, and you will understand what real treasure is."

*

It was barely dawn next morning when the witch doctor arrived.

He had two tribesmen with him and all three were dressed in ceremonial costume. Kalabulay had his beads and grass skirt, and his headdress. The others had grass skirts and their bodies and faces were painted. They were carrying heavily carved spears. Kalabulay explained they were the official keepers of the treasure. No one went into the caves unless the keepers of the treasure went with them.

He insisted Kofi wear his regalia of office, his palm woven crown and the decorated spear. Any visit to the vaults was a ceremonial occasion.

There were three boys too, slightly older than Kofi. They had tallow candles slung around their necks.

But Kalabulay frowned when he saw the Imam.

"He can't go, boy king. Only Nam-Nams. It is death for an interloper to visit the treasure houses."

"But he's my baba," Kofi said. "He's my teacher. I don't go anywhere without him."

The witch doctor and the keepers of the treasure glanced at the

Imam and then they went into conclave, and it was some time before Kalabulay broke free. But the barriers were up now. His arms were folded and his face was grim.

"Very well, Kofi King," he said. "If it is your command. But, if this man goes in, he must swear the oath, and should he breathe a word of what he sees, then the Nam-Nams will take out his eyes and cut off his head, and we will use his scull as a drinking jug."

The Imam obliged by swearing the oath, and they were able to set off, but the flickering candles hardly touched the edges of the cave. It was only when Kofi lifted the talisman that they really saw. The talisman's light became so bright, Kalabulay and the two guards had to shield their eyes. The boys made a dash for the entrance, but Kofi and the Imam held them back.

"It's all right," Kofi said. "You can put your candles out. The talisman will show the way, and it won't hurt you."

"Just cover your eyes until you get accustomed," said the Imam.

They wound their way, following the uneven floor as the cave doubled back. Untapped seams of ore crazed the walls, reflecting in the talisman's light.

They could make out shafts where miners had excavated. Gold, and among the scars made by the pick-axes and dynamite, diamonds and emeralds, rubies – raw, protruding, uncut, gleaming with a thousand facets.

It took more than an hour to delve into the mountain, and, as they went deeper, the air became more stale. But then there was a refreshing restlessness, a freshening wind, and suddenly the walls parted.

Their footsteps began to reverberate, and, as they pressed forward, Kofi gasped, because they had come to a cavern, and it expanded in all directions like the vaults of a cathedral.

And never had any of them, not even Okomfo Kalabulay, seen the place as they saw it now, because the talisman searched every corner.

Seams of untapped gold meshed the walls, and made patterns like gothic filigrees, and there were precious stones, green, red and white, cascading from the roof, gleaming like threads of living fire.

From roof to floor, stalactites and stalagmites stretched and they were impregnated with precious stones. The diamonds sparkled like galaxies of stars.

There were lakes of water between the pillars, burnished with a golden fire, and, on islands between the lakes, piles of uncut stones where the miners had hoarded treasure.

There were no words.

It was as if they were in a holy place, and for a full half hour no one spoke.

Finally, Kalabulay said, "This, King Kofi, is the treasure of the mountain. This is what the Nam-Nams guard. No one knows of this place and no one will know of it. It is the secret of the Nam-Nams."

But Kofi looked at the Imam, puzzled.

Secret? Not known by anyone?

The caves were littered with shafts. Uncut piles of precious stones had been hoarded. They'd been mined and he didn't believe the Nam-Nams had done it.

"But, how is it a secret, wise doctor?" he said. "Who dug the treasure and cut the shafts?"

"White men," Kalabulay said briefly. "Miners from beyond the forest."

"Well, how is it a secret known only to the Nam-Nams?"

Kalabulay's smile bared his blackened gums and the monoliths of rotting teeth. "The Nam-Nams," he said, "know how to silence white men."

*

There were more uncomfortable truths to come.

The reputation of the Nam-Nams had suggested some of them. The discovery of the gold and the precious stones – and the tribe's self-appointed guardianship of the treasure – no one could have anticipated that, but there were things that Kofi found troubling.

He was with Kalabulay one day.

Kalabulay had taken it on himself to initiate him, and they'd been talking, walking across towards the Baobab tree.

Kalabulay lived in the tree. It was completely hollow, and, inside, it was dark. It took some time for Kofi's eyes to adjust.

When they did, he saw a rug of animal skins in the corner where the witch doctor slept, and, hanging from the walls, various implements of his office – the headdress, grass skirts, brushes of animal hair for putting on ceremonial paint – other implements forged into shapes that meant nothing to Kofi.

There wasn't much, but at the back of the tree he could make out a loosely accumulated pile of shapes. At first he thought they were twigs and branches for some fire-lighting ceremony, and he was curious. The fragments were bleached and they had a brittle appearance. ... Then he stopped, because he could see what they were – bones – limbs and vertebrae ... and skulls ... and the skulls weren't animal skulls.

He turned and he could see Okomfo Kalabulay watching him.

"White men's bones, Kofi king'" he said. "– Men from other tribes, and old ones bones – bones of those who have passed to the other place."

"You killed these men in battle?" Kofi said, but the old man shook his head.

"That is not the way of the Nam-Nams King-prince. The white men and those from other tribes, we eat. They make good food, full of nourishment, like suckling pigs."

There'd been rumours, but Kofi hadn't wanted to believe them.

"And the old ones?" he said "You keep their bones in this pile too?"

Kalabulay came closer and he could smell the putrefaction on his body.

"One day I will be there," he said. "On that pile – and you will be the one to put me there."

Kofi stared. "But, wise leader – these bones are all picked bare ... when you die ..."

"When I die, they will eat the roasted flesh from my body, so my flesh will be one with the young again, so that I will be perpetuated. It is the custom Kofi king. None of the Nam-Nam tribe dies. Our mothers and fathers live in us."

Kofi felt an overpowering urge to vomit. "I have to go," he said suddenly and he staggered to the entrance, his stomach retching and his lungs screaming to be out in the fresh air.

Eating other humans – and eating their own parents and

grandparents … it was like him eating his baba.

That night he had terrible dreams and he woke late.

He still felt sick, and, staggering to the mouth of the cave, it was as if he hadn't woken at all, because, over by the Baobab tree, Kalabulay had lit a fire and there were supports of wood holding a spit over it – and he could see, roasting, slowly turning, burnt red on its flesh and dripping with fat, something that didn't have the shape of an animal.

His stomach lurched. He couldn't help it. They were roasting a human – and it wasn't just an ordinary human. They were roasting a child.

He tore across the clearing, pushing Kalabulay away and screaming with outrage. With one sweep he knocked the fat-dripping carcass to the ground, and all around, men, women and children came from their caves to see what was happening. At first they stared, hardly believing what they saw.

Kofi was shouting at Okomfo Kalabulay, holding the talisman so the words came clear to the old man and he was shouting, "It has to stop. That is a child. It's hardly started its life and you are roasting it for food. No. No, old man. No!"

Kalabulay's head turned slightly, and there was a bewildered anger on his face. "This is no child, great leader. It is fully-grown. No ape child would be that big."

The watching villagers started laughing, and the children rushed to the Baobab tree, baring their teeth, snapping their jaws and nipping at the half roasted flesh. They took bites at the fleshy buttocks, chuckling with delight. Kalabulay pushed them away and picked the carcass up, returning it to the fire, and slowly he turned the spit again, with a look of triumph and Kofi was confused

An ape was not a human.

There could be no case for stopping them killing and roasting apes, but, in Kofi's heart, he knew … that tradition had to stop as well. It was a mess. The whole thing was a mess.

He fetched his prayer mat and sat cross-legged by his baba at the mouth of the cave. "What am I going to do?" he said.

"Tell me, Kofi, what have you found?" the Imam said

Kofi pulled a piece of grass from beside him, and ran it between his fingers. "They eat their own," he said.

"You mean they eat humans," said the Imam.

"They eat their own," Kofi said again. "Not just other humans. Not just white men and people of other tribes. They eat the flesh of their dying relatives."

"I have heard of this, Kofi," the Imam said. "To perpetuate the flesh of the old in the young. It's their way of defying death."

"But it mustn't be, Baba. It can't happen. I'm king of the Nam-Nams. I can't be a king to a people that do that kind of thing. I hate it. It's like ... I ate you!"

"Why do you hate it, my little prophet?" said the Imam.

Kofi started. He'd expected support from his baba, and the question unnerved him. "Because ..." he said. There were thousands of thoughts in his head – doubts and revulsions, and it was almost wrong to say 'in his head'. They were everywhere, in his head, in his heart, in his stomach. His instinct screamed that this was wrong.

"Because ..." he said again.

"Because ..." the Imam said.

"Because men are special," said Kofi. "Because they talk. Because they think, because they dream, Baba. They try to understand the stars and planets. They tend the trees and animals. They sing songs. They make poetry ... they love and they cry."

The Imam grabbed hold of Kofi's hand and looked into his eyes, and Kofi didn't think he'd ever seen such love. "Tell the people that, my little Kofi. Tell them what you've told me," he said.

"But what about the apes? The witch doctor is roasting an ape."

"And that's wrong too?"

"They are my mama, my suckling mother, my brothers, and my sisters. They are my aunts and my uncles. They are my cousins, Baba. For the first five years of my life ..."

"We will refuse to eat the flesh of the ape," the Imam said.

"But they will ask us why."

The Imam looked at him. "Kofi Musa, tell me?" he said. "Who is leader of the Nam-Nams? Who has the talisman? Who came to the foot of the Baobab tree on a rainbow?"

"Me, Baba," Kofi said.

"Then you do not need to give them reasons. One day you can

take them to your troop. Show them your brothers and your sisters. Then they will understand."

"You will stay with me, won't you?" Kofi said. He held the Imam's hand more tightly. "You won't leave me will you?"

But the Imam looked troubled. "I have my flock, Kofi Musa."

"But these people. How can I lead them without you?"

"There are many things you are destined to do without me, my son," the Imam said. "And the boy who can tell his tribe what makes a man a man – the boy who can tell his tribe about stars and poetry and love, that boy can lead the Nam-Nams far better than this old Imam."

Kofi couldn't speak. There was something in him that defied words. It pumped tears into his eyes and made his throat ache. "I love you, Baba," he whispered.

"I know, my Kofi Musa."

They watched the children playing, and around the edges of the forest the women were at work with berries and fruit. Men stood in knots looking across the arid lumps of earth towards the hills, watching the plume of smoke from Kalabulay's fire twisting across the trunk of the Baobab tree.

"We will teach them husbandry, my son," the Imam said. "We will teach them to graze cattle and raise deer and wildebeests. We will teach them to rear animals for food and milk, to keep chickens and eat eggs – to grow crops, maize, wheat and barley, to cultivate fruit."

Kofi nodded, and he watched Okomfo Kalabulay turn his spit.

"You won't go until we've taught them all that. Until they know not to eat their own," Kofi said.

"I won't go, Kofi Musa, not while you need me."

Suddenly Kofi felt easier. "We won't have to eat the ape, Baba," he said. There was a gleam in his eye.

"No?" the Imam said.

"No," said Kofi. "No one will have to eat the ape."

He lifted the talisman and aimed it at the base of Kalabulay's spit. There was a startled cry, and a gurgling as muddy water oozed from the stones around the fire. It welled to a fountain, dousing the flames and sending geysers of steam into the air.

The gasses sizzled to silence and the startled Kalabulay stared at his ruined feast.

Then Kofi felt something shake beside him, and he looked up. The Imam was laughing.

*

But how did you obliterate generations of culture and tradition?

"You must talk to them, Kofi," the Imam said. "You are their king. Tell them what you told me."

Kofi wasn't sure. He'd never spoken in public, but he knew the talisman would help. If his voice faltered, the talisman would cloak the anxiety.

When he called the people to the Baobab tree though, it was easier than he expected. There was an excitement, and when he raised his hands, every eye was on him. Only Okomfo Kalabulay hovered in darkness.

He breathed deeply and began. "You have been expecting me for a long time," he said. "For years your wise men have foreseen my coming, and now I am here."

Even the children playing on the periphery were silent. "And, because I have come, things must change. If you are to become a great people – if you are to become the people of Kofi Musa, then you must learn new skills, develop new ambitions. You must have a new wisdom. My baba and I are here to teach you. We will show you how to become great.

"But first you must break with some of your customs, because, Nam-Nam people, they are bad."

He stopped, and looked at the upturned faces, and he sensed a tremor of resentment in some of the men.

Okomfo Kalabulay shook his head and spat.

"There are things that displease me," he said, and in the people's eyes he could see they didn't understand.

For the most part they were ready to go with him, but not Okomfo Kalabulay. Straight away he shouted, "What things?" and there was anger in his voice. "Tell us which of our cherished traditions are not to your liking, master."

"To start with, you must stop eating people," Kofi said. He said it simply, because he wanted no doubts. "People are not food. People are special. You cannot eat them."

Kalabulay snorted, but Kofi pressed on. "Let me explain why," he said. "People are different from animals. They laugh, they cry. They dream dreams, they plan and invent, they create … they write … music and poetry. They make beautiful things. They feel pain and sorrow. They love and they care. They have souls that lift them above simpler creatures. They must be valued and respected. They must not be eaten."

"What about our loved ones?" Kalabulay shouted. "What about the perpetuation of the old and dying. What about their assimilation into the young? Do you want us to abandon that as well?"

Kofi wasn't scared. He had the talisman. He had a power that was greater than anything Kalabulay could throw at him. "That tradition must stop too," he said.

"So the flesh of the old becomes nothing more than the flesh of an animal," Kalabulay said. "– Left to rot in the ground like the flesh of common rats. Is that what you want? Is that what you mean by humans being special?" But Kofi did not flinch.

"They *will* be assimilated, Okomfo Kalabulay," he said. "And in a far better way. Bury them with dignity. Mark their burial ground with signs of respect. Then learn to cultivate plants, wheat, barley, maize – cultivate the fruits you gather from trees and bushes in the forest."

For a moment his eyes strayed and he saw his Imam. And there was such a look of approval on his face that it spurred him on.

"Plant these things on the precious graves of your dead, and the beautiful cycle of nature will begin. The bodies of your loved ones, even the bits you cannot consume, will be assimilated into the maize, and into the wheat and the barley. The crops will grow strong, and when you gather and eat them, you will be taking in the flesh of your old ones, and their bodies will be perpetuated. You do not need to gnaw at their bones; you do not need to put your loved ones through fire. Just let them rest in peace. Nature will bring them back to you.

"You must not eat human flesh," he said again. "Let the Imam and me teach you ways that run with nature, not against it, and then you will be great."

There was an expression on people's faces now that sent a shiver through him. Many of the women were crying, and he could see they adored him. Some of the men needed more time, but none were hostile, except Okomfo Kalabulay.

Kofi knew though, if he'd got the people, Kalabulay was powerless.

The Imam tried talking to Kalabulay. He explained to him that some traditions must die with the times, no matter how painful it was. He explained how even he had to release his grip on some things in order to let people progress. He challenged him. He said it was his own cherished tradition that foretold Kofi's coming. It was his own ceremony that made him king. It was he who blessed and crowned him. He couldn't be seen to go back on his own declaration. He couldn't turn against the ancient tale of a saviour coming on a rainbow just because the saviour's message was not to his liking.

Kalabulay couldn't accept it, but he couldn't fault the Imam's argument, and he retreated from open hostility.

Kofi knew, though, there was resentment, and he had a nagging thought that, one day, Kalabulay would bite back.

In the meantime he and the Imam taught the people. They showed them how to catch deer and wildebeest. They took them, with a few treasures taken form the periphery of the caves, to barter at a town on the edge of the forest. It was not the Imam's town. Kofi was uneasy about going there, but, at another town, they traded for chicken, for guinea fowl, for ducks and goats. The people learned how to use eggs in their cooking, and milk from the goats. Some eggs were allowed to gestate so that baby chicks hatched, and that delighted the people. Later the pregnant goats gave birth and they saw their flocks increase, and, whereas, before they had pilfered fruit from the forest, now they took the healthiest trees and planted them around the village. They mulched and nurtured them, so the fruits were richer and more plentiful, and slowly the chance existence of the hunter-gatherer gave way to the certain plenty of the farmer and Kofi and the Imam watched, as the people grew strong and content.

*

"I couldn't have done it without you though, Baba," Kofi said. They were watching men dig around newly planted melon trees. "You're the wisdom in my head. You're the strength behind my judgements, and I wouldn't be anything without you."

The Imam knew it was not going to be easy.

"My little Kofi Musa," he said. "You are the dearest novice, but you have already learned more than I can teach you. None of this is my doing. I have been a crutch for you to lean on, but ... you sometimes leaned when you didn't need to. You know what to do. It is you who has the authority. It is you who has the power, and it is you who has the wisdom. You're the person the people listen to. It is you they learn from. You are their leader, not me – and, Kofi ..." He took Kofi's hand and his heart was aching. "My boy," he said. "My dearest son – the only one ..."

Kofi looked up, wide-eyed. "Baba?" he said.

"I have to go back, my son. My people need me."

"But Baba, the people of the village – they hate you, like they hate me."

"The people want me, my boy. They need me. I saw their faces when we rode the rainbow that night. There was awe, there was fear ... but there was respect, Kofi Musa, respect for me and respect for you. They will welcome me, and, for your peace of mind, in two weeks, when I have settled, you must send a party of Nam-Nams to my house, and I will give them seed. Then, my son, you can show them how to grow crops, and how to make flour, and bake bread. The talisman is *your* mission, Kofi, not mine. I know about the mission and there will be a friend to work with you – but it's not me. Your friend will be young and soon you will meet him, but, in the mean time, the Nam-Nams are your challenge. You have everything you need to lead them – wisdom, respect, the power of the talisman. You will do well, my son."

They both knew it was right, and at last the Imam set out, waved off and cheered by the villagers.

He only turned once and Kofi steeled himself, taking in every line and crease on the old man's face, consigning every gesture to memory, burning images of him into his brain, the eyes, the grizzled beard, the gentle smile. And he did what he had to do, for his baba's sake, leading the people, guiding them into ways of conservation and husbandry. And after two weeks he sent a party to the village, and they came back laden with seeds. Then he knew his Imam was safe and he set to work teaching the villagers to cultivate the ground, watching their excitement as the long rows of shoots began to appear.

The river was too polluted for them to catch fish, but the sea was nearby. He took them to the coast and showed them how to cut down tree trunks to make dug-out boats. He taught them about fishing, and he showed them how to spit-roast their catches.

But there was still Okomfo Kalabulay.

He did not like what was happening, and he was beginning to build up a following – a small group of elders who saw this domestication as a betrayal of the people's strength. They didn't rebel openly, but, occasionally Kofi would see, on the spit by the Baobab tree, the carcass of an ape with the men standing by, cutting off slices, eating, with a recalcitrance that defied Kofi to challenge them.

It was difficult. After all, apes weren't human. To the Nam-Nams they were just creatures of the forest.

He wasn't sure what to do; but one day, when the men were with Kalabulay by the Baobab tree, he decided.

"I want you to come with me," he said. "I want you to come, because I want you to understand. You are right. Apes are not humans. They are just like goats and wildebeests ... but ... I want to show you something. I want you to see why it hurts me to see you roasting apes on your spits.

*

He wasn't sure he could find the place after such a long time. He wasn't even sure his troop would be there, but they made their way through the forest, following the river's course, until he could see familiar landmarks, and he knew where he was. Things had changed. Many of the trees were blighted, and scrubland and choking weeds had strangled the natural growth. Old fruit trees had withered, but the hill was still there, and the clearing, and, as he drew nearer, he could hear chattering.

The apes were startled to begin with. They stared at the boy with his dark skin and white eyes. But then a wizened female let out a cry and staggered towards him, forelimbs outstretched, and her leather face was transformed with an expression of such love that even Kalabulay gasped.

The female flung her arms around Kofi and there were tears seeping from her brown eyes. Her mouth twisted and, with her hand, she began grooming his hair, whimpering, frantic with love.

There were others then, mature apes that had been cubs when Kofi was with them. They rushed forward, wanting to touch him, chattering, clapping their hands, and Kofi chattered back, conversing with them, understanding their language. They brought berries and yams from their depleted store, and he turned to Kalabulay and said, "This troop of apes saved me from drowning in the river and they brought me up." He patted the head of the aged creature nestling into him. "This was my suckling mother for the first five years of my life."

When the troop saw him speak to the men, they ran to their store again, to fetch more yams, offering them to Kalabulay and those who were with him and, for the first time, the men looked uncomfortable.

They took the fruit, but they'd been shamed.

Through the day Kofi learned of the apes' survival, and their hardships as the forest became more polluted.

He told them about his new tribe. He told them there would be food set aside for them from the Nam-Nams' harvest. He told them where to find him and when they left, none of the men spoke, except Okomfo Kalabulay.

"So, Kofi king," he said. "This is why you don't like us eating apes."

"They reared me," Kofi said. "If it was not for the apes I would have died."

The men nodded; but there was still something about Kalabulay. He understood, certainly, but his thoughts were running ahead. "You were reared in the forest?" he said. "You did not have your beginnings in the heavens. When you came to us on the rainbow ..."

"Kalabulay," Kofi said. "Do you remember where you had your beginnings?" He knew where the old man was leading, and

Kalabulay was dangerous.

"I know what I was told – by my mother – and by others in the village."

"Well I know nothing of where I came from," Kofi said. "Where I began is a mystery known only by the Imam, by the great Mr Mandela and by the ancient leader of India, the leader Gandhi. Do you know these people, Okomfo Kalabulay?"

The witch doctor scowled. But there were no more roasted apes and Kalabulay knew there was no point in challenging Kofi for the moment.

He decided he would bide his time and, for a year the people developed their skills. They watched the cereals grow, they harvested the seeds – some for new planting, some for flour and bread. They reared chickens and ducks. They tended their guinea fowl and they grazed the goats and cattle, using the milk, selecting and killing beef, and they grew fat and healthy.

They still lived in the caves, but they learned to make wool from goats' hair, and began to trade and barter with the surrounding villages.

And all the time Kofi Musa kept in touch with his baba. When the people traded with the Imam's village, he sent him letters, and the Imam sent letters back.

The witch doctor's traditions became a thing of the past. Only Kalabulay remembered them.

He still lived in the Baobab tree, and he still performed his ceremonies, but now they had no meaning. The ceremonies were empty. It was essential that the people tasted human flesh. Without that great tradition they had become soft.

Kofi knew what Kalabulay thought – but he saw no prospect of him ever gaining control of the people's minds, and it was because of this that he allowed his guard to drop, so, when Okomfo Kalabulay saw his chance, and when Okomfo Kalabulay struck, Kofi was asleep.

*

It had been a hot day.

The hum of the afternoon was soporific. It was too much for Kofi. He was curled up in his cave, on his prayer mat and it wasn't long before he'd drifted into a hazy doze – then into the deep sleep of a baking afternoon.

And it was from the depths of this sleep that he became conscious of the disturbance.

From the bowels of his subconscious he could hear an urgent cry, and there was shouting. Sounds swirled around him, and then the tramp of military step – and the rhythmic chant of some unfamiliar ritual.

He could hear cries and jeers and he knew something was wrong.

Still drunk with sleep he staggered to the entrance of the cave, and then he stared in disbelief, because…

Marching around the Baobab tree in feathers and grass skirts, painted with the paint of war, and wielding their spears, were the warriors of the tribe.

Women stood on the periphery, watching, and children were dashing around, baring teeth and gnashing, their eyes wide with excitement and Okomfo Kalabulay, in his full ceremonial dress, was in the throes of a ritual that rooted Kofi to the ground.

There was a pyre.

There was a spit.

And bound to the spit was a white boy, about Kofi's age, blonde haired, curls hanging from his forehead, his arms struggling, his mouth gagged, and his blue eyes wide with terror.

With chants and rituals, Kalabulay was crouching, his ceremonial glass directing the rays of the sun, focusing them onto the pyre, spawning flames.

And Kofi grabbed at the cave wall. He couldn't breathe, and he couldn't move. They were spit roasting a white boy.

***

Chapter 8

The NASA Suit.

It was early spring in Washington.

Jesse Tierfelder was carrying a box onto the lawn.

It was an unusually hot day, and he was stripped to a tee shirt and pants, with his Yankees baseball hat to shade his head.

The box had the word NASA inscribed on its sides, and stamped across the lid in red type were the words: *Top Secret. For Jesse Tierfelder by authority, Everett Tierfelder and The President of the United States of America.* It was a present from his dad. Dad had arranged for NASA to make it, and it was just about the most amazing thing ever.

Jesse put the box on the grass and removed a suit. It seemed to be made from a metallic membrane, and it looked like a space suit – only smaller – a space suit designed for a twelve-year-old.

He laid it out and began examining it, checking the gadgets, the inter-active Internet link, the meteorologist assessment unit and the PH testers. He checked the back to see the propulsion units were okay, and the helmet for the webcam.

In the hazy distance he could hear the monotonous growl of the Washington traffic. A solitary plane droned across the sky and instinctively he covered what he was doing.

You couldn't trust people. He knew that.

There were people out there spying on his dad. Industrialists, jealous of the huge developments he was making in computer science, and envious of his company's success. His dad had worked with NASA in all the computer technology for the space industry. That's why NASA had developed the suit. It was a prototype, and it was revolutionary.

Planes flying over, people engaging him in innocent chat, telephone calls, texts and emails, spy-ware on his computer, there was nowhere that was safe,

The drone faded and he resumed his preparations.

But he'd got stuff on his mind, and it was playing around his head. He couldn't give the suit the enthusiasm it deserved.

His mum's cancer was getting worse.

For the last few months she'd been in remission – but yesterday, when she went for her scan, there were worrying signs. It would mean more chemotherapy.

It was hard for him. He wanted to resist the knowledge that there might not be a cure for his mum – that soon she wouldn't be there anymore – but it was always at the back of his mind. And it was not just that he might be without a mum in a few months. For him she was a guru. She was a powerful force in the world, fighting against pollution and corruption and, more than anything, he wanted to be like her.

That was one of the reasons why he had the suit. He wanted to go to Africa.

Africa was the country she was targeting. It was being devastated by pollution and Mum was at the forefront of the battle to put things right.

If she wasn't able to do it herself, then he wanted to take over. It was in his mind that a trip to Africa – just two weeks – with his NASA suit to collect data – would give him background knowledge, so he could talk to Mum properly about it.

He lay on the grass, stretching out beside the suit and pulling his hat down over his eyes.

But if the motivation for this trip to Africa was just philanthropic, it wouldn't really have been that important. There was something else – and that 'something' was much more personal – much more disturbing, because it wasn't founded on logic and logic was the mainstay of Jesse's life.

He'd had dreams about Africa, and there was a native boy – some kind of prince – someone his own age – and Jesse was convinced it was his destiny to find this boy. He believed, if he went on a trip to Africa, he would find him.

Night after night he had the dream.

He was in a forest with a tribe of cave dwellers, and the prince was there, sometimes by the mouth of a cave, sometimes by a broad trunked Baobab tree, smiling, and it was as if Jesse already knew him, as if he was his friend.

In the dreams he saw a disc hanging around the boy's neck, radiating all the colours of the rainbow. His head told him the disc could unleash miraculous powers – powers of purging and purifying – and his heart told him the disc had a power that would cure his mum, if only he could get to it in time.

It was irrational – he knew that. It was so irrational it was off the scale ... but he believed it.

He hadn't told his parents. He didn't know how he could.

He stared as a small cloud blotted the sun, sweeping a shadow across the lawn.

It was such a big thing.

He knew his dad had faith in him. Even though he was only twelve, dad involved him in all the projects and developments in his company. Jesse understood computers as well as his father, and there was no invention or research project where he wasn't consulted. He went with dad to conventions and conferences. He even addressed conventions, but ... to go to Africa on his own. ... His dad's enemies were always watching. Even if he went somewhere in the States, he had to have a minder. There had been a couple of kidnap attempts already ... and ... Africa?

He pulled himself up, brushing grass from his tee shirt, and he gave a rueful grin.

Dropping his hat to the grass, he slipped off his trainers and clambered into the suit. If he was going to Africa he needed to be proficient in every manoeuvre. He'd designed the suit himself. He didn't know Dad was going to get it made. When he'd shown Dad his plans all Dad had said was: "Good idea, son. But it would need the likes of NASA to produce something like this." He hadn't said anything more, and then – there it was – in its NASA box, and with the say so of the president himself.

He touched a button to activate the magnetic zip, and he felt the soft material closing to the nape of his neck.

It was his first flight, and his immediate instinct as he rose from the ground was to grasp out for support, but it was mind over matter. Adjusting the stabiliser he let himself fly higher, and he watched the grounds and the house drop away. The whole estate was spread out like a reality map, acres of lawn, mosaics of flowerbeds and water features, paths webbing to the ground's extremities, the long, meandering drive, and the glinting glass houses where the gardeners worked. The sky stretched to a tantalising haze. He could see the White House and its grounds, and the traffic crawling on the freeways.

Down by the glasshouses was a solitary figure, working on some rhododendrons, and he focused the camera. It was Mr Anansi, the head gardener, a man from Sikaman country. He always insisted on being called 'Mr'. Even Mum and Dad called him Mr Anansi, but he was a great guy. Jesse believed all the wisdom of Africa was inside that man, and he was Jesse's main confidant.

He zoomed in with the camera and the detail was amazing. From up here he could see the silver threads in the old man's sideburns, and he could make out rivets on his glasses. He played back what he'd filmed. What he'd be able to get in the African forests would be unbelievable. He'd be able to chart the pollution, he'd have records that he and Mum could mull over. He'd be able to plan out strategies. It was just what he wanted.

He focused onto a flower in the bushes where Mr Anansi was working. He could even see a honeybee crawling among the stamens.

Then he drifted across the grounds and began his descent.

The first thing Mr Anansi was aware of was a dark shadow crossing the shrubs. Then Jesse spoke and the gardener sprang around, staggering back. The voice had been processed through a microphone system. It sounded metallic, and all Mr Anansi could see was this silver humanoid with a goldfish bowl of a helmet, and that wasn't the type of thing you'd expect on a warm spring day in Washington DC.

Jesse laughed and took the helmet off while Mr Anansi wiped his forehead with a rag of a handkerchief.

"You scared the life out of me, boy," he said. "I thought it was the Angel of Death coming for me."

Jesse put an arm around the old man's waist. "Don't worry, Mr Anansi. The Angel of Death won't be coming for you yet. Not for a very long time."

The gardener withdrew so he could see the suit properly. "I don't know Mr Jesse. A couple more scares like that … what is it, anyway, that thing you're wearing?"

"It's my NASA suit," Jesse said. "Dad got it made up for me. I did the designs for it myself." He began to show Mr Anansi the gadgets. "See this. It's video footage I took when I was flying."

Mr Anansi stared at the replay and then looked skyward.

"You've been up there?" he said.

Jesse nodded, "Yep. I took pictures of you, look?"

"You got in mighty close, boy," Mr Anansi said. "My grey hairs. You could have taken something about me that was a bit prettier."

"But look at the detail, Mr Anansi, from way up, hundreds of feet. See that honeybee in the rhododendrons?"

Mr Anansi shook his head. "That's amazing Mr Jesse. But what you going to do with it? All this equipment just to fly round your garden taking pictures of bees in flowers and photos making a handsome man look like nothing but a decaying wreck."

Jesse ambled towards the glasshouse. "Come over here, Mr Anansi," he said. "I want to talk to you. And you don't look anything like a decaying wreck."

"You got things on your mind, then boy?" Mr Anansi said.

Jesse nodded. "Yeah, big things."

There was a wooden bench by one of the glasshouses. Behind it pot plants fanned out, and the humidity misted the glass. "You shouldn't be thinking big things – not a boy your age," Mr Anansi said. "Your dad – he let you grow old too soon. Boys your age should be thinking baseball – home runs, that kind of thing."

"I don't want to do that stuff, Mr Anansi, I want to do stuff like Mum and Dad," Jesse said. "I want to take this suit to Africa – take pictures – get information about the pollution out there, so, if Mum goes, I can carry on her work"

"That's a very good thought, boy," said Mr Anansi. "But you're dad isn't going to let you go off to Africa, not on your own. You're just a kid – twelve years old."

Behind his glasses, Jesse's eyes flicked. "That's got nothing to do with it, Mr Anansi. Dad lets me do grown up stuff. You said so yourself, so, why would he stop me going to Africa?"

"That's a country full of dangers, boy, believe me."

Jesse sniffed. "Wild animals can't harm me – not when I've got this on. I can get away from any animal."

"It isn't just animals," Mr Anansi said. "You got to understand that. It's uncharted forests, countries with cultures that don't work your way. It isn't cars and freeways out there, boy. And, in some of these places, there are leaders, and they don't care. A boy on his own, son of the richest man in America – there's a pretty packet for a kidnapping, and they won't think twice about killing you if they don't get their money, you know that, don't you?"

Jesse frowned. He did know that, but he couldn't let stuff like that get in his way.

He paused, looking out across the lawns and then he said, "Mr Anansi. Do you believe in dreams?"

Mr Anansi grinned. "You asking an African if he believes in dreams, boy? That's like asking a Chinaman if he eats rice."

"Well, I've had dreams, and – I know it won't make sense to Mum and Dad – but it's because of the dreams I've got to go." He told the old man, about the boy prince and the disc, and about his belief that, if he could find the boy, he could release powers from the disc that would cure his mum.

Mr Anansi nodded. "You try herbs to cure that snake that's eating your mom, Mr Jesse – remedies from back home? I got them in plenty. I could grow the stuff here. I've told your dad about it often enough."

"Herbs might work, Mr Anansi, but then again, they might not. If I could get this disc ... I know that'll work."

"It won't be easy. Asking your mom and dad when she's like she is. It's going to hurt. It's going to hurt you, and it's going to hurt them," Mr Anansi said.

"I know that, Mr Anansi. It's hurting now – but I've got to go. You understand don't you?"

"Where did you say you saw this prince?" Mr Anansi said, and Jesse described it, the hills, the honeycomb of caves, the scrubland and forest, the Baobab tree – and Mr Anansi nodded. There was a far-away expression on his face.

"That sounds like the Gemstone Mountains in Sikaman country, boy," he said. "You seen pictures of that place somewhere?"

Jesse shook his head. "No, Mr Anansi. Only in the dreams." He looked up at the old man. "You believe me, don't you?"

"I've seen that place once," Mr Anansi said. "The Nam-Nam tribe, they guard the caves. People say they're cannibals."

Jesse gulped. "Are you saying this African prince with the disc could be a cannibal?" he said. He hadn't thought. In his head he'd pictured a guy very much like himself – an all-American African prince. Hearing Mr Anansi say that made him do a sharp re-take.

"If he's a Nam-Nam prince, more than likely," Mr Anansi said. "You see now why I said it's dangerous. Why you're dad won't let you go."

But Jesse had dreamt of a place that really existed. It gave his dreams an irrefutable authenticity. This boy and his disc were really out there.

"I've got to go, Mr Anansi. What you said proves it. I mean, I dreamt of a real place."

"You did," said Mr Anansi. "And like I say, dreams are the life-blood of the truth, but your mom and dad aren't going to let you go seeking out no cannibalistic African prince."

"Well, what am I going to do?"

Mr Anansi looked at Jesse intently. "Now let me see, boy, it's your birthday soon – right?"

Jesse shook his head. "Not till November."

"Ah, November – that's a long time." He was silent again, and then, "I tell you what, son. You're going to have to tell a little sweet lie to your mom and dad. If you want to go to Africa, you're going to tell them you want an early birthday present. You want to go on Safari – now – when the Easter Vacation comes. You can say about fact gathering to carry on your mom's work, but what you don't say is anything about the Nam-Nams. You tell them you want to use your space suit so you can do research, and you tell them Mr Anansi'll go with you, because Mr Anansi knows Africa like the back of his hand."

Suddenly two silver-clad space suit arms were around Mr Anansi's neck and the all-American space boy, Jesse Lincoln Tierfelder was planting a fat kiss on the old man's cheek. "That's real cool, Mr Anansi. You're a star," he said. "You'd come with me and everything? You'd back me with Mum and Dad. You'd do all that?"

"Sure, boy, if you can see you're way clear to releasing me from this hold you got me in."

Jesse laughed.

"But, first, you put that space suit helmet back, and give me a demonstration of what you can do. I can watch you properly now," the old man said. "Seeing as I know you aren't no Angel of Death."

Jesse grinned. "You're a top guy, Mr Anansi," he said, and, moving a few yards away, he activated the suit, lifting himself gently into the air.

*

He was going to take Mr Anansi's advice and not say anything about the dreams.

If Dad or Mum knew he was going to Africa in search of some tribal prince they'd never agree. The Safari sounded okay, and he knew his parents trusted Mr Anansi. But he needed to broach the subject soon. The Easter vacation wasn't far away and there'd be arrangements to make. He knew it wasn't going to be easy either.

As the unseasonably hot spell dragged on, Jesse's mum and dad took to going out by the pool in the evening. They would chat, with their drinks, and Jesse would go for a swim. He was an accomplished swimmer and they often watched him from the poolside, shouting for him to do things, change strokes, somersault under water, perform fancy dives. It kept Mum amused, and he was happy to do that.

And one night he decided to give Africa a go. Mum had been feeling better and he thought it would be the best opportunity.

He was towelling down and Dad said, "How was the suit then, Jesse?"

"Cool," he said. "I took some amazing close-ups of the grey bits in Mr Anansi's hair."

Mum laughed. "Didn't he mind?" she said.

"I was hundreds of yards up. He didn't know I was doing it till I showed him on the VDU."

"Yes, but did he object when he saw the pictures?" Mum

persisted. "Mr Anansi's very particular about being respected, Jesse."

"He didn't say much, to be honest. I guess he was in a state because I caught him unawares when I landed. He thought I was the Angel of Death."

Mum smiled, but her eyes clouded and he wished he hadn't said that. "I'd like to give it a bigger try now," he said.

"In what way?" said Dad.

He took a deep breath. "I want to go on Safari in Africa – try it out where it was meant to be used."

There was an awkward silence. Mum and Dad looked at each other.

"When are you planning to do this trip?" Dad said.

"I want to go in the Easter vacation – it could be a very early birthday present." He looked at Mum and wanted to say all the stuff he'd planned. He wanted to give her the arguments that would convince her ... but the words wouldn't come.

"Wouldn't you rather be with your mum this Easter?" Dad said, and that hurt him. He knew he was giving them grief, and he knew what he'd said sounded heartless.

"It's hard to explain, Dad," he said. He looked at Mum again, in her wheel chair, her knees wrapped in an over blanket, her face lined and the once thick hair thinned to a wispy shadow. "It *is* for you Mum," he said, and he nearly choked. "I want to carry on with your conservation work in Africa after you've ..." But he couldn't bring that word to his mouth, and then he did choke. His glasses misted over and Mum propelled her chair across and put a hand on his knee.

"After I've died, Jesse," she said. "It's okay to say that. It's an event as natural as being born. It'll happen to us all. Just – it happens to different people at different times."

"But it's hard, Mum," he said, and he knew he wasn't doing it the way he'd planned. "Yeah okay – after that than, and I thought, if I went over to Africa now, to get data and pictures, to get my head around stuff while you were still – sort of – like – still here." He paused, and gulped. "So, when I came back you'd still be well enough to talk – help me plan ..." He tailed off again and stared miserably at the pool. He got the feeling it was hurting all three of them, and he longed to tell them about the prince and his disc.

But when he looked at Dad's and Mum's faces there was no hurt there. It was more like a glow of pride. Dad still sighed and shook his head though.

"It's a great thought, son. But … the risks … for your safety and everything. You know there are folk out there who don't see me as the most popular guy in the States just now, what with the new humanised robot I'm working on. My competitors are desperate to get their hands on the plans – especially Howard Tyson. He'd do anything to get at me." He shook his head again. "We've talked about it often enough, and it's bad enough over here. But out in Africa … you'd be a sitting target."

"Mr Anansi said that, Dad," Jesse said. "He said he'd go with me. He reckons he knows Africa like the back of his hands."

Dad smiled. "Mr Anansi's a very dear man, son, and I'd trust him with my life – but we're talking armed gangs. Mr Anansi's no defence against that kind of stuff."

"What do you think, Mum?" Jesse said.

"I want you to do it, Jesse," she said. "I know you're only twelve, and, by rights you shouldn't be thinking about this sort of thing … but fate's kind of changed that for us. You want to do it and I think you should."

He squeezed her hand. It was all bone and that hurt him, but it was hearing her say such stuff made him realise just why he had to get his hands on the disc.

He watched as the water in the pool dimpled in a soft breeze. After what seemed like forever Dad said, "Okay then son – if it's what you want, and your mother's happy … we'll go for it – but not with Mr Anansi. I'll contact the embassy out there. You'll stay with Joe Weinberg, the consular-general, and we'll have bodyguards to go with you. And we'll keep this thing hush-hush. You don't say anything to anybody. You got that? Not to the kids at school, not to the teachers or to the staff here."

"I got that Dad," Jesse said.

"We'll have to plan routes – so you're away from other Safari parties. I'll instruct the embassy. If it leaks out you're over there, they'll have to keep the press off till you get back. And when you're

74

up in that space suit you've got to give me your word you'll stay within range of your bodyguards. I don't want any wacko taking pot shots at you."

Jesse was silent. He was going to do something now that went against his every instinct. He was going to make his dad a promise he'd no intention of keeping. He'd never done that before – not to his dad or to his mum – and he hoped with every fibre of his being he'd never have to do it again.

"Sure, Dad," he said. He shook dad's hand. "That's my word I'm giving you."

But, behind his back, the fingers of his left hand were firmly crossed, and he hated himself with a passion.

***

Chapter 9

Into Africa

They didn't use the chauffer to get him to the airport. The less people knew about this the better, and Jesse was beginning to find the secrecy unsettling.

He sat in the back of the car with Mum.

The weather had broken and the city's skies were featureless. Rain glossed the roads and cars slashed through, thrusting a mist across the freeway. He watched as tyres hissed and the mood outside matched the bleakness in the car.

"You will say if you don't want me to go, won't you, Mum?" he said, and Dad laughed.

"You're not crying off now, kid – not after all the work that's gone into this."

"I *do* want you to go, Jesse," Mum said. "It'll be great, planning strategies when you come back. We'll miss you though. And Africa isn't easy. You take care out there"

"Sure I'll take care," Jesse said. But the reassurance was painful. There'd be risks that neither of his parents knew about. "I'll keep in touch like I was home. Every day, emails, and I'll talk to you Mum, whenever I can, and we'll use a web cam so it'll be like I haven't even gone."

Dad turned into the airport's main thoroughfare. "That might not be so easy, Jesse. We'll be talking on an encrypted site, remember. We can't risk anyone knowing you're there. You've got to be careful about that."

"I know, Dad," he said. "I will be careful … about everything."

He looked at his mum. It was almost as if she wouldn't last while he was away. But she'd been like that for months, and the doctors were in there all the time, with every medical devise known to man. "It won't be long – just two weeks," he said.

"You have a great time," Mum said.

They turned into a side road that led around the back of the airport, and, when they stopped, there was a group of men there – security guards. The operation was planned with precision – even the act of getting Mum from the car to her wheelchair was executed within seconds, and the VIP lounge had been cleared.

They watched the Boeing being boarded and it was only when the last passenger was secure and the last piece of luggage had been stowed that Jesse went on board. His entourage was ushered into first class, and again, there was no one else there.

He hugged his mum, and, as the plane taxied away, her drawn face haunted him. The disc, the African prince, say they were just dreams? He was losing two weeks of his mum's life … for what?

If he'd had the authority, he would have commanded the pilot to turn back, but, even with his clout, he knew he couldn't do that.

He didn't feel any excitement though, and, for some time, he just sat, gazing out of the window, watching the sea of frozen clouds and the occasional muddied patchwork of green.

Eventually he dozed. And that changed things, because, in his dreams he saw the village in the forest again, and the Baobab tree, and he saw the prince with the rainbow disc. The guy was smiling. Even his eyes were smiling, and he was beckoning. And, when Jesse woke up, he knew.

Whatever he found in the forest would bring life back to his mother – and, with the backing of his dad's silicon empire, he would unleash something so revolutionary, its impact would be unparalleled in history.

The excitement began to grow. He chatted to the cabin crew and guards. He went onto the flight deck and watched the computerised controls moving free of human touch, and he thought, "My dad developed all that."

There were moments of reflection. … He knew there'd be problems. He'd have to give the security guards the slip for one thing, and, even with the protection of his space suit, there would be danger.

He'd asked Mr Anansi where the Gemstone Mountains were and he'd studied them on maps, and on line. They were within comfortable reach from the embassy.

Dad had arranged accommodation. He knew Joe Weinberg, and

he knew his kids. Before they'd gone to Africa it was almost like they'd grown up together.

Carl and Samantha the kids were called, and they were twins. They'd been good mates in Washington, and he was looking forward to seeing them again.

The plane had been re-routed to avoid detection. It followed a course that brought them across the Atlantic into Central Europe.

It lengthened the journey, and, for a long time, the tedium got to him. When he wasn't being entertained on the flight deck or by his guards and the cabin crew, he played video games, watched films and dozed, but, as they crawled over France, he glanced out of the window occasionally. Although he was well travelled there was always a thrill at crossing a different continent.

Then they turned south towards Africa.

The undulations and plains of France gave way to the foothills of the Alps. Peaks tipped with snow passed beneath him and, as they moved further into Switzerland, the peaks changed to the crags of the High Alps.

He put his headphones to one side and gazed down. No matter how many times he flew over this, it always thrilled him. The jutting summits shaded pink where the tips caught the early sunlight, plunging, ice blue, into deep snow-filled ravines. It was still early in the year, and some of the valleys were so stacked with snow, they looked impassable. Others crept into view nestled with towns and villages, and he could pick out veins of roads winding down them.

The peaks gave way to lowlands and the sweep of the Mediterranean. Then there was the sea. Boats, like tiny water boatmen trailed threads of wake. After that they came to the coast of Africa, and Africa was completely new to him – irrigated, green and flat. Then dunes of the desert – miles of sand, mottled with shadows where the wind changed its contours. Sometimes, he could make out rashes of green and the glint of water. Then, once more, desert. There were skeins like threads of a spider's web, beaded with black, moving as slow as an hour hand. That, he guessed, would be camel trains.

For two thousand miles they flew, with uncharted dunes passing and, again, he dozed, until one of the cabin crew shook him. "We're coming near the tropics," she said. "It's quite something to see, the tropics."

This was his destination – the tropical forests of Africa. Scrubby trees were littering the desert, and the land was beginning to tinge towards green. Then, like the edges of lace-work, it darkened into acres of trees. He'd never seen anything like it – a steamy intensity of thick foliage.

It was full morning now, and he continued watching until they began their descent. As the grasslands passed below him, there were still clusters of forestation and there were traceries of blue where rivers meandered into a huge lake.

The land got nearer, until they were almost touching the tops of the trees – then the wide sweep of the runway and airport buildings. There was the screech of tyres on tarmac and they were down.

He watched the passengers from business class and economy emerge. Some were wandering, disorientated by the length of the flight and the brilliance of the heat.

Trucks towed by diesel cabs took the luggage, but still he and his guards waited.

Only when the airport was completely empty did Jesse see the convoy of cars moving towards them.

Then he shook hands with the cabin crew, and stepped out of the plane, breathing the air of Africa for the first time.

Joe Weinberg was waiting. Carl and Sam were there too and he was glad of that. With their dad it was a solemn handshake and a "Mr Ambassador", but with Carl and Sam it was high fives and a hug.

Sam was pretty. He'd always thought that, but now she was shaping out and he grinned. "You've got a different shape on you," he said. Her face coloured up – but she wasn't displeased. She had dark hair, shoulder length and loose, and her eyes were blue. And she'd got a smile that lit up the world. Carl wasn't pretty. He made sure of that. He'd got close cropped black hair and a diamante stud in his right ear. He shoved Jesse.

"She fancies herself enough already. She doesn't need you telling her that stuff," he said, and Sam laughed.

The security guards were ushering him across the tarmac. It

annoyed him. He could see these guys were going to be a problem.

But it was his first glimpse of Africa and he was curious.

It wasn't so much different from back home. There were broad streets leading off the main highway, with trees planted out for shade, and people milling under them. The houses and office blocks were set back, angular and modern. There was a cosmopolitan bustle everywhere and the sun glinted off open windows.

But, on closer observation, there were differences. There was an indefinable hint of the carefree, and women had their hair scraped back in tight knots. They were carrying stuff on their heads, balancing pots, and baskets filled with bread and fruit. There were oranges piled to peaks, and melons and bananas. They moved with elegance. Nothing seemed to be dropped or spilled.

Traffic moved up and down the road, and here there was a certain happy chaos – and there were vehicles unlike any he'd seen. Bedford fronted, while, at the back, they looked like wooden-slatted vans – a cross between a minibus and a cattle truck, and they were literally bursting with people leaning out, waving, shouting, and the roofs were bulging with produce, tied down with a carefree abandon. And all around was the raucous blaze of horns.

He laughed. "What are *they*?" he demanded and Carl grinned.

"Mami-wagons. They're like a cross between public transport and family limos gone crazy."

They were happy vehicles though, something grown out of the old traditions, and they had texts on them – proverbs. One slid past and it had, emblazoned on its front, "Had I known". On the back was inscribed, "Always at last".

"African proverbs," Carl said.

Jesse liked it. It gave the city character – the old traditional flavouring the modern. "It's great," he said.

The convoy drove into the ambassador's residence and that had all the splendour of American colonialism. It was such a contrast from the Mami-wagons. The American flag was fluttering, and the entrance was guarded by marines, watchful, slightly confrontational and with a hint of hostility. Jesse understood, but, after the contagious confusion outside, it seemed wrong.

He still felt a thrill of excitement though.

His quest had started and the whole of Africa was out there waiting for him.

*

Steve Da Silva, head security guard, had lined up the first Safari for the next day.

But when Jesse turned up, Steve took one look at him and shook his head. "You can't go dressed like that, kid," he said.

Jesse had put on his space suit. He frowned. "Can't go like this?" he said. "That's why I'm out here, to trial this suit. I've got to go like this. I need to get up close and take aerial photographs – I've got the camera in the helmet."

Steve looked at a couple of marines who were going to accompany them, but they shook their heads too. "No way," they said. "Things are real tough out here. Anyone seeing you going off like that would be thinking 'espionage' straight off. They'd be down on us like a ton of bricks."

"Can't I take it and change later?" Jesse said.

But they wouldn't have it and, without his space suit, he was stymied. He was smart enough to know negotiation wasn't on the cards though.

The space suit had to go back.

He put on Khaki shorts and a T-shirt – and, in spite of everything, it was hard not to feel excited. He was in Africa. He was going into the wilds to see for himself. He was about to share his mum's passions.

When they set off dawn was only a hint, and the stillness was breathless. To the east, the skyline dropped to serrated mountain peaks, and there were touches of pink and mauve everywhere.

They took a fleet of jeeps and straight away Jesse started noticing things. He kept glancing at the direction indicator in the dashboard, and he was watching the miles click by. If this convoy was heading towards anywhere significant, he needed to know, so he could find it again. He'd been frustrated by Steve Da Silva, but he wasn't beaten.

They were in deep scrubland now, on the edge of the plains. The guards said they were to stay off the plains because that's where the popular Safari routes were, but there were sightings of wildebeest, and a water hole where he watched transfixed as elephants let rip rolling in ungainly confusion, churning the mud.

There were other sightings, lions, and, in the distance, giraffes stripping bark from the highest treetops.

Then they drove on, bordering the edge of the high plains, and all the time he noted the compass readings and mileage. It wasn't long before he could see trees thickening into a forest.

"Where's that?" he said. But he knew. He could recognise the foliage. He could recognise the trees' structures and the intensity of growth. These were the trees he'd dreamt about; the ones growing around the cliffs and caves of the Gemstone Mountains.

"We're getting close to the river," the guide said. "And that's the Sikaman forest."

"Would the Gemstone Mountains be in there?" he said, and the guide looked at him.

"What do you know about the Gemstones?"

"Only what our gardener, Mr Anansi, told me. He comes from round here."

"Yeah," the guide said. "The Gemstone Mountains are in there, but the Nam-Nams live around the Gemstones, and you don't want to mess with the Nam-Nams. It's reckoned they eat white men." He grinned and added: "That's what I've been told anyway. Never been there myself, and never want to."

But by now Jesse was seriously excited. Now he knew where he had to go. He'd kept a note of every directional change and every mile they'd clocked up.

It was late when they got back, and, because of the early start, Da Silva decided they would have a rest, next day.

Jesse couldn't see the point in spending a day loafing around the grounds of the embassy. But Da Silva wouldn't give and he suggested a tour of the city instead.

Jesse could see merit in that – for his other mission. It would give him information about big business in urban Africa – and it would show him how western civilization was undermining African culture – but it wasn't going to lead him to the breakout he wanted. The tour wasn't scheduled until the afternoon either, and that meant he'd got a whole morning to kill.

Fortunately Carl and Sam were free, and the three of them were sprawled under the trees, chatting – about times in the States, and about Everett's business. Carl and Sam knew about Jesse's mum, and he was comfortable with that. He told them about his ambition to carry on her work.

He couldn't tell them about the disc and his hopes to keep Mum alive – but the space suit was well at the forefront of his mind.

"I designed it," he said. "Dad got NASA to make it for me – I was hoping to use it – you know – fly around collecting data."

"Can we get a look at it?" Sam said

It would give him the chance to show off – to get into the suit and fly again, and his brain was so addled with jet lag that the long-term problems faded for a moment, and straight away he leapt to his feet.

He had to run the gauntlet of marines first. They were stationed around the ground and were watching every move he made.

"Where're you going, kid?" they said. They weren't happy when he told them either.

"Don't take it too high. Not where you can be seen from outside. If the local militia see anything flying, they'll take pot shots at it."

Back with Carl and Sam he climbed into the suit. "I'll take some film if you like," he said. "You lie out under that tree or something, Sam, and I'll get shots of you, so you can sell them to *Vogue*."

"What about me?" Carl said and Jesse grinned.

"You want to be in *Vogue*?" he said.

"No, but for some male model mag." He stuck an attitude, and Jesse laughed.

"You wouldn't even get into 'Wimps Anonymous' looking like that," he said and Carl aimed a kick at him.

Then Jesse lifted off. He hovered, first filming Carl as he strutted his stuff. Carl had stripped to the waist and was holding a pose he thought looked provocative, but Jesse had other ideas. He featured close-ups of his naval. Carl wasn't slim like Sam. The folds of flesh around his shorts were Jesse's prime subject, and he made the pictures as unflattering as he could.

Then he descended – but Carl was a great guy. He laughed when he saw them.

But he'd promised Sam photographs as well, and that meant going up again.

This time he was much kinder, looking for the flattering angles, shouting from the sky to direct her poses. They wanted him to take more, but, as he hovered for the third time, he became more interested in the grounds.

The marines had satisfied themselves there was no danger, and they were talking to Steve Da Silva.

He swept around while his friends looked on. But, as he flew, something happened.

He heard a voice in his head – as clear as glass, and his spine tingled, because it was the African prince, and it seemed to come from away in the south.

"Jesse," it said. "Come now. This is your time. You will find me in the caves of the Gemstone Mountains. I will guide you."

He breathed sharply, and immediately he looked across towards the boundaries of the ambassador's residence.

He glanced towards the marines, but they were still engrossed with Steve and he knew the voice was right. It was now or never and he looked at his friends watching from under the tree and signalled for them to be quiet. Then he waved, touched the controls, and he was off. First upwards, then out towards the perimeter trees, and then on over the city.

There was shouting. The marines and Steve were waving. But he'd broken loose and in another second he was over the city and riding above the plains.

Half of him wanted to film, but he had no time. Ahead, shimmering like the clouds of a weather front was the edge of the forest, a hazy expanse encircling the horizon. He adjusted his direction, moving towards it. But he knew, back at the residence there would be pandemonium. They'd be mobilising marines. The security guards would be out, and here on the plains he was an easy target.

Increasing his speed he headed for the forest. He needed to make cover before they got helicopters into the air.

Then he lowered his height and swooped to the south east, until he was flying above the trees.

They were massive, – leaf-laden branches stretching to touch the sky, and beneath him he could hear screeches of birds and animals.

Then though, … the deadly drone, growling in the air at his back and he turned. There was a fleet of helicopters, like bees creeping out from the distance, and, straight away, he ducked down searching for a space to land.

But things were different in the trees. Up in the sky it all seemed navigable, spread out in a richly foliated plain, and the sky was full of space. Down here it was dense and there were no features. Trunks stretched into a gloom of overbearing branches and they closed in like walls. If he could make out a path, it meandered straight into shrubs and, as he stared, he heard a slight rustling in the undergrowth. A snake slithered into the scrub and he shuddered.

There were other heavy-footed disturbances, and noises in the branches, and every sound carried a menace. Lions? Panthers? There was something out there watching him, he could feel it, and he had no protection for this kind of thing. A pouncing predator would leave him no time to activate the space suit.

He moved back to where he'd landed, aware, even here, of danger. There was no way he could begin his search for the Gemstone Mountains down here, and the helicopters were scouring the skies above him. That meant he dare not venture above the trees.

This wasn't how he'd imagined it, and he remembered Mr Anansi's warnings.

Then there was another rustle, and he cowered. He was convinced there was something out there. He could feel its eyes boring into him.

Then he heard the voice again – the voice that had called him from the ambassador's residence lawns. "Follow the river to the sea," it said. "My brother will help you." And, immediately, from the undergrowth, there was an ape staring at him.

He gasped and stepped back, but the ape didn't move. First it looked at him, and there was an almost human recognition in its soup-like eyes. Then it bared its teeth, more in a smile than a threat, and, without making a sound, it raised its forepaw, and Jesse distinctly saw it beckon, and the voice came again. "This is my brother. Follow him."

He could hardly believe it. He stepped into the forest, locked in a trance, and the ape began making chattering noises, nodding its head. When it turned, it looked over its shoulder to see if he was following.

There was no other way, but he couldn't get his head around it. The ape seemed to know what he wanted. It darted among the trees turning to check he was there, and each time it beckoned. At one point it came back and pulled him against a tree, and Jesse breathed sharply, because, where he'd been standing, there was a snake, full of venom.

They beat away the branches until he saw glimpses of water.

Then it was as if the ape had done what it had to, and, having led him to the river's brink, it leapt into a tree with a peal of chatter, swinging away, losing itself in a conglomerate of growth, and he stood, unable to grasp what had happened.

He could still hear the grinding drone of the helicopters – but they were more distant now, and he felt safe to use the space suit again.

For a while he followed the river's course. The voice in his head had said he was to go to the sea, and a brief glance showed the flow of water moving south. He stayed well below the tree line and hugged the bank, always watchful, and listening. When a helicopter drew near he landed and hid under the canopy of trees.

One of them swept low, just down river from where he was. It was a good half an hour before he ventured out again.

But while he waited, he took in the river. There was an oily film staining the water, and thick weed clogging the banks. He didn't see any movement in the river itself – no activity that indicated fish, and he knew the river was dead. He'd have to do something about that.

This time he filmed, because there was something here to talk with mum about.

When he began flying again, the river began to widen, and soon he could sense the tang of salt in his nostrils. He could see the water was turning from oily green to grey, and he noticed it was flowing in the other direction, as if the river had become tidal.

The helicopters continued to scour, but they'd gone further north. He was confident he wouldn't be seen, so he swept on across the river, and then he saw the broad sweep of the sea.

The settlement of the Nam-Nam tribe and the boy prince were close by, and, with a touch of a button, he rose, scouring the tops of the foliage as the woods rolled inland. And a mile or so across the forest he made out the jagged contours of the Gemstone Mountains – just as he'd seen them in his dreams, and his heart was racing.

He flew, watching the canopy of trees fall away, until he saw a settlement – caves honeycombing the mountain cliff, and land, tilled and cultivated. There were animals, and it was clear this was a farming community.

Children were playing. Men working the land. He could see women at the cave entrances, grinding corn, making dough. Some lazed in the cave's mouths, and, to the edge of the settlement he saw the huge Baobab tree.

Then the people saw him.

The children's play stopped. Men stared, women left off work, while more appeared from the cave entrances, and then, emerging from the Baobab tree, he saw an old man, gnarled and wearing a headdress of peacock feathers.

He heard a sharp command and saw men dropping their farm implements and running to the caves. And, in the next moment his body stiffened, because the men re-emerged, and this time they were wielding spears.

*

Okomfo Kalabulay was in full regalia. In a gesture he'd not used in over a year he raised his hands, and his voice was cold and scheming. "People of the Nam-Nam tribe, attend," he said. And, with half an eye still on the silver creature coming out of the sky, they turned.

"Nam-Nams – my people, guardians of the Mountain Treasure, there is a legend; our king descending from the sky – but our king is already here – he came on his mat – riding the rainbow. This thing is an impostor – a counterfeit. He knows of our legends and would dupe us. He is our enemy. Kofi Musa is our king. This creature will plunder our treasures and destroy our king."

His voice rose to a rasping shriek and he turned. "People, summon the ancient custom, the fire and the spit," and, stretching his arms in an act of invocation, he uttered the ancient incantation,

"Impostors must be consumed."

Then, as the silver clad creature plummeted, frenzy erupted in the village and the people closed in shouting and baring their teeth.

*

Jesse could see the people scurrying around – men making formations with their spears, and he wanted to retreat, but he couldn't move.

He was dropping uncontrollably into a feeding frenzy and he was going to die. Mr Anansi had warned him.

There were chants. Women waving fists and cursing, children snapping their teeth, men menacing with spears, and on the periphery, cold and isolated the old man, directing from the Baobab tree.

The moment his feet touched ground he ran, diving for the trees, but he was grabbed by the warriors, and he could feel their breath on his back. He kicked, but they had him pinned, and they dragged him towards the Baobab tree. There were children pushing forward, nipping at his space suit. Women were shouting, and in the seething chaos he could barely register his own thoughts.

By the Baobab tree the old man was waiting, and, as Jesse lay there, one of the warriors wrenched at his helmet. And when they saw his face, his blonde curly hair, the wide blue eyes of a white boy, they let out a yell of fury.

In a moment his suit was off, and he was lying, naked in front of the old man. And, as he looked up, he nearly passed out, because never had he seen such mendacity.

They were all shouting now until the old man raised his hand, and that was the moment of heart-stopping terror, because, in the awful silence that followed, Jesse knew what they were going to do.

They brought stripped branches, and they tied him down. Then they lifted him to rest on two stakes above a pyre of wood. He saw the old man produce a magnifying glass. He watched as he stooped to focus the sun's light onto the dried tinder, and then, as the first flames crackled there was a roar of hate.

His heart was crying and a dark mist clouded his head.

He could feel the scorching pain of the fire.

And then, from among the turmoil of yelling cries, he heard his own voice, frantic, calling above the pandemonium.

"Kofi, Kofi – Kofi Musa. Where are you Kofi?"

***

Chapter 10

Smoke and Fire

The marines searched until it was too dark to search anymore.

Steve Da Silva had been certain Jesse had gone into Sikaman forest. When they first got airborne he'd seen a hint of silver hovering over the trees. But the forest was so dense. If he'd gone in there, chances of finding him were practically non-existent.

All day they'd thought he'd go airborne again. But he hadn't, and eventually they went north, hoping he'd made for the plains to film animals.

But the kid had disappeared and Steve was in a mess. He'd been put in charge of the boy and already, on the second day, he'd given him the slip.

He went back to the ambassador's residence.

"Kid got away before we could get near him," he said. He looked at Sam and Carl. "Did he say anything before he went?"

Carl shook his head. "He took pictures – me and Sam, then we got him to go up again, and before we knew it, he was heading out over the city. It was like, he signalled us to keep quiet – then he waved, and he'd gone."

Sam was crying, and her dad put an arm around her. "We'll get him back, Sam," he said. "I'll make sure of that."

But getting him back wasn't what was registering on Steve Da Silva's face. He knew what they were up against.

"He's got gadgets," Carl said. "Computers, cell phones and stuff. Say he's sent out some kind of message."

They checked the Internet and they checked phone lines and voicemails, but there was nothing.

"We'll have to tell his dad," Joe said. "And that's not going to be easy."

*

Ursula had been low since Jesse had gone. Everett would have been with her, but there were projects he was tied into. He had to work, and, when the phone rang he thought it would be Carole, or one of his co-directors, and he was shaken to hear Joe Weinberg.

"Is something wrong?" he said, and he listened, grim faced.

Then he said, "Okay, Joe. He's got a microchip inserted. I can locate him. I'll do it now – call you back. And I'll come out, but wait till I get there before you do anything."

His first instinct was for a stiff whisky, but he'd need a clear head. He'd have to tell Ursula, and God knows how she'd take it. He spoke on the internal line to Mr Anansi. He'd see Anansi before he told Ursula anything. That guy knew the terrain. He would help him locate Jesse, no trouble, and that way things would look more hopeful when he told her.

But Mr Anansi looked anxious.

"I can trace him okay," Everett said. "He's got a chip implanted." He looked at the flashing images on his VDU and Mr Anansi sank into a chair.

"I should have gone with him," he said. "I knew I should have gone with him."

Everett was staring at the screen and he was hardly listening. "It was my decision," he said. "And there's no time for recriminations. What we've got to do is find him and get him out."

The computer had opened onto a map and there was a tiny flashing blip. "Is that him?" Mr Anansi said.

Everett nodded. He enlarged the picture until the terrain of Sikaman country filled the screen. Then he brought the curser onto the flashing beacon.

"Do you know that place?" he said, and Mr Anansi's eyes glazed.

"Are you sure that's him, Mr Tierfelder?" he said. "You're sure that's Jesse? That's where he is?"

"Yeah. It's all done by satellite. I can zoom right in, see it like a photo if you like."

"You can zoom in all you want, but you've no need on my account," Mr Anansi said. "I know that place, and I knew the boy was going there."

Everett looked up sharply. He drew the curser down onto the

flashing point and dark shadows touched by moonlight filled the screen. "If you knew about it, Mr Anansi, why didn't you say?"

"He didn't want me to. It was a fantasy thing. He said he knew about that place. He'd dreamt about it."

"How so?" Everett said. "It isn't like Jesse. Going into a fantasy world. He's got his feet more firmly on the ground than I have. How come he's gone out there in search of a dream?"

"He thinks there's something out there that'll cure his mum. He described the place to me like only someone who's seen it could. And he wouldn't have me tell you."

"He's seen it on some internet site," Everett said. "It must have been getting to him, his mum being so sick and all. But where is the place, Mr Anansi?"

Mr Anansi stood up and walked slowly across to the screen.

His little Jesse was in there with the Nam-Nams and he didn't know what to say. Mr Tierfelder was worried big time. There was no point in telling him about the tribe's cannibalism. He leaned against the desk and said, "You got to get him out, Mr Tierfelder. That's not a good place for young Jesse to be."

"Yeah, sure, but where is it?" Everett said.

"It's the Gemstone Mountains. There's a tribe there, the Nam-Nams. Jesse knows about them."

Everett had heard enough. He picked up the phone and dialled Joe Weinberg. "I'm going out there, Mr Anansi," he said. "I've got to tell his mum first though. After that, I'm out to Africa on the first plane."

He didn't know how he was going to tell Ursula. But she was amazing. "He'll be okay, Everett," she said "Jesse's a survivor. He'll be back just like he said he would. He must have gone out there for some reason and when he comes back, he'll have done what he wanted to. You've got to trust the boy. Just go out there now and be there for him, that's all."

*

It was dark when he touched down in Africa, and it was grim – Joseph Weinberg and Da Silva were waiting.

"Anything new?" Everett said.

Joe shook his head. "There's a problem Everett – with the government. They've already objected to us deploying helicopters. We didn't tell them the boy was here, and now, if we're going to launch any kind of search, we'll have to clear it with them first and they're not going to be happy."

Everett eased himself into the embassy car. "If you do tell them, how likely are they to keep it under wraps?" he said. "I don't want the world's press out here, and any hint that Jesse's missing is going to galvanise every hustler on the planet."

"We can try it through diplomatic channels," Joe said. "We might get away with clearing it through their secret service – it shouldn't be such a big deal that the Colonel needs know, and … you reckon the kid's in the Gemstone Mountains? That's a pretty remote area. No one's going to notice any searches going on around there. We can negotiate a bit of help from their ground forces. We'll say it's a combined exercise – The States and the local militia."

By the morning Weinberg had everything arranged. Everett met the local Chief of Staff at the embassy, and he was impressed. The guy had been trained in the UK – Sandhurst, and he had his head well screwed on.

"You think you can locate him?" the Chief of Staff said.

Everett pointed to a flashing point on the computer in Joe's office. "The boy's right there," he said.

They checked the co-ordinates.

"There's a small tribe out there," the Chief said. "Very aggressive. They could be hostile. If their reputation is anything to go by, they're not going to give him up through sweet talk and negotiation. I think it's going to be a military operation."

"I don't want the boy put in danger," Everett said.

"The safest way is to do it big," the chief said. "Helicopters with machine guns, and we'll bring in troops, small tanks on ducks – we can get them in via the Sikaman River." He touched the point on the map where the Gemstone Mountains were located. "You can see. The settlement is close to the estuary."

Everett went in the lead helicopter next day and they flew swiftly over the plain. They could see the ducks already beached when they came to the estuary, and the tanks were forging in land. The helicopters swooped low; guns ready.

The plan was to land the lead helicopter, and Everett and Da Silva, along with the Chief of Staff were going to demand Jesse back, with the backing of the tanks and the helicopters.

But, as the terrain unfolded, they couldn't see any mountains. There were no caves, no cliffs, no clearing and no village – just miles of trees and the tanks ground to a halt.

Joe Weinberg looked at Everett. "This tracking device," he said. "Accurate is it?"

Everett was puzzled. According to his equipment Jesse was directly beneath them. But Mr Anansi had said he was with the Nam-Nams. He'd identified the place, and they'd seen it on the screen back home. There had been a clearing where the Gemstones rose above the forest. But now they were here, there was nothing. "Pinpoint accurate," he said.

There was a brief discussion between the Chief of Staff and Joe while the helicopters circled. Tank operators and troops stood motionless and radio waves burst with confused voices.

Then Joe said: "According to all our maps these are the co-ordinates for the Gemstones. Chief of Staff reckons their ordnance is as good as any in the States ... but these Gemstones ... this tribe, there's no sign of them. Do you reckon they're more legend than fact? There's an outcrop further down. We could take a look down there."

The lead helicopter flew off towards the outcrop, but there was nothing there either, just a cluster of cliffs pushing up from the trees.

"If that's it," Joe said. "It's not exactly the range of mountains we were lead to expect. Like I said – is it more myth than reality?"

"Well, at least," Everett said. "It means the kid hasn't been captured by any tribe. But he's down there. He's at the original co-ordinates. He got lost more than like. Put me down and I'll find him."

They flew back and strapped Everett and an armed guard to safety harnesses. The helicopter's engine gave a deep-throated roar, and slowly they lowered the men into the trees, manoeuvring to find a clear patch of ground.

It was darker down there – darker than Everett had expected, and it was steaming. The noise of the forest was something he could never have anticipated; shrieks, cries, chattering, a chaos of histrionics. It even managed to drown out the helicopters' roar.

He pushed through the growth, following the location on his computer, struggling to hear its bleep above the strident forest cries; but there was no sign of Jesse.

Then he tried calling, but still nothing and he could see no indication that the boy had ever been there, no footprints, no broken branches, no flattened areas, only the maddening bleep of a disembodied microchip.

It didn't seem right and he couldn't understand it. He'd seen the Gemstone Mountains back home with Mr Anansi, and there'd been a settlement.

He called again, but the only answer was the cacophony of forest cries.

"You want to come up?" said Joe.

"Not without the kid," Everett said.

There was a pause. Then Joe's voice came again. "We don't think there's any point. I know it's hard, Everett, but we've got to be pragmatic about this. You haven't got the stuff to make a proper search. Come up and we'll put the marines in. They'll turn the place inside out. They'll find him. Your best place is back at the embassy, directing operations."

Everett took a deep breath. He looked around and called again. He didn't want to leave – not without Jesse, but … Joe was right, and besides, he was too involved. This needed clear thinking – best leave it to the professionals. He still couldn't understand why he was getting a signal without there being any sign of the boy though, and that worried him.

The marines tore the place apart. They scaled trees, burrowed under shrubs, turned the place upside down, but there was nothing. Like Everett, they couldn't even find a footprint in the undergrowth.

By nightfall it was clear to everyone that nothing else could be achieved without the Colonel's agreement.

They were on the patio after dinner, at the Weinberg's residence. Steve Da Silva was there, and they'd had a full report from the Chief of Staff.

"We'll have to make a visit to the palace," Joe said.

"I can't figure it out," said Everett. "The signal's strong."

Joe held his whisky glass, watching traces of alcohol trickle down its side. "You don't think someone's got the kid," he said. He watched Everett's face. "You know – detected the chip – took it out – dumped it in the forest or something?"

"I can't think of any other explanation," Everett said.

"It could be," said Steve. "This place is in political turmoil. And they don't like you Mr Tierfelder. Not wishing to be insensitive – but, your wife's activities, highlighting the poverty and the exploitation, they're not happy about that."

"What's new, Steve?" Everett said. He gave a wry smile. "I'm used to that kind of stuff. You can't make omelettes without breaking eggs … but … it's hard if they get to you through your kid." He looked at Joe. "Ursula's certain he's okay, you know. She's convinced he'll show up."

"Can't leave it to blind faith though," Joe said. "We'll have to go in and talk to Colonel Mamba. We've got to face him down with this. We'll go over there tomorrow. I'll get my staff to fix it. And don't worry, Everett. Jesse's a good kid. We'll get him back even if we have to move heaven and earth."

But Everett wasn't listening, because, while Joe had been talking, he'd had a most peculiar sensation. He didn't know if it was stress – or the whisky, but, he'd just seen Jesse, back in the Gemstone Mountains, and the settlement was there, just as it had been on the computer back home. There was a black kid too, and, in Everett's head, there was an overpowering sense that Jesse was okay. He couldn't explain it, but it was there, pulsing through his head, and the weird thing was, he believed it. Jesse was all right. Suddenly it made him more eager to get to Colonel Mamba – to renew the search.

But getting to see Mamba wasn't easy. Mamba was angry that the boy was in the country. He wanted to know why he hadn't been told, and it was three days before he agreed to see them.

*

His palace was imposing, constructed mainly of marble and situated just outside the city. It had a pillared façade and it was bursting with opulence. The hall was like some Greek temple, with statues and sculptures, and the political incongruence struck Everett.

A smartly dressed concierge led them to a room with a richly woven carpet. There was an ornate chair, raised on a dais. It looked every bit like a throne and they were ordered to wait.

Mamba kept them waiting for over an hour and, when he did arrive, he was dressed in full military regalia. He sat on the raised chair, and signalled seating for Everett and Joe. And it was clear he was looking for a fight.

Joe told him that Jesse's visit was an early birthday present, a Safari, as the boy loved Africa. The trip had to be taken now because his birthday wasn't for months, and because of his mother's illness. He said this in the hope the personal touch would get to Mamba. But the colonel's eyes just glazed into affected boredom.

Everett couldn't fault Joe. His patience and restraint were beyond criticism … but how could you couch accusations of kidnap in diplomatic terms?

"Trouble is, we think someone's taken the kid," Joe said and they saw Mamba's eyes narrow.

"*Someone's* taken him?" he repeated. "And who might you have in mind for this 'someone', Mr Weinberg?"

Joe shrugged. "Could be anyone. It's got to be someone big though. The boy had a microchip implanted in him and we believe it's been taken out."

Mamba's voice was heavy with ill disposition. "*Someone* big," he said. "Mr Weinberg, are you suggesting my government has something to do with this?"

Joe didn't flinch. "Someone with power and know-how," he said. "Someone looking for political or financial gain. Someone who recognised the boy and knew his family had influence. It could have been your opposition, Colonel Mamba. We only approached you because we knew of your amazing intelligence network."

By now Everett could see Mamba's face set. He wasn't swallowing anything Joe was saying.

"Imperialist rhetoric, Mr Weinberg," he snapped. "You're

accusing me. You think I kidnapped the boy. That's why you've come here. I tell you, sir. You have no grounds … and, to add insult to injury, you've had my Chief of Staff helping you." He smirked. "You didn't think I knew about that did you? I know everything that goes on in this state Mr Weinberg. Read my lips. Nothing slips my notice, and do you think I'd have permitted his involvement if we'd been responsible for the boy's disappearance?"

"Colonel Mamba," Joe said. "It would be absolutely inappropriate for me to make such an accusation."

But Mamba wasn't into taking on slippery words. "You may not *make* such an accusation, Mr Weinberg, but that's what you think. I tell you sir, going to my Chief of Staff behind my back, making veiled accusations to my face. You don't like my regime, and your country never has. I don't know why I've allowed you on my soil for so long. But this is the limit of my tolerance." He snapped his fingers and stood up.

He wasn't a big man, and his face was beginning to show the ravages of age. At some time his nose had been broken. His hooded eyelids masked a streak of meanness and, at the snap of his fingers, a group of soldiers came forward.

"Escort these men from the premises, will you?" he said "And Mr Weinberg, you have three days to remove yourself – you and your embassy staff. I will not nurture a nation of imperialists that harbours a false accusation."

Then he turned, his heels snapping, and he marched out of the room.

Joe looked at Everett and shook his head. "I've been expecting it," he said. But then he sighed and added; "It'll make locating the kid real tough though."

*

For once in his life Everett didn't know what to do. His son was missing. They'd been kicked out of the country where he'd last been seen. He had to go back to the States and tell Ursula. It was the very worst of times.

But he was determined not to be beaten. He was going to set up search and monitoring units. He'd contact friends in Britain, and he'd locate other Secret Service agents – people he knew. He'd go public. There was no point in keeping Jesse's expedition secret any more. He'd activate a universal search, offering big bounty. He'd do anything. The only thing in his head was getting Jesse back.

Ursula took it all more calmly than he'd expected. She was still convinced he would turn up, and it was unnerving, seeing her unrelenting faith.

But faith wasn't Everett's scene. He had to do something.

He contacted everyone he knew, and he fixed an astronomic bounty.

He had to. If this had been done by a political faction, or some country, then the incentive would have to be massive and, for Everett, any price was small change.

It wasn't long, either, before the bounty brought a response – a phone call, and that seemed to confirm everything he and Joe Weinberg had suspected, because the call was from Colonel Mamba.

If the bounty was guaranteed, he said, and this did not imply he knew where the boy was, but, if the bounty *was* guaranteed, then his Chief of Staff would continue the search, take tanks in and comb the forest.

Mamba's protestations of innocence didn't wash with Everett. He was convinced Mamba had the boy.

… But if he hadn't, then his men were the one group in a position to find him.

Either he was still in the forest, or he'd been abducted, but one thing was certain. his microchip was there, and, if that was still there, then there would be other clues.

He was still convinced something about this wasn't right, though.

When he got home, the first thing he'd done was feed the co-ordinates back into the computer, and, in his office, the picture that came up was cliffs and mountains again, caves and a clearing – and, quite clearly, the dwellings and scattered outbuildings of the Nam-Nam tribe. It didn't make sense, and it made him uneasy.

***

Chapter 11

A Touching of Destinies

Kofi stared.

It didn't take long to assess what was happening.

Okomfo Kalabulay was about to roast someone, and – what was worse, he recognised who he was roasting.

He'd seen him in his dreams. He knew the curly blonde hair, the face, and the striking blue eyes.

In a second he'd shinned up the trees and was swinging from vine to vine. "Stop. Leave him. Kalabulay, no!" he screamed.

Then he was in the Baobab tree suspended above the burning pyre, and Kalabulay looked up baring his ancient teeth, and he leered in defiance. He was wearing ceremonial dress and, to Kofi, it looked grotesque and anachronistic.

But the flames were taking hold by now. He could feel the heat even up in the Baobab tree. The boy on the pyre would be feeling it even more and, with all the power of the talisman, he made water surge up around the pyre, drenching the wood, dousing the flames and sending steam hissing into the air.

The warriors stepped back, but it wasn't the warriors he was gunning for. His fury was directed at Kalabulay.

The old man hadn't moved and Kofi's first instinct was to raise fire just like he had, to burn him. But … destruction – re-enforcing the old ways – his Imam would not condone that, and he doubted the white boy would either.

He looked at Kalabulay again, and suddenly he knew what he was going to do.

He aimed the talisman and an avalanche of water gushed from the centre of the Baobab tree. It rocketed into the air and fell directly onto the witch doctor. Kalabulay was soaked, and so was his tribal finery. His peacock feathers were flattened and his strands of long hair reduced to skeins of bedraggled grey.

He darted away, and then Kofi laughed, because the waterspout was chasing him. He was ducking and diving and, wherever he went, the water followed.

When the tribe heard Kofi laugh they started laughing too, watching the wizened old man gyrate under the torrent. Even the white boy was laughing, and Kofi increased the force of the waterspout, so that it knocked Kalabulay to the floor. Then he turned his attention to the four acolytes and flattened them too.

The people cheered, and suddenly Kofi's anger was gone.

In a moment he leapt from the tree and ran up to the soaking pyre. He tore at the thongs that bound the white boy and lifted him down, hugging him.

"Akwaaba! Welcome, friend," he said.

*

It hadn't happened as Jesse had expected it to – but – this was the African prince he'd seen in his dreams. He had the disc around his neck and, already, he'd done amazing things with it. What was more, the prince was clearly overjoyed to see him.

He was still unsteady on his feet, but he held out his hand. "Hey, it's just great to see you, buddy" he said – and, considering just a couple of minutes earlier he was being roasted, that was something of an understatement.

"I will speak to the people, and then you must come to my cave," the prince said, and his English was perfect. He said something in the local dialect, and Jesse watched the people slink away. The witch doctor picked himself up, and he was muttering.

Jesse saw him glare at the prince, but the black boy didn't seem bothered. He just turned, and, with his radiant smile, he said, "Come with me. We will talk."

"I need my glasses first," he said, holding back. "When they trussed me up, they ripped them off."

He stumbled towards the bundle of silver fabric where his space suit had been chucked to the floor. The prince followed, grubbing around in the grass, and it wasn't long before he'd spotted the glasses. "Are these what you're looking for?" he said.

Jesse took them, and he could see the boy was curious about the suit. "Is this what the people in your country wear?" he said, and Jesse laughed.

"My dad had it made specially," he said. "It's a sort of flying suit. It can do plenty of stuff. I'll show you later, if you like."

Then he bundled it into his arms and followed the prince across the clearing.

It took a few minutes for his eyes to adjust when they'd got into the cave, but when he could see he was speechless.

"You like it?" the boy said.

"It's like nothing I've ever seen," Jesse whispered. "It's awesome, man."

"You can sleep here," the boy said, pointing to the bed carved into the cave wall. "I always sleep on the prayer mat. It was given to me by my baba Imam."

Jesse tried the bed. There was some kind of feathered mattress and he was surprised. It wasn't bad. He could sleep on this with no problem.

"It's real weird," Jesse said. "I don't know how to explain it, but I know about you. I've had dreams. I came here specially to find you. I know about that disc hanging around your neck and everything. Can you believe that?"

The boy laughed and he leapt up from the prayer mat where he'd been sitting, landing beside Jesse on the bed, and his eyes were sparkling. "I've known about you for ever," he said. "I knew your face the minute I saw you. I've always known you'd come. You had to. You and me, and the talisman – it's our destiny."

"I've known you like a brother," Jesse said.

"We are brothers," said the boy, and, although it was so unreal, Jesse was more at ease with him than he'd been with anyone in his life.

He laughed. "Yeah," he said. "Like you say, we're brothers, and yet ... I don't know what your called and that's real bad form."

"I'm Kofi. Kofi Musa," the boy said

"Kofi Musa," Jesse repeated, and then he stopped. His eyes widened. "I called that name out – when I was on the pyre. That's the weirdest thing."

"It's the talisman," said Kofi. "It does things like that. Sometimes

I control it … but … sometimes it almost thinks for itself."

They shook hands. "I'm Jesse. Jesse Tierfelder," Jesse said.

"Jesse Tierfelder," Kofi said. "Kofi Musa and Jesse Tierfelder. They go well together."

He stood up. He was slighter than Jesse – wiry, muscular. "We have a lot to catch up on," he said. "There's a lot to tell … but now I must speak to the people. I want you to come with me, though I'll have to talk in the language of the Nam-Nams." He unhitched the disc from his neck and passed it to Jesse. "Hold this," he said. "And, when I talk, direct it at my mouth. You'll understand what I'm saying then."

Jesse took it and Kofi watched him closely. Then his eyes danced. "I knew it," he said

"Knew what?"

"Until now, no-one except me has been able to hold the talisman. It's only for the chosen. Me, my mother, Mr Mandela, and the great Gandhi … and now you. You are able to hold it just like us."

"Mandela and Gandhi?" Jesse said.

"It's a long story," said Kofi. "There's so much to tell you. But we'll have time."

Then he stopped and looked slightly embarrassed, and he said: "What must you think of me? We've been talking – so much to say, and you've got no clothes. I should have offered you a wrap. You must forgive me. I was so excited, I forgot."

"That's okay. Truth is, I was so excited I forgot I'd got no clothes on," Jesse said.

Kofi picked up a fabric from a pile in the corner. "Put this over you."

Jesse pulled the wrap around his waist, tucking it in like a beach towel. He winced slightly as it touched his skin, but he didn't say anything.

Then Kofi threw a ceremonial robe over his own shoulder and put on a headdress of feathers, and they went to the mouth of the cave.

The Nam-Nams were already gathered, sitting, crowded across the clearing, and they were like kids at school, caught in a prank.

Kofi didn't say anything for a while. His eyes were wide, with those deep brown irises. He had his arms folded, and Jesse sat at his feet, directing the disc towards his face.

At last he said, "I do not see Okomfo Kalabulay. Has he left the village?"

One of the tribesmen stood up. He had his head bowed, and Jesse turned the disc towards him. "Kalabulay is in his tree, Kofi Musa. He is wet and angry. He will not come out."

"I want him," Kofi said. "Fetch him."

Four men at the back of the crowd stood up and every head turned to watch the Baobab tree, and Jesse could see Kofi's eyes dancing, and his mouth was twitching, because a string of high pitched yells came from the Baobab tree, the pipings of the old man. They could hear scuffles and various bits of furniture flying as the men struggled with him. At last he came out, and he was kicking and fighting.

Jesse watched as Kofi's expression changed.

"Hold him firmly," Kofi said, and then he stood silent, scanning his subjects, and not even the smallest child moved.

"You have done a very bad thing," he said. He gave every Nam-Nam the same accusing eye, waiting for the message to sink in. Then he said: "You have tried to roast a fellow human being. You were going to eat him, because he is not of your tribe, and because he does not share your colour."

He waited again, and it was stunning. The guy had hardly started, and, already, Jesse was spellbound.

"This person is a human like you – someone with a mother and father, with friends, with people who love him and people he loves. He has a heart that beats like your hearts, eyes that weep like your eyes, a voice that laughs as you laugh. He is everything that you are … and … you were going to eat him like a roasting pig."

He used eye contact like Jesse had never seen it used before. "Not only that," he said. "But this person came to visit you as a guest, with nothing but good will. He came to be welcomed, to be shown your hospitality. He came from across the sea and over the oceans, from the other side of the world, as one friend would come to visit another."

When he paused the only sound you could hear was the sigh of a branch high in the trees, and the persistent curses of Okomfo Kalabulay crouching, pinned down by the four warriors. "And, what is your welcome to your visiting guest?" Kofi said. "You sharpened your teeth to consume him."

For the first time, his voice rose above controlled moderation.

"Further to that, Nam-Nams," he said. "This guest – who flew across the world to be with you, this guest, who you set on a spit like a wildebeest, this guest is my greatest friend. It was me he came to visit. Me, Kofi Musa, your king.

"And look at him, Nam-Nam people. Look long and hard, because this white friend holds the rainbow talisman, just as I hold the rainbow talisman. This white friend is a prince, just as I am a prince. He is as much the King of the Nam-Nams as I am. This great, white friend is someone I have dreamt of since I could dream dreams. My Imam has dreamt about him. He is known by the great Mandela and Gandhi. And what would you have done to him? You would have roasted him."

It was like watching a great actor deliver some speech from Shakespeare. It was the tops.

"And you would have *roasted* him." Kofi said again and Jesse could see the people wriggling in their skins. Then he heard a faint mutter, in the vernacular, soft at first, but swelling and he turned the disc on the people. They were chanting "No. No, King Kofi. Never. We would not do it. Forgive us Kofi Musa. Forgive us, white friend of Kofi Musa."

Kofi held up his hand, and, when everyone except the high piping Kalabulay was silent, he spoke again, quietly this time. "Nam-Nams," he said. "This is not your crime. These were not your actions. You are not to blame."

There was a sigh from the crowd, and Jesse watched, because, if what he'd seen up till this minute had been an act, the expression on Kofi's face now was one of genuine ferocity. "The evil carcass that gave birth to this villainy is the witch doctor Okomfo Kalabulay," and suddenly his eyes flashed. "Bring him here," he said.

Kalabulay may have been old, but he was strong, and the struggle he put up was astounding. He kicked and shouted, he wrestled to free his arms, and all the time the villagers jeered. He was screaming something too, but it had no meaning for Jesse because he was so transfixed he forgot to turn the talisman on the old man. Whatever he was screaming though, it was heavy-duty cursing.

When Kalabulay finally reached the front, the villagers began clustering around. Some of the women lifted their children to their shoulders and only when the pandemonium had settled did Kofi speak.

Then he said. "Mr Kalabulay," and his voice stung. "*Mister* Kalabulay, you know what I think of the old traditions. You know what I think of roasting white men – of eating your fellow humans. You know how I have striven to stamp out this practice."

Kalabulay glared, his tiny eyes glinting, and his sunken mouth chewing on the few stumps of teeth that remained in his head.

"I know, Mr Kalabulay," Kofi said, "that you have always fought my wishes. You have always longed to bring back those barbaric ways. Today you saw your chance. While I was asleep you pounced. But, in so doing, old man, you set upon my dearest friend."

Still Kalabulay glared, and Kofi glared back.

"Until now I have left you with the dignity you held for so many years, as wise man of this tribe, because it was you who welcomed me into the tribe. It was you who proclaimed me king. But I have had enough, Mr Kalabulay."

He punctuating each word, and then he turned to the elders close by him at the front of the crowd and pointed towards the Baobab tree. "Get into that hole where he lives," he said. "And bring the rotting bones that fester in the corner, take the trinkets of his office and bring them out. Pile them on the pyre where he tried to roast my friend."

A group of elders headed for the Baobab tree, while Kofi turned to the soldiers holding Kalabulay down. "And you …" he said. "Strip him. Tear his clothes of office and put them on the pyre as well."

It was as dramatic as anything that ever came out of Hollywood – the elders disappeared into the tree and re-emerged with armloads of bleached bones and sculls. They were human bones, human sculls. They brought out spears and ceremonial clothes, headdresses and shields, and everything was dumped in a pile.

The crowd wanted to watch the purging of the Baobab tree, but they also wanted to watch the struggle that was going on at the front, because, if Kalabulay had fought earlier, what he was putting up now made that look like ballroom dancing. His piping voice yelled, he

106

chanted curses, his face was contorted, he kicked, he scratched and it took all the strength of five men to hold him down. Eventually they ripped his robes away and tossed them from hand to hand until they reached the pyre.

When the old man had been stripped to a loincloth, he lay pinned by the five warriors. But his eyes still burned and his old mouth still chewed on his gums.

Kofi watched until the last vestige was on the pyre. Then he turned to Jesse. He took the talisman.

"As you know, Mr Kalabulay," he said. "The ground around the pyre is sodden with water. But no water is powerful enough to withstand the talisman. Watch, and learn, old man." And, as he spoke, a fireball came screaming out of the sky. It took hold of the pyre, and it was fiercer than anything Jesse had ever seen, burning white through to purple, licking up the old bones and the headdresses, the spears, the shields, the clothes of office, and, in a cloud of smoke and steam, the heap of corruption was reduced to ash.

But Kofi wasn't done. As soon as the fire had spent itself he held up his hands and stared at the old witch doctor again.

"That is the end of you Mr Kalabulay," he said. "You are no longer wise man in this village. You are a source of corruption, and I will not have my people corrupted."

The old man looked up, his mouth still distorted with mendacity.

"Because you are old," Kofi said. "I will let you stay in the village. You can live in your Baobab tree. But you will no longer have authority. What is more, I promise you, make one move to reintroduce your barbaric ways and I will throw you to the forest animals … and remember, Mr Kalabulay, those animals are my brothers and my sisters, my mother and my father, and, if I throw you to them, they will know what to do with you."

He was supreme. He was a master leader, greater than any man Jesse had known, and, as the warriors led Kalabulay back to his tree, he felt a glowing pride.

But Kofi turned and grinned, and this time it was the artless grin of a boy. "Right," he said. "That's him sorted. Now … let's go back to the cave and talk."

*

Jesse eased the wrap from his waist. The contact with his flesh still hurt.

"Did the fire burn you?" Kofi said. "Did I not get there soon enough?"

"It is a bit sore," said Jesse. He let the wrap fall and his skin was red. But there were no blisters.

"Does it hurt?" Kofi said, touching a red patch with his finger.

Jesse laughed. "A bit," he said, and Kofi went to the back of the cave.

"I'll find something to take the heat away," he said. "We'll wash it and then you must wear the wrap loosely, so it doesn't touch the burns."

When he came back he had a bowl of water. "There's a spring. It's my personal water supply, you know?" He gave a sheepish grin. "As king I get privileges."

"So you should," said Jesse. "You get this, Kofi. I've seen presidents, prime ministers, religious gurus – I've seen the lot, back in the States, but I've never seen anything like the stuff you put up today. It was really moving. You were awesome, kid."

"I think I learned it from my Imam," Kofi said. "– The man that brought me up."

"You said about him," Jesse said.

"He reared me from when I was five" Kofi said. "Before that I was brought up by a troop of apes."

Jesse caressed his burns with the water, and he could feel Kofi's eyes penetrating him. He had that way of looking, deep – silent and thoughtful. "I think you have a story to tell too," he said at last. "How did you get here for one thing."

"My space suit?" Jesse said. "It flies. Do you wanna see?"

"I fly on my carpet," said Kofi. "But I use the power of the talisman. In a suit though – you'd fly with nothing, no wings, nothing."

The suit lay in a heap near where they were sitting. The ill treatment didn't seem to have damaged it, and Jesse opened it carefully. "I've got cameras," he said. "They take pictures – you know, like paintings, and it takes paintings that move too." He looked up to see Kofi laughing.

"It's okay," Kofi said. "I know about cameras and TV. Just because I'm king of the Nam-Nams doesn't mean I'm stuck in the dark ages. When I was with my Imam, they had TV in the village, and people had cameras."

Jesse turned hurriedly to explain the jet packs and stabilisers.

"What's this bit?" Kofi said.

"That's the computer," said Jesse. "That's the kind of thing my dad makes in the States. It's the nearest thing to magic. You can talk on computers and send messages. You can see images of anywhere in the world. They can think and they read information; they can store stuff and remember it forever. A computer's like a human brain. Some bits it doesn't do as well as a human, but other bits, well, computers do it better."

"These we didn't have in the village," Kofi said. "But … you said it reads. I don't see any eyes."

"It reads discs," Jesse said. He released a disc from the drive and Kofi's eyes widened.

"My talisman looks like that," he said, and Jesse nodded.

"That's why I'm here. I told you – I've had dreams. I knew about your talisman. It *is* a computer disc – a bit like the one in the drive. There are things on your disc that only a computer can read."

"That would be its power to heal the world, and the powers of regeneration," Kofi said. His eyes were alive with excitement now. "I've always known about that, and I always knew I couldn't unlock the powers on my own. That's why I knew you'd come." He touched the computer and his hand trembled. Then he looked at Jesse.

It was as though they'd known about this moment all their lives – and suddenly there was such a special feeling; … it was almost like the creation of the universe. The two boys had met. Their potential and their destinies had touched and it was as if the spirit of Gandhi and Mandela, of Kofi's Imam and his mother were all hovering in the cave, watching the amalgamation of their dreams, and Jesse leaned across. He took the talisman and held it in his hands, seeing the diamond cut transparency flash rainbow fires across the cave. It was perfect – a disc radiating to the circumference, pulsating with a potential as powerful as the universe. For a while his fingers trembled.

"This is a great moment," Kofi whispered.

"It's *the* great moment," said Jesse. "When we unlock the secrets of this disc the world will change."

"Can your computer read it now?" Kofi said, but Jesse frowned.

"The disc's too big. It'll need adapting, and, even then, I can't be certain this computer will read it."

"It's our destiny to know and use what's in there," Kofi said.

"It's got to be," said Jesse.

And then ... there was that holy silence again... and it was almost more than a human body could bear. Jesse could see tears in Kofi's eyes, and he knew his own eyes were misting up. They looked at each other ... and, for a while they couldn't break the silence – until Kofi laughed, because the intensity was more than he could cope with. "It's as if the Angels are singing," he said and Jesse gulped.

"They are," he whispered.

"And these Angel songs, they're bursting in my chest," Kofi said.

Jesse laughed too now and the tears were running down his cheeks. "Mine too," he said.

"It's too much, isn't it?" said Kofi. "I think we must forget about computers and talismans till we get used to it. Perhaps we should go outside. You could show me how your space suit flies."

They staggered to the mouth of the cave, and threw themselves on the ground, laughing, wiping the tears from their eyes and Jesse said, "That was something else."

"I thought I was going to explode," said Kofi. He lay on his back looking at the infinite blue above him. "I'm wiped out."

"And me," Jesse said. "I've hardly got the strength to put the suit on."

But he did, easing the fabric cautiously over his body and the suit was amazing – the fabric so fine and the insulation so perfect, it seemed to sooth the soreness rather than irritate it.

Then he put the helmet on.

Most of the tribe were out now; men back working on the land, children playing, and women at the mouths of the caves preparing food. Jesse noticed how they stopped what they were doing ... and suddenly, as he rose into the sky, he was playing to the audience, hovering over the Nam-Nam village again; although, this time they were watching in admiration. And Kofi was following his every move. Jesse glided and hovered, rising into the air, putting on the most impressive display he could, but he was careful not to fly too high. He knew Steve Da Silva and his helicopters would be out there, scouring the forest.

He took video footage of the village, and, for sheer devilment, swooped low in front of the Baobab tree.

He cart wheeled, did back flips, and he was amazed to see how well he could manoeuvre the suit.

Then he landed, sweeping across to Kofi's cave, taking off his helmet and grinning. "How's that?" he said.

"That was amazing," said Kofi. "Like a bird with no wings."

"I designed it myself," Jesse said. "I took video pictures, look."

He showed Kofi the pictures of the village and the shots where he'd focused in on Kofi and Kofi laughed. "I'm a TV celebrity and see how handsome I am?"

Jesse nodded. "Yeah. Do you want me to go up and take some more?"

But Kofi shook his head. "Not just now," he said. "I think your space suit is amazing. We must use it often … but … when you use your suit I am left on the ground. I want to take you on my prayer mat now. With my mat we can fly together. You'd rather fly with me, wouldn't you? I want to show you the sights of the forest."

"Prayer mat it is then," Jesse said. "But, should I wear my space suit for safety, in case I fall?"

"You can't fall," said Kofi. "The power of the talisman will keep you safe. Even my Imam has flown on the prayer mat with me."

Jesse slipped his suit off, packing it neatly in a corner of the cave. Then he draped himself in the wrap while Kofi took the mat and laid it at the cave's mouth.

They sat cross-legged and, as Kofi held the talisman, the mat moved. Jesse grabbed the corners for support and Kofi laughed.

"You don't need to," he said. "Go with the flight. You won't fall."

In the distance Jesse could see Da Silva's helicopters but Kofi directed the mat up river, in the opposite direction.

They flew to a point where he said his mum had left him on the day of his birth. Then down river to where the apes had rescued him. Then on to the raised ground where his troop still lived. He swooped and waved, and, to Jesse's amazement, the apes waved back. They were smiling, baring their lips.

After that he took him to the edge of the forest, to the village where he'd grown up, and they flew over the Imam's house.

"One day I will introduce you," he said. "To the apes, and to my baba Imam."

He manoeuvred the mat, and they flew back across the trees, into the depths of the forest, following the river to the shoreline.

It was like a dream, looking down from the Imam's prayer mat on miles of trees, following the ribbon of white sand, seeing water lacing the shore, being here with the African boy-prince, talking, laughing.

"Are they canoes?" he said, leaning over the mat, peering down at the beach below.

A line of logs, carved to the shape of elongated torpedoes lay regimented at the top of the beach, pulled up under the palm trees. There were a few still in the water, with men working fishing nets.

"It's our fishing fleet," Kofi said. "That's what I taught them. I showed them how to hollow the trunks. It's a long tradition in Africa."

"And are they steady in the water?" Jesse said.

Kofi grinned. "It's a skill. Sometimes they roll and the men get wet. But the water's warm."

He tilted the talisman and the mat lowered itself towards the beach. Then they ran across the burning sand to the overhang of palms.

"It's sheltered here," Kofi said. "And quiet. It's where I come when I'm looking for peace."

They flung themselves under the trees and Kofi looked up to the palm fronds. Then he grinned. "Hang on," he said, and, as deftly as an ape, he shinned up the nearest tree, throwing down a couple of coconuts. Then he leapt back onto the sand and removed their skin with a flint stone. Then he smacked the shells together, cracking open the tops. He handed one to Jesse. "Drink it," he said. "It's the most refreshing drink in the world."

Jesse lay back, staring at the undulating palm leaves, listening to the waves, and he could feel an ecstasy seeping into every limb.

"This is like heaven," he said.

"It is heaven, Jesse Musungu."

"Jesse *what*?"

Kofi laughed. "Jesse Musungu – it means Jesse *white boy*."

"I like it," Jesse said. "Jesse Musungu – but shouldn't there be something I could call you?"

"Like what?" said Kofi.

"Well – like *black boy* I suppose," Jesse said.

Kofi chuckled. "It had better be Kofi Bibini then – and now we should swim." He rested on his elbow, looking down, smiling. "The salt in the water will sooth your burns – take away the heat. Besides, I love swimming in these waters … and after that, Jesse Musungu, I'll tell you the story of my life."

*

The next day they went to the caverns in the Gemstone Mountains.

They had to take the torchbearers, even though the talisman would have given them all the light they needed, and they had to take the official guardians of the treasure. There was a confrontation with Kalabulay, because he turned up, dressed in nothing but his loincloth and an old drape he'd commandeered from one of the village women.

"You're not coming, Kalabulay," Kofi said. "I told you, you're nothing in this place anymore. Go back to your Baobab tree."

Kalabulay's mouth began working, and he started his querulous whine. But, instead of retreating, he lay on the floor.

"Go," Kofi said again. He stamped his foot, pointing towards the Baobab tree.

Then there was an interlude, where the old man tried to stare Kofi out, but his defiance was more comedic than authoritative, and Kofi didn't stir.

113

At last he gave in. He let out a final curse, and, muttering all the way back to the tree, he dragged himself down the slope. And all the time he was looking back over his shoulder, glaring, like a naughty dog, skulking back to his kennel, and it was hard not to laugh.

But Kofi didn't take his eyes off him until he was out of sight.

Then they went into the caves and Jesse had never seen anything like it. He couldn't begin to put a price on the wealth embedded in the rocks.

There was an impulse to imagine it being used for good in the world ... Yet something of his mother told him ... if they mined the caves – for whatever reason – it would be one more assault on the world's recourses – a raping of its most amazing phenomena.

These caves, open to everyone, would rank at the top of the world's wonders. Leaving them in their natural state for generations to admire ... that's what his mum would do.

For the next two days they were drunk on euphoria. It was only on the third afternoon that the spell was broken and it was broken in the most unnatural way – with a happening that was beyond anything that was normal, even for a guy who'd flown in a space suit and who'd explored the African forest on an Imam's prayer mat.

They were outside, contemplating another trip to the beach, when the talisman began to pulse. Both Kofi and Jesse noticed and they stared. Then they heard sounds roaring above the forest – a storm, Kofi thought – but Jesse knew better. He recognised the growl of helicopters. But they didn't sound like normal helicopters. They had a disembodied echo to them, thin, metallic, as though they were coming from somewhere outside the world, and the strange thing was, none of the villagers noticed the noise at all.

Then they saw helicopters, only they weren't real helicopters, just faintly etched hints. They had guns mounted and the guns were trained on the village. Yet the whole fleet was nothing more than a shimmering heat haze. And the villagers still didn't notice anything.

It sent an uneasy shiver down Jesse's spine.

There was something biblical about it, and he couldn't understand. Then there were more disturbances, and he looked across to see tanks pushing through the trees. But they weren't real either, just shimmering mirages and they seemed to stop as if some invisible

114

obstacle was barring their way.

The boys stared, as one of the helicopters turned and headed south. And, while it was gone, those that remained circled in random paths. It was the most unnerving thing. It was as though it was all happening in a parallel universe, and all the time, the talisman blinked and flashed sending shards of light across the clearing.

"What's happening?" Kofi whispered.

"It's like a vision," Jesse said. "Like, they're not here, even though we can see them."

"But ... why?" said Kofi.

Jesse shook his head. "I don't know. I don't see any sense in it."

Then the reconnaissance helicopter came back. It hovered and Jesse gasped. He gripped Kofi's arm – because there were two figures being lowered from the hatch – they were as spectral as the helicopter – just a shimmering shapes. But immediately Jesse recognised one of them.

"That's my dad," he whispered.

They stared as the figures landed.

Jesse's dad seemed to be searching, groping around the villagers – and still they didn't see him. He was ducking as if there were trees and shrubs obstructing him, and he kept checking a locator of some sort, and then Jesse heard him shout – a hollow whisper of his father's voice, and he was calling Jesse's name, feeling around.

"Dad," Jesse shouted back. He darted forward, but there was no response. His dad seemed to be in a different world. Dad continued diving under non-existent undergrowth. He talked to the phantom helicopter and it looked as if they wanted him to come back. But he didn't want to. Jesse heard him call his name again, cupping his hands, and again Jesse responded, but to no avail.

Eventually they winched both figures back into the helicopter, and suddenly, the talisman sent an explosion of light across the clearing and the whole thing was gone – the helicopters, the tanks, the guns, the noises. There was nothing – just the stillness of the afternoon, and Kofi stared at Jesse.

"What is it?" he said. "What does it mean?"

Jesse shook his head. "I don't know. Something ... a vision ... like ... telling me my dad's searching for me I guess. Someone out there reminding me about my family – why I came here – because – I've sort of got over excited in the last couple of days – finding you and everything … and we've been having this great time … and the vision was telling me that's not what it's about. I'd almost forgotten about my mum and dad. My mum's dying of cancer and … I forgot …

"They'll have realised I've disappeared by now. They'll be worried, and all this was like … telling me. I mean – we can't go on just playing like kids. We've got the talisman, and that's for the people – people like those we saw just now. I've got to contact Dad, that's the first thing, because one thing I know now is: my dad's looking for me … and then, you and me, we've got to figure out what we're going to do with this talisman – how we're going to get it into the world."

The halcyon days were over, and neither Kofi nor Jesse moved for a few minutes.

At last Jesse got up.

"I've got to fetch my computer," he said. "I've got to let Dad know I'm okay. I'll tell him I'm with an African prince. I'll tell him we've got the cure for Mum's cancer and we're working out what to do."

He looked at Kofi for his agreement. Then he headed up the slope and into the cave.

***

Chapter 12

Behind the Firewall

It was a hot afternoon and the atmosphere was heavy. It even managed to suppress the children's play. The women were clustered in the shade of the caves. Some of the older ones were dozing.

There was no sign of Kalabulay. He had kept himself in his Baobab tree since the trip into the treasure caves, although there was no comfort in not being able to see him. He was still a threat, and there was something sinister about the stillness shrouding the entrance to the tree.

Kofi watched Jesse tapping at the keyboard of his computer.

"It's like a television," he said. "What are you doing?"

"You build up layers of programs," Jesse said. "Like you're preparing the computer to do its job. Its got to have a lot more layers this time, because the message I'm sending has to be encrypted."

Kofi frowned.

"It means it has to be kept secret." Jesse said. " My dad's got rivals in the computer world – enemies, especially a guy called Howard Tyson. He's ruthless. Dad reckons he'd kidnap me if he knew about my suit and my computer. If I sent a message to Dad and Mum in the ordinary way, his spies would read it. They'd know where I was and come looking for me. Tyson's men are like a Mafia in the computer world. They'd do anything to get what they wanted."

"You're safe here though," Kofi said. "No one can get to you here. The Talisman won't let them."

Jesse laughed. "Yeah," he said. "But we didn't know too much about the talisman when we set this stuff up. Anyway – it's kind of 'belt and braces' isn't it? Double protection."

As they talked, the computer was flashing interminable messages until the screen cleared leaving just a curser and Kofi watched. He was captivated, seeing Jesse tap out his message and Jesse was quick. He'd learned to touch type before he was five, and the message scrolled across the screen like lightning:

"Hi Dad – Mum. I'm OK. I'm in Sikaman forest. I've found a cure for Mum's cancer – a computer disc – it's amazing. I haven't sussed how it works yet, but I know it will cure Mum. Tell Mr Anansi I've found the boy prince. He'll understand, and he'll explain to you.

"I'll be back with you soon. Don't worry. I'm safe. The prince, Kofi, is looking after me. He's the one with the disc and he's a great guy, real cool and a real good buddy.

"See ya. Love you both and missing you.

"Jesse. xxx."

"You can write all that just by tapping keys?" Kofi said. "And how's your dad going to read it?"

"The message will go through space," Jesse said. "It uses wireless networks –cyberspace, and Dad will pick the message up on his computer. It travels at the speed of light so he'll get it as soon as I press *'send'."*

"And the encryption will stop the others reading it?" Kofi said.

Jesse grinned. "You're a smart kid. You learn real fast,"

He touched the screen, negotiating the *send* icon and then he leaned back.

"It's gone. Dad will have it on his screen already." But as he looked, he noticed the screen was blank. There was a discordant clash and words flashed out: *"Message not sent."*

He tried again, and still the message failed.

"Is something wrong?" Kofi said.

"Something's blocking it," said Jesse. "It may be Howard Tyson's got into to my computer. He must have bypassed my firewall."

"You can still get a message to your dad though," Kofi said.

Jesse looked at him. "How?"

"The talisman. You can send your thoughts with the talisman."

"Like – telepathy?"

Kofi nodded. "I do it with my Imam some times. Take it now and try."

But Jesse didn't want to, not yet. He was gutted his message had failed. "I want to try again with my email first," he said. "There

118

could be a virus – something Howard Tyson's put there. I want to run my scans and do some diagnostics. It should work then. If it doesn't I'll try the talisman."

Scanning took some time and it was early evening when they tried again, but, although the scan hadn't found anything, the message still failed.

"Now use the talisman," Kofi said and this time there was no point in refusing.

He positioned the rim of the disc into Jesse's hand. "Hold it like this," he said. "Then think hard about your dad and mum – visualise their faces, and tell them what you've got to say."

Jesse wasn't convinced. He could think till he was blue in the face, and there would be no way of knowing that Mum and Dad had received his thoughts. And, even if he imagined a reply, how did he know it wasn't something he'd just dreamed up?

But he did have a go, basically thinking the things he'd put on the email … and then the weirdest thing happened, because, the moment he'd thought the words, he experienced an out of body sensation that almost put him in shock.

A glow, like an infusion of warm liquid, filled him, and he felt he was floating. In his head he saw the patio at the ambassador's residence. His dad was there and Joseph Weinberg fingering a glass of whisky. He saw Steve Da Silva too, and, as he thought the words, he saw his dad tense up. For a second, there was a startled expression on his face. Then he smiled and said something to Weinberg. The next second, the image morphed to his Mum, at home in her wheelchair. Mr Anansi was with her. They were beside the swimming pool, and he saw his mum smile suddenly. She spoke to Mr Anansi, just as Dad had spoken to Weinberg and Mr Anansi smiled back.

Jesse didn't know what either of them had said, but he knew. The message had got into their heads. They knew he was safe.

"It's worked, hasn't it?" Kofi said. "It has its way of letting you know."

Jesse handed the talisman back. He was reluctant to let go.

"Yeah. It worked," he said. "They got the message – no doubt about that … and, my dad, he really is in Sikaman country. I saw him on the patio at the embassy with Joe Weinberg, and Steve Da Silva.

It seems like that thing we saw this afternoon was – like – they really are looking for me."

"They won't find you though," Kofi said suddenly. "I think that's what this is all about. The talisman doesn't want them to find you. It's not ready for you to be found yet."

"What do you mean?" said Jesse.

"That's how it works. It wants you to stay here. We've got something to do before you go."

Jesse sat up then and looked at Kofi. "Before *I* go?" he said. "I don't think I'll be going back to the States on my own. Whatever we've got to do with this talisman, we've got to do it together. When I go back, I reckon you've got to go back with me."

*

That idea hadn't occurred to Kofi, but ... Jesse was right. To do what he needed to do with the talisman he would have to leave his tribe – and they weren't ready for that. Their quick descent into potential cannibalism was proof, and, if Kofi left now, he didn't know what would happen.

"We've got to prepare the people for this," Jesse said later.

They were sitting at the mouth of the cave and groups were gathered around their fires, talking, laughing among themselves. The flames shone on their faces.

"They really depend on you," he added.

"They're good people," said Kofi. "But they do need a leader, someone who knows where to take them. The trouble is, they follow without thinking. It's okay as long as it's me, but they'd follow Kalabulay just as well if I wasn't here."

"The stuff you've taught them isn't in their system yet," Jesse said. "That's the trouble. We've got to get them deep into farming. We've got to get them seeing the benefits of it – believing in it so much, Kalabulay won't be able to shift them."

"But they've had a life time of Kalabulay," said Kofi. "And he's such a scheming man. I know he'll be at them as soon as I've gone."

"Then we'll have to find some guy to replace you," Jesse said. "Someone we can train up. Is that why the talisman is blocking us, do you think? Because it wants us to set up a successor before we go?"

They lay back. There were millions of stars in the sky, probing the depths of infinity. You never saw anything like that in Washington. Here the sky was deep and pure and every star had its own place. It was hard to grasp, but some of that light had been generated thousands – even millions of years ago, and the sight filled Jesse with awe.

"Who do you think could do it?" Kofi said.

"I think it should be someone young," said Jesse. "The older ones have had Kalabulay for too long. A younger guy wouldn't have so much dross to get out of his head."

"There's Kwami," Kofi said.

Kwami was one of the boys who'd been chosen to bear the lamps into the treasure caves. He was a clever kid. Before Jesse had come, he'd been closer to Kofi than any of the other boys. He seemed to understand what Kofi was doing.

Jesse nodded. "I was thinking Kwami," he said

"We'll have to train him," said Kofi. "Teach him how to be strong with the tribe, teach him a plan to lead them forward."

"It'll take time," Jesse said. "Trouble is, my mum – the cancer – she's really bad ... and ... I'm just scared, if we spend too much time here, it'll be too late."

"The talisman won't let that happen," Kofi said. "Don't be afraid for your mum Jesse Musungu. The talisman won't let her die."

Next day they called Kwami to the cave.

He was a handsome boy, strong, muscular, his eyes clear and quick to respond. He had a broad smile, and it constantly animated his face.

"We have big things to tell you, Kwami," Kofi said. "And big stuff for you to take in."

The three of them made their way into to the cave and Kofi and Jesse sat on the bed. Kwami stood. He'd often sat with Kofi before, but now, with Jesse here, he felt he had no rights. There was no jealousy. He just felt it right to show deference to his king. But when Kofi saw him standing, he laughed. "Sit down, Kwami. There's no need to feel uneasy because Jesse's here."

Kwami wrapped his cloak around him and sat cross-legged on the floor, close to Kofi, but still with the deferential gap between them.

"You are princes of the talisman," he said. "I am just an ordinary Nam-Nam."

Kofi patted the bed. "We must talk in English," he said. "That way all three of us can understand. Besides, it'll stop the others in the tribe listening."

Jesse looked up, puzzled. "But Kwami can't speak English," he said, and Kofi grinned.

He took the talisman and held the rim. "Kwami," he said, and he spoke in English directing the surface of the talisman towards Kwami's face. "Hold this with me."

Immediately Kwami shrank back. He'd seen others try to touch the talisman, and they usually ended up flying across the floor in big pain.

"Trust me," Kofi laughed and cautiously Kwami put a hand out, touching the edge of the talisman and then pulling back again.

But there was no pain and Kofi urged him on, "Touch it again," he said. "Grip it with both hands."

Jesse watched. He knew, when he'd held the talisman, it was a sign to Kofi that he was one of the chosen … but this guy wasn't one of the chosen. He was just a Nam-Nam. He had no rights over the talisman. All the same, when Kwami gripped it, nothing bad happened. In fact the light seemed to shudder for a moment, and Kwami's face glowed. Then, when he spoke, he spoke in perfect English, and he seemed to understand "You'll be going away," he said. "To a place where you can release the full power of the talisman. You won't be here to guide the people anymore."

He let the talisman go and sat back.

"When we go," Kofi said, "you must become king of the Nam-Nams. You have to carry on our work."

It came as a shock. "I'm not like you two," Kwami said. "Especially with Kalabulay around. They won't accept me with him here."

"They will," Kofi said. "Because, from now on they will see you as one of us. You can bring your stuff up here and live with us in the Gemstone cave. We'll work together, teaching the people, and, over the next weeks, we'll show you all our plans. You'll learn all we know. Sometimes you'll hold the talisman with me and it will give you its strength. You'll still be a Nam-Nam. You won't be prince of the talisman, but in every other way you will be like us – Kofi, Jesse and Kwami."

Kwami swallowed and glanced at Jesse. "Won't you mind?" he said.

"'Course not. We planned it together," Jesse said. "We've got to go back to America, – me and Kofi, and, when we go, we need some guy like you – someone we can trust – some kid that understands what we're about."

"It's a big thing," Kwami said. "I'm only a simple peasant boy."

"There's nothing simple about you," said Jesse, but Kwami just stared at his hands.

"The thing is, I've never thought of such things. All I am is a torch-bearer to the Gemstone caves."

"Give it time," said Jesse. "You'll get used to it, and we won't be leaving any time soon."

*

During the next few days Kwami moved into the cave. The villagers took note, but the general speculation was that Kofi and Jesse had taken a servant, and that pleased them. It raised their status, and the fact that the servant was so high up the hierarchy as to be a torchbearer pleased them even more.

Kofi and Jesse let the speculation run. It wasn't in their interest to tell the tribe what they were planning and Kwami was a good companion. He was bright and he learned quickly. He had a great sense of humour, and it didn't take him long to be completely comfortable, especially with Kofi. He didn't see himself in any way as a rival to Kofi and Jesse. In fact he gave them space. There were times when they went off together, to the palm beach, or into the forest with Jesse's space suit.

Meanwhile they groomed him in every way. They told him the story of the talisman. He heard the history of Kofi's life. Both he and Jesse went to meet the apes, and that set up a bond between them, because, with the apes, they were both out of their comfort zone. They were awed by the way the creatures greeted Kofi. They saw them bring him gifts and feed him with bananas and nuts. They watched them groom him and talk with him. They were equally incredulous to see the way he chattered at them, gesticulating with his arms, beating his chest, climbing and swinging with them in the trees.

When they were introduced to the apes they were both hopeless, trying to articulate their gestures. It made them laugh and Kofi was hysterical. By the end all three of them were aching, especially when the apes started laughing too. The apes even held their sides and that completely creased them up.

Kofi took them to meet his baba too.

They travelled on the prayer mat, and, to get there, they needed to take evasive action.

In spite of the Imam's assurances, Kofi was still unsure of the villagers. On his last encounter they'd been screaming for his blood. He wanted his visit to be a secret and so he got the talisman to throw a cloaking device around the prayer mat.

"They won't see us," he said. "There's a wall around us that will deflect their vision. It's like an illusion. In their eyes we will be sky and clouds. We'll replicate whatever is between us and them."

The disc flashed as the cloak came down, and suddenly Jesse gripped Kofi's arm. "That's like a computer Firewall," he said. "Do you think the talisman could do that without us knowing?"

"I told you," Kofi said. "Sometimes it takes over. It'll do anything to protect us."

"It flashed like that the day the tanks and helicopters came – when we saw that vision of my dad," Jesse said. "Those tanks, and those helicopters, they could have been real – from the embassy, and that vision of my dad. He could have really been there. He couldn't see us because the talisman had thrown up a cloak – a Firewall and the others in the village wouldn't have seen anything because, for them, the firewall was total."

He glanced at Kwami. "Did you see big machines," he said. "In the trees and flying, hovering over the village?"

Kwami shook his head.

"That's it, then," said Jesse "It was the talisman. It cloaked us.

We saw a bit for a while, just so I'd know my dad was looking for me – but then … it created a virtual world all around us – so we couldn't see the embassy stuff and they couldn't see us."

"It could do that," Kofi said.

"And they might still be looking for me?" said Jesse.

"Why do you say that?" said Kofi.

"Because I think the Firewall is still up. That's why I can't get emails through to my dad. I can't break through the Firewall. It'll be like that, I guess, until they stop searching."

"You're soooo clever," Kofi laughed. "You are beginning to understand the talisman better than I do."

They swooped into the Imam's courtyard, cloaked still from the townsfolk and the Imam was caught completely off guard. When he saw the prayer mat and the three boys he gasped. But he couldn't hide his delight at seeing Kofi. "My boy," he said. "My dear Kofi Musa."

Kofi introduce the other two. "This is Jesse," he said. "He is my brother from America. He's a son of the talisman. He flew to me in a space suit."

"I know all about you," the Imam said. "You have been destined to assist Kofi since the beginning. You will unlock the wisdom of the talisman together – but …this other boy? It was not ordained that there should be three of you."

"Baba," Kofi said. "We need your wisdom. We have to talk."

They went into the room at the back of the courtyard and seeing it caught Kofi. It was so full of memories. As soon as he walked into it he recalled – the first day, the day his baba kidnapped him. He saw himself screaming and fighting – he saw the gentle persuasion of the old man – the long days of learning – the siege when the villagers attacked the house. It was as if whole pages of his life were being re-opened.

They settled at the table and Kofi told the Imam about the Nan-Nams. He explained the progress he'd made, and the regression when Jesse had arrived – he told him about the roasting – about the demolition of Kalabulay. He relished recounting that but, although the Imam smiled, he looked anxious. "It might have been better if you'd banished him, Kofi Musa," he said. "He has a long memory and he'll strike back. The moment he sees an opportunity, he'll be there. You must be very wary of him, my boy."

Kofi nodded. "That's why we've got Kwami," he said. "Jesse and I have to go to America. It's the only way to unlock the talisman. Kwami is going to be my successor. He's strong and he's clever. He can outwit Kalabulay. Kwami has always been my closest friend. He has always understood what I am trying to do. He knows how to follow in my footsteps, Baba."

"But, he'll need support," said the Imam. "Kalabulay has scores of years in cunning. He will attempt to wrap Kwami around his little finger. You must make sure your reforms are so deeply embedded that Kalabulay won't be able to manipulate the people."

For the next few hours they devised more improvements for the Nam-Nams. There were potential trade links. They could encourage outsiders – people who would barter farm machinery for grain and fruit, and who would trade for fish and meat. They would teach the women how to make bread to sell. They would introduce them to money.

"We must teach the children to read and write," the Imam said. "And, for that we'll need a teacher, with books and slates, and pencils. It will cost money."

Kofi glanced at Jesse. The treasure in The Gemstone Mountains – they'd discussed it before and they were reluctant to take anything. The mountain had to be preserved. The treasures had to be kept secret. But – a couple of well picked diamonds – on the black market – that would raise all the money they needed, and a couple of diamonds wouldn't cause suspicion. Besides, with all that wealth, you wouldn't notice the loss of a couple of diamonds.

Jesse nodded. It was as if he knew what Kofi was thinking, and Kofi reached out, grabbing both his and Kwami's hands. "We must be in agreement," he said. "But ... if we took just a couple of diamonds ... what do you think, Kwami?"

"We must," Kwami said. "The kids must be able to read and write, and we can never pay for that with farm and fishing produce."

"I can arrange it for you," said the Imam. "Just get the diamonds to me. Then I'll find a teacher. We'll get books – bring them up by boat. I'll come and set it up for you."

The Imam was as good as his word. He traded the diamonds and arrived with a young teacher. He brought books, and pencils, and slates, and chalks and styluses, and the children took to learning as if they were born to it. It excited their parents too. You could see the pride in their eyes as they watched their children scratching out letters on the slates and struggling over words in the books.

Both boys and girls went to the school. The elders wanted it to be just for boys, but Jesse insisted. In the outside world equality ruled, and if the Nam-Nams were to be integrated, then they were to take on the full force of modern thinking.

For weeks they worked on their projects, and practically every day Jesse tried to get through to his dad.

But the weeks slid into a month, and then two months – then three.

"Your mum won't die," Kofi kept assuring him. "The talisman won't let her. You must believe that."

He continued to attempt messages, although, after awhile, it became a meaningless ritual.

Then, just three months after he'd arrived in the Nam-Nam village he called up the message again. It was basically the same message he'd tried on that first day, only embroidered through time.

"Hi Mum, Dad. I'm OK," he said. *"I am with the Nam-Nam tribe in Sikaman country. I am with a friend – someone I always knew was here – Kofi. He is King of the Nam-Nams. He's the same age as me, and he has a very special computer disc. It has amazing powers. It will need a massively powerful new computer though. Kofi and I will come to the States as soon as we can so we can develop the computer.*

"Give Mum all my love – and Mr Anansi.

"I hope you're well Mum. The disc will cure your cancer.

"See you soon,

"Love you lots,

"Jesse."

It was a tired formality.

He was so used to failure he barely looked at the screen and he was about to close the program when Kofi started.

"The message has changed," he whispered

Jesse looked and across the screen he saw the words, *"Your message has been sent."*

Suddenly he felt his heart jump.

The talisman must have taken down the firewall.

He looked at Kofi and he was beaming. "Now we can make plans," he said. "Now we can get this show on the road." He gave a sigh and then, for a while, just lay back, looking at the vast expanse of stars in the African sky.

***

Chapter 13

Enemies

Everett was uneasy.

Since getting back to the States weird things had been happening. He'd had visitations, almost like visions – from Jesse.

Normally he'd have dismissed them as anxiety dreams. But these weren't dreams. They happened when he was awake, and they weren't prompted by thinking about Jesse. They just happened, and they left him with this irrational feeling of well-being. Not only that, but Ursula had them too. In them Jesse was safe and he was with a tribe in Africa, with a boy – a tribal leader. They even knew the boy's name – Kofi – and there was always the insinuation that some kind of enchanted talisman was involved.

They got to know the tribe was called the Nam-Nams, and that confirmed what he had already deduced from Mr Anansi and the map co-ordinates.

Another strange thing was that, although back here in the States, he could locate the tribe, using satellite surveillance, whenever Mamba instigated a search in Sikaman forest, he couldn't find anything.

Mamba's search was giving him other problems as well.

Mr Anansi had friends in Sikaman country, and some of them were on Mamba's staff. Mr Anansi had been warned in letters that there were other people involved with Mamba. He was receiving finances from someone, and everything Mamba knew about Jesse was being passed on to this person.

Everett believed it was Howard Tyson.

It was all very unsettling. He didn't believe in sorcery, or in any other kind of magic, but his visions and these rumours tied in so explicitly, he couldn't help feeling something was going on.

What bothered him most though was, Mr Anansi's sources told him that Tyson had some line on the enchanted talisman.

Something had to be done. If Tyson traced the kid down before Everett did – then God knows what would happen.

But there was no way he could get back to Sikaman country.

Since diplomatic relations had been severed, it was a no-go area for everybody who was American. The nearest he could get was through the US embassy in nearby Sabon Zongo. But even that wouldn't help him reach Jesse, and he needed to be certain the boy was safe.

Emails weren't getting through. Wherever Jesse was, there was a blackout. His only information came from these weird visions, and the rumours.

Ursula's faith was unshakable. "He'll turn up," she said. "And you can't dismiss this talk about sorcery and enchanted talismans. I've been to Sikaman country. I know about these villages. And those visions we get, of Jesse – they've got something to do with all this, and he's safe."

"I want to believe it," Everett said. "It's just ... I'd be so much happier if we had concrete proof."

Then, one morning ... it was there ... a message on the Internet, and that was just about the biggest thing that had happened to Everett in ages. When he read it he let out a whoop of joy, and Ursula thought something was wrong.

She came rushing into the study, propelling her wheelchair, and when she read the message she was overjoyed. "I knew he'd be all right," she said.

Straight away Everett replied.

"Jesse," he said. *"We are so glad to hear from you and to know you're okay. Your mum is fine – missing you, like I am – but she's all right. Mr Anansi's been worried. He'll be real proud you thought of him.*

"You say you'll be back 'as soon as you can'. Have you any idea when that will be? We have your passport back here. I'll set up arrangements for you to come home.

"Let us know more about Kofi. He sounds like a great guy. Tell us about the disc, too, but only on this channel, and be careful. Tyson is already on to you, and he's got intelligence on Kofi.

"Can't wait to hear from you.

"God bless, and see you soon.

"All our love,

130

"Mum and Dad."

He wasn't sure how he'd get Jesse back to the States. He certainly couldn't get him back directly from Sikaman country. He'd have to leave via Sabon Zongo. Everett could get his passport and other documents to the ambassador there. But getting Kofi back would be a different matter. He'd need a visa and Everett would have to keep all the preparations secret. If one whiff of this got to Howard Tyson, there'd be real trouble.

The question was: how were the boys going to get out of Sikaman country?

He'd have to talk it over with Jesse.

He sat back in his chair, and he was smiling. He couldn't help it. He'd just thought – something he hadn't been able to think in months – "I'll have to talk it over with Jesse."

Even thinking those words warmed his spirit.

*

The email was with Jesse next morning and seeing it sitting there, the words of his dad, after all this time, sent a thrill shuddering through him. He was relieved. Mum was all right still. That was the biggest thing. But he hadn't really doubted it. Mum was a fighter. It would take something bigger than cancer to snuff her out. Besides, Kofi had said the talisman wouldn't let her die, and now he was beginning to believe it.

But renewing contact with Dad and Mum had another effect.

For some time, he'd been losing his grip on the real world – this paradise of tropical forests, the beaches and palm trees, the seas – his friendship with Kofi – being with the Nam-Nams, flying on carpets and meeting with the Imam. Although he still felt anxiety about his mum – the mission with the rainbow talisman and the need to get back to America – they hadn't been at the forefront of his mind. He and Kofi had been through the motions of planning their departure, they'd chosen Kwami, and they'd started training him … but – even Kwami had become part of Nevada. The three of them managed to create their own idyllic world, and, although Jesse had missed his

131

mum and dad, and worried about his mum, although he had tried to send emails daily, there was no urgency in his heart when they failed.

But when he had this first reply, something inside him clicked. Suddenly he was missing his parents again. Suddenly he was pining for his mum. The need to get the talisman back to the States became vital and curing Mum's cancer became the most urgent thing in the world.

"Kofi, we've got to move," he said. "Now the talisman's released its grip and I can contact Dad, we don't need to stay here. Our work with the Nam-Nams is finished."

"But it isn't, Jesse Musungu." Kofi said. "Kwami isn't ready to take over. We haven't set up trading links with the outside world. We need a meeting with the elders. There's still oceans of stuff to do."

And Jesse's head told him Kofi was right … but his heart was back with Mum and Dad, and he was impatient. "Yeah, okay," he said. "But don't you think, up till now, focusing on the Nam-Nams all the time, we've kinda lost sight of the bigger picture? What I'm saying is, from now on, whatever we do we've got to have that in our heads – a deadline to get back to the States and get this talisman working. We've got to push harder, Kofi Bibini. We've got to be working with my dad to get us out."

Kofi leaned across and read Everett's message.

"You're dad seems happy to leave the timing to us," he said.

"Yeah, but Howard Tyson's on to us, and you've got no idea what that guy's like. If he gets hold of us, we're sunk."

Kofi shook his head. "This man Tyson won't get hold of us. The talisman won't let him. He might be able to break your codes, but he can't break the force of the talisman."

"Well I still figure we've got to work harder to get out. I mean, this is what brought us together. It's what your mission from Gandhi and Mandela was about – to use the talisman to change the world."

Kofi was thoughtful for a few minutes. "Sometimes," he said at last, "having the Nam-Nams to sort out, I lose sight of the big stuff," and that made Jesse laugh.

"Don't worry, buddy. I'll keep reminding you," he said. But then he became more earnest, because what he was talking about was really serious. "See" he said. "If I don't keep reminding you, my mum will die, and, you know what? Until this email came, I was beginning to forget about that."

That night, before they turned in, Jesse sent an email.

"Hi Dad, Mum,

"It was great to hear from you and to know Mum is okay. Lots of hugs and kisses.

"You asked about Kofi. He's an amazing guy. I can't tell you too much about him now. There's so much to tell. You'll just have to wait until we get back.

"We've got a load more work to do here though, if Mum's alright with that. Kofi is king of this tribe in Sikaman country. They're a bit primitive to say the least, and there's this guy – Kalabulay who's a really bad guy. If we go before we've finished bringing them into the twenty-first century, he'll have them back to eating white men again. We're working hard on it though, and we're getting big help from Kofi's mentor – a wise man from a village outside the forest. He's like a Guru. The guy's an Imam in the Muslim church. We've also got a boy lined up to take over from Kofi – a chap called Kwami. He's great too.

"But we want you to go ahead and make arrangements, so the minute we're ready we can come home. There'll be no problem getting back to the embassy – and you just wouldn't believe how we travel. In fact I'm not going to try and tell you. All I'll say is, we can get there, no sweat.

"Let us know how you're doing.

"Don't worry about Tyson. This disc I told you about – even now – before we've read it – has amazing powers. No way will Tyson get his hands on us. My big worry is Mum.

"Email again soon,

"Loads of love,

"Your son,

"Jesse. xxx"

Over the next few weeks they worked hard, bringing Kwami to the fore.

Up until this point the villagers had seen him as Kofi's servant, but now, whenever Kofi spoke in public, both Jesse and Kwami flanked him – both dressed in ceremonial regalia ... and, occasionally Kwami made his own speeches. He talked about trading with other tribes and he explained how they could get hold of money and how it could be exchanged for goods and commodities, and it was when Kwami started appearing that Kalabulay made his presence felt again.

For weeks he'd skulked in the Baobab tree. But when Kwami appeared he shuffled to the mouth of the tree, chewing his gums, and mumbling oaths.

At first Kofi ignored him, but the people didn't, and when Kwami was making his speeches, those near the tree became restless, because somehow, although they hated Kalabulay, he was voicing their own reservations. Kwami shouldn't be there. He shouldn't be addressing the elders without their consent. He was just a Nam-Nam kid.

"We've got to do something," Jesse said. "Those guys just can't figure Kwami."

"We can't tell them," said Kofi. "Not that we're leaving."

"Say we give him the talisman to hold," Jesse said. "– When he's making a speech. Do you think it would let us do that?"

"We could try."

Kwami was tidying the bed at the far side of the cave and Kofi called him. "Here, try holding this," he said. "– On your own. See what happens."

Kwami's face tensed. The sight of Kalabulay crouching in the tree entrance had knocked his confidence. He wasn't sure how he'd manage when Kofi and Jesse weren't there. He didn't trust himself holding the talisman either, and he fully expected to be hit skywards.

But, to begin with, there was no reaction.

Then the most amazing thing happened. The talisman started showering sparks – like fireworks – and there were stars shooting around the cave. They exploded into rainbows, and as Kwami held the disc, you could see his face light up.

When the display had finished he handed the talisman back and he was breathless.

"Kofi Musa," he whispered. "I have seen things I can't begin to describe – You and Jesse – you are kings, and you will rise above everything in the world. You will be above kings – above angels. You will be gods in the universe."

Jesse stared at Kofi. All they'd wanted was confirmation that Kwami could hold the talisman. And, really, it was that message that mattered. The Talisman had told them choosing Kwami was right. It told them that giving him the talisman would work. ... And it did ... even more spectacularly than they could have hoped.

When they addressed the people a few days later, Kwami spoke, and, as he held the talisman, its light grew.

By this time the rainy season had come, and, when Kwami began speaking, the sky was dark.

Just as he began, the rain exploded, and, as he continued, the talisman radiated more light. It lit up the space around the boys creating an aura of colours. Then it started with the fireworks, shooting rainbows into the air, setting a light dancing among the raindrops, crackling in the storm's electricity, and, with the darkness intensifying, it was mind-blowing. The people weren't listening to what Kwami was saying. They just stared at the pyrotechnics, and, from his Baobab tree, Kalabulay let out a yell of fury, and, without moving from his lotus position, he dragged himself back into the darkness.

*

They were visiting the Imam often now. He advised them on setting up contacts and he arranged meetings with leaders from other villages. They were able to negotiate food in exchange for farm machinery. The villagers built a holding for a fuel tank by the river. They cut a road through, so the motor driven machines could re-fuel. They had diesel delivered, and, over the weeks the settlement changed.

Kofi and Jesse knew opening out the tribe to the wider world was dangerous. The Imam said Mamba was still searching, and his men were everywhere. The fact they couldn't find the Nam-Nam village was making them desperate.

They were beginning to turn nasty, so it was vital to keep

developments in the village as secret as possible. With the installation of the tank and the refuelling, everything had to be done at night, and when the track wasn't being used, they camouflage it with branches and uprooted trees.

The Nam-Nams hated being in the forest at night. They felt it was dangerous. But Jesse and Kofi insisted. The tribe's location had to be protected at all costs, and everyone was excited by the changes. Ploughing and cultivating became so much easier. They were able to turn more of the wasteland into fields. They cut down trees to build pens for the animals. They used chainsaws and dragged the trees with tractors. Jesse insisted they work ecologically. They got their wood by thinning out dense areas of the forest. He was determined they would grow closer to modern civilization in an eco-friendly way.

But Kalabulay didn't like it. He dragged himself to the mouth of his tree again, and, as he chewed his imploded jaw, he scowled, denouncing the machines as engines of the devil. Every day he was there, from early morning.

It was so disconcerting they decided to take their worries to the Imam.

They always used the prayer mat to get to him, but, with Mamba's men still after Jesse, they cloaked now for the whole journey.

As they flew in this time though, they could sense something was different.

Usually there would be villagers milling around the plain with cattle grazing up by the house; but this time the whole hinterland was deserted.

"That's not right," Kofi said, and, as they got nearer, there were other things. They could see the front door of the Imam's house swinging open, and some of his windows had been smashed. There was debris in the front garden.

As they swooped over the plains they could see men hiding – Men of Mamba's militia – crouching behind bushes, with rifles trained against the Imam's house, and, instinctively Jesse knew. Howard Tyson was at work.

If he and Kofi stayed in Africa much longer Tyson would get to them. He must have made the link between him and the Imam, and there was a stunned horror as they swept across the plain. Towards the village, there were dead bodies and Kofi gasped. There'd been some kind of a battle – Mamba's men and the villagers. They swept to the village outskirts, and in the shadows they could see village men, armed and training their rifles onto the plain.

"Something really bad's going on," he said.

There was only the grim clank of a swinging door and the occasional rustle of dry leaves as they dropped into the Imam's courtyard, and they were cautious.

There could be militia in the house. This could be a trap. As they advanced, they held hands. That way the talisman still cloaked them.

But there didn't appear to be anyone there. The house had such a feel of emptiness that it made Jesse's blood freeze.

They searched until they'd convinced themselves there were no soldiers ... but there was no Imam either.

When they got back to the room by the courtyard, they dropped hands and, for a moment, they just stood there, looking around, listening, but there was only the sound of their own breathing, and the thumping of their hearts.

After a minute Kofi whispered the name: "Baba."

It hardly disturbed the dust it was so quiet, and he called again: "Baba," – louder this time. Then they heard the slightest rustle in the corner of the room. It came from behind the wall and Kofi knew. There was a secret cupboard – a place of final refuge. The door had been disguised by the panelling and straight away his eyes widened and he called again. "Baba."

Then they heard it – a dry whisper. "Kofi? My Kofi Musa?"

He rushed to the panel and thrust the door open, and there, crouched in the corner, hunched into a foetal ball was the Imam.

Smears of blood stained his head and his face was bruised. As the door opened, he threw an arm over his head to protect it, crouching deeper into the cupboard and the sight made Kofi cry out: "Baba – my Baba, what have they done to you?"

He had been hiding there for days without food – and with hardly any water, and he was stiff and weak.

They helped him to the table and Jesse fetched water. He found a few scraps of food in the fridge too.

"They are searching for you, Kofi, my boy," the old man said. "They want the talisman. And they want your friend."

"Who's searching?" Kofi said. "Is it Mamba's men?"

"Mamba, yes. And there's money on your heads – some American."

"Howard Tyson?" said Jesse.

"I don't know. But Mamba is desperate to find you, and they know a lot about the talisman. They questioned me. The village people tried to defend me, but Mamba's men beat them off. They know I've got links with Kofi and the Nam-Nams. They're trying to find the Nam-Nam village, but it seems they can't."

"That'll be the talisman," Jesse said. "It's put up a firewall."

"But they did more than just question you, Baba," Kofi said. The sight of the old man was ripping him apart. He was tending the cuts. "How could they do this to you, holy man?"

The Imam touched his hand. "They want answers, Kofi," he said.

"They'll come back?" said Jesse, and the Imam nodded.

"Every day. I hear them searching, calling my name. It's only Allah that has stopped them finding me."

"You can't stay here," Jesse said.

Kofi looked at the old man. "No. You must come back with us, on the prayer mat. You'll be safe in the village. The talisman won't let them find you there."

Cautiously the Imam struggled to his feet.

"That will mean leaving my flock," he said.

"You couldn't serve them, even if you stayed," said Kofi. "Not with Mamba's men camping outside your house. It's the only way. You've got to come back with us."

"It'll be great if you do," Jesse said. "You'd be on hand to advise. You can help get Kwami ready for when we leave – and it'll be one in the eye for Kalabulay, having an Imam around the place."

The Imam didn't offer any resistance and they lead him into the courtyard, but when he saw the prayer mat he held back. "Kofi Musa," he said. "I usually occupy a prayer mat alone, and when I do, I'm facing Holy Mecca. I'm implanted firmly on the ground. But … four of us … on one mat, flying through the air? I know I've flown with you before ... but ... there were just two of us then. – Four people, my child, on one prayer mat?"

"We can do it, Baba," Kofi laughed. "Holding each other, in a ... what do they say in American football? In a huddle."

"But won't we overbalance?" said the Imam.

"You gotta trust the talisman, father holy man," Jesse said. "You gotta trust in the disc."

"Ahh," the Imam said and he hobbled towards the mat. "It's faith is it? A blind step into the unknown."

"I'll hang on to you," Kofi said. "And no one will see us leave. In fact, no one will see us all the time we're flying."

The Imam smiled again. "Kofi Musa. After the last few days, that sounds a very sweet idea," he said.

*

Having the Imam in the village was a huge help.

He supported Kwami. He was there to oversee the links with the other tribes. He knew much more about farm machinery than the boys did.

Kalabulay retreated to his tree the moment he saw him.

There were daily emails between Jesse and Everett and it soon became clear that Sikaman country was a very hostile place, especially for Americans, and Jesse had been right about Mamba's fellow conspirator. It was Howard Tyson.

"The US embassy in Sikaman country has been closed." Dad said. *"You can't come back that way. You'll have to leave the country and come back through Sabon Zongo. I have sent your passport and a few effects to the embassy there. I don't know how you intend to get to the border. You'll be seen if you use your space suit, and the suit wouldn't be any use if Kofi comes with you."*

Jesse reassured his dad ... and he told him it was only a matter of time ... as soon as Kwami was ready ...

One thing comforted them more than they could say.

There was no way the Imam could go back to his village. He'd have to stay here, and Kalabulay wouldn't try anything while he was around. The longer he stayed, the more established Kwami would be.

139

The trade with other tribes grew, with more land being cultivated and more crops being sown. The villagers increased their fishing fleet. They even began trading using money. But they were always careful, covering their tracks, hiding their boats, making sure they couldn't be discovered by Colonel Mamba.

And eventually Kofi was ready.

Jesse emailed his dad.

Their plan was to fly to Sabon Zongo on the prayer mat, maintaining a cloak until they landed. Jesse didn't tell Dad that. Dad's feet were too well rooted for him to cope with enchanted prayer mats, but he did assure him their journey would be safe. He also said they wouldn't need to be met at the border.

They located the American embassy, and the ambassador's residence on Jesse's computer. They planned to use that on the flight as a satellite navigation system.

They even packed their belongings ready to leave, but then Dad sent an email that exploded like a bombshell.

"Send details of Kofi's passport," he said. *"So I can get a visa set up for him."*

Jesse's reply was immediate. *"Kofi doesn't have a passport. Kofi has no documentation at all. There isn't even a record of his birth."*

There were a few minutes before Dad replied, and, when he did, the message blew them apart.

"Jesse," it read. *"Without a passport Kofi <u>cannot</u> come to the USA. He will have to wait in Sabon Zongo while I sort out documentation. You must come back on your own. We'll get Kofi here as soon as possible. Contact me when you reach the American embassy in Sabon Zongo."*

Jesse stared at the message.

He hadn't thought about passports, but, if Kofi couldn't come with him, it would paralyse everything they wanted to do.

There'd be no talisman, and, with no talisman, there'd be no cure for Mum's cancer, and, having to get a visa sorted without documentation – that could take months – by which time it would be too late for Mum.

***

140

Chapter 14

Out of the Web

Letting Kofi stay in Africa was fraught with danger, Jesse was convinced of that.

Sikaman country was right next to Sabon Zongo. Mamba must have untold spies there and Howard Tyson had as much influence around these parts as Jesse's dad.

And there was another thing. Kofi raised it that night. "If I haven't got any identity, Jesse Musungu, won't they send me back from Sabon Zongo?"

Jesse didn't know, but the Imam saw no problem.

"Tell the ambassador your story," he said. "Tell him Jesse's dad is arranging documents for you. Tell him Mamba and this Tyson fellow are after you. Ask for asylum, and ask for secrecy. If people get to know where you are – either of you, then you *will* be in danger."

But the day they set out was a dreadful day.

The Nam-Nams had grown to adore Kofi. He'd brought them wealth and fine living, he'd brought them education and links with the outside world, he'd brought them money and security. To them he wasn't far off being a god.

There'd been no hints that he was leaving either, and now, here he was, with Kwami and Jesse and the Imam, all arranged in their ceremonial clothes.

Kofi had intended to give Kwami a coronation, but when the people realised what was happening, they threw their hands in the air, they cried, they beat their chests, they threw dust into the sky and thrust themselves to the ground. They pleaded, and the grief on their faces was so heart breaking, Kofi was in tears, and so were Jesse and Kwami.

It was the Imam who took the sting out of things.

He held up his hands. "Good people of the Nam-Nam tribe," he said. "Listen and bear this well. You have seen the power of the talisman. You have seen how Kofi can use it to protect you. You have seen the miracles he can do with it; but the talisman can do so much more. It can cure your sicknesses. It can take away your pain. It can heal the dieing forests and take the poison from the rivers. And not only for you, Nam-Nam people, but for the whole world. So it was ordained. That is why the great Gandhi received the talisman from the sky. That is why he passed it to Mr Mandela. That is why Kofi was born – and why Jesse came to the village. It was ordained that the great powers of the talisman should be released. But it cannot be done here in Sikaman forest. To release these powers, Kofi and Jesse must go to America, where they will build a machine that can make the talisman perform its greatest miracles. But do not be afraid, good people. When they have unlocked the power, they will come back, and they will heal your sicknesses and your forests and your rivers. First, though, you must let them go. You must bear the pain Nam-Nams. And. you will not be doing it just for yourselves. Your great sacrifice will heal the world."

He looked at the upturned faces and, from the crowd, a single elder began to clap. It was a lone sound to begin with, but after a while more joined in, until the noise swelled and the whole clearing rang with clapping and cheering.

The Imam looked at Kofi and Jesse and whispered, "Go now. Go, boys. It is time." And, as the people clapped and cheered, they rose gently into the air. Then, in the wink of light they were gone, cloaked … and a stunned grief fell over the village.

Only one person, crouched at the entrance to his Baobab tree, showed no grief. Kalabulay, the fetid, one time leader of the tribe, smiled, and his evil eyes gleamed as he watched the two boys disappear.

*

They materialised in Sabon Zongo, on the lawn of the ambassador's residence at approximately two forty five. They'd set Jesse's computer to guide them to the residence because that was where they would stay. And the first people to see them were the ambassador's daughters.

There were three of them, enjoying a teddy bears' tea party with

142

their German nanny. And the boys appeared just a few yards from where they were playing, sporting peacock feathers in their hair. Their faces were painted. Their almost bare bodies were draped in loose robes, and, when the three girls saw them, they screamed, racing across the grass towards the embassy building.

The Nanny didn't move. She just sat, staring and one of the embassy staff looked out to see what was going on and immediately alerted the security guards,

In a matter of seconds, three armed men were haring across the lawn, guns trained.

"Don't move," one of them shouted. "Just stay put and raise your hands."

Jesse and Kofi deemed it wise to observe the latter of these instructions and raised their hands.

"What's your game?" the same guard said. "And how come you broke through security without being detected?"

Still with his hands raised, Jesse said, "I believe we're expected. You could get the ambassador, or one of his senior staff to verify it. I'm Jesse Tierfelder – son of Everett Tierfelder, and I guess you know who that is. This is my friend, Kofi."

The three guards kept their guns trained and they didn't move.

One shouted over his shoulder, "Gretchen, get Nick out here. Find out if these guys are expected."

Nick was a young secretary, fair-haired and he was wearing a dark suit. He came across the lawn, brisk with determination. "Who did they say they were?" he said.

"I'm Jesse Tierfelder, and this is Kofi, my friend – from Sikaman country."

The secretary stopped in mid stride. "We *are* expecting a Jesse Tierfelder," he said. "And an African boy, but we weren't expecting them to turn up here on the lawn. We planned to pick them up at the border in an embassy staff car."

"I told Dad we wouldn't need picking up," Jesse said.

"Well, how did you get here?" said Nick.

"On the prayer mat," Jesse said. He grinned. "I know you're not going to believe that, but if you hang on for a minute we'll show you how we did it."

The guys with the guns were jumpy. "Don't move," they snapped – but Nick nodded.

"Leave them be. Because, two kids on a flying carpet – this I must see."

Kofi and Jesse sat cross-legged again, and, gently the prayer mat lifted while the guards leaped to a kneeling position, training their guns. Nick's mouth was open and the three little girls let out more screams.

"We can cloak," Jesse shouted. "Wanna see?"

"Yep," Nick said. "Go on. Cloak" … and, to even more hysteria from the girls, the mat and the boys disappeared. They did a quick flip across the lawn, and re-emerged twenty yards to the guard's right and Jesse shouted: "Over here."

By now, the guards were too edgy. It was risky playing games any more, so they stepped off the carpet.

"That's how we did it," Jesse said. "It's all to do with this disc Kofi's got. It's top secret – but I'm trusting you guys because I know you're officials. You've signed the official secrets act."

His tone took some of the angst out of the guards. They lowered their guns and led them off into the residence while Nick stayed back. He crossed towards the girls and knelt beside them. "What you've just seen is magic," he said. "And you've got to keep it a big secret. You mustn't tell anyone, because these boys are escaping from a really bad wizard. If he gets to hear about this, he'll come and get them, and he'll do awful magic – on all of us."

The girls nodded as Nick put his finger to his lips. Then he winked at Gretchen.

"Not a word, mind," he said.

Then he followed the guards into the building.

By this time the office staff had established from Jesse's passport that he really was Jesse Tierfelder. They called the ambassador back from the embassy and led the two boys into a room where he was waiting.

He was young – a lot younger than Joe Weinberg, and his hair was fair. It was thinning, and he had strands of it dragged across his head in a comb over. His gold-rimmed glasses added to his sallow complexion and seeing him made Jesse despair. There was no way this guy was going to bend the rules – not like Joseph Weinberg would. He noticed how he gave a slight wince when he saw them in their peacock feathers and ceremonial paint.

But then he smiled and somehow that brought humanity to his face. "Welcome, gentlemen," he said. "I guess the appropriate greeting would be, 'I've been expecting you,' but that would only be a half truth. I *was* expecting you – but I imagined your arrival might be somewhat more traditional. I certainly did *not* expect you to materialise on my lawn – riding on a carpet, dressed in such splendid regalia.

"But, then again," he added. "Everett Tierfelder's son ... why would anyone expect Everett Tierfelder's son to do something ordinary?" He stood up, leaning across the desk and extending a hand. "Jesse isn't it? Welcome to Sabon Zongo, Jesse Tierfelder."

Then he turned to Kofi. "And this is the young African prince? Everett told me about him."

"Yeah," Jesse said. "Kofi Musa. He's a kind of tribal leader in Sikaman forest – he leads the Nam-Nams, but now he's got to get to the States. If he goes back to Sikaman country or stays here, he's in danger from Colonel Mamba and Howard Tyson. I think there's a bounty out on us."

"Your dad did fill me in on that," the ambassador said. "But I was under the impression Kofi wanted asylum while he sorts out papers in the States"

Jesse was gaining confidence again now. He didn't think the ambassador was going to be so bad. "Yeah," he said. "That's exactly it. He does ... but we need secrecy." He glanced around at the three security guards and the secretaries.

"You want to tell me something off the record?" the ambassador said.

"It would help if we could," said Jesse. "I want to put you in the picture as much as I can, but it's top secret. I don't want stuff getting out."

The ambassador nodded and the security guards, Nick and the secretaries left. Then he leaned back more relaxed. "Your dad's filled me in on quite a bit," he said. "– Fanciful stuff, but – well, if you can make carpets fly and you can turn invisible ... I guess it's not that fanciful."

145

"We have a disc," Jesse said, "And it can do a lot more than fly carpets and cloak. But we have got to get it back to the States. We have to unlock it. To do that we need to build a new computer. The trouble is Howard Tyson's desperate to get hold of the disc. That's why I've got to get back with no one knowing, and that's why Kofi needs asylum. We can't do anything without Kofi."

He stopped. It had all come out in a moment of impetuosity. No one had ever been told this much before, except for the Imam, and Jesse'd dad ... and, in their simple way, the Nam-Nams. But he re-assured himself – this man – an American ambassador ... he had to know, otherwise, how could they be certain Kofi would be safe? "The disc – the talisman ... it's been entrusted to Kofi and that means I can't take it with me, not unless Kofi goes too."

The ambassador nodded and suddenly Jesse felt uneasy again. He wondered if he'd said too much, because there was a gleam behind the ambassador's glasses, and it unnerved him.

"Don't worry, kid," the ambassador said. "Kofi and his disc will be safe with us till your dad gets the papers sorted."

Jesse relaxed a bit, but ... still something unsettled him.

Now though there were more pressing things to attend to. Nick was getting in drinks and sandwiches, and, then the boys had to be taken to their rooms.

They'd been given single rooms, adjacent to each other. There were clothes and towels laid out, and, for Jesse, a small travel case for when he flew home.

They were left to shower and change, but Kofi had never seen a shower like this before, and Jesse had to show him how it worked.

Then Kofi joined him. He looked strange in trousers and shirt and he still had nothing on his feet. He said he'd never worn shoes.

"I guess they'll have to find you a pair of sandals," Jesse said. "Because it's pretty clear you and shoes are never going to be happy bedfellows."

"Do I have to wear them in bed?" Kofi said, and that made Jesse laugh.

"It's just a saying," he said. "Don't bother your head about it."

But something did bother their heads.

"I shouldn't have told that guy about the talisman," Jesse said. "I mean, say he's in league with Howard Tyson. Tyson's as much an American as Dad is, and this ambassador guy could just as well be in with Tyson. I tell you what, Kofi, I don't like the idea of leaving you here."

Kofi was on Jesse's bed, leaning forward, his hands clasped between his legs. He wasn't happy either, but not just because of threats from Tyson or Mamba. Everything about the place bothered him – the showers – the air-conditioned rooms – the plush furnishings – the boxed in feel. It was like a prison.

"I don't like any of it," he said. "I don't like it even when you're here." Then he looked at Jesse, and there was a hint of awkwardness. "I don't even want to be on my own," he said. "Would it be all right if I came in with you tonight?"

Jesse grinned. "I guess that's not a problem. I'll get someone to move the other bed in here."

"I'm not sleeping on that," Kofi said. "I'll sleep on my prayer mat, like I always do, but I'm going to hate it when you've gone."

If he was honest, Jesse was even more worried about leaving Kofi now. He really wanted the papers sorted before they left, and, when he emailed his dad that night, it was an email pleading to let Kofi come back to the States straight away.

But there was no hope. Apart from expressing amazement that they'd managed to get out of Sikaman country so easily, all Dad did was preach. There was no way Kofi could come back. Even fast tracking and using all his influence, it would take more than a month, and Jesse should be more concerned about his mum. He needed to be back in the States, which was why the ambassador had arranged for him to be on the first flight next day.

That news tore him apart.

He wanted to get back to his mum. He wanted it more than anything, but he wanted Kofi with him, and Kofi's face fell when he heard.

"So soon?" he said.

"You'll be okay," said Jesse. "You've got the talisman. And you've got to keep in contact – with the telepathy thing, every day, every hour, all the time."

But, on the way to the airport, they sat staring ahead of them and

147

neither of them could find time to spend on their minder's fatuous conversations.

Kofi's face was ashen, and it shook Jesse, because, for the first time he saw a small, frightened kid, vulnerable and alone. And he felt desolate on the plane. There were no feelings of excitement at the prospect of seeing Mum and Dad. He didn't watch the films or listen to the music. He didn't read the magazines. All he did was stare into the emptiness outside the plane window.

But if he hadn't been staring out, he wouldn't have noticed the speck tracking the plane. He wouldn't have seen it as it got nearer. He wouldn't have watched it run alongside and he wouldn't have recognised Kofi flying adjacent to the window on his prayer mat. He wouldn't have seen the white flash of teeth, and he wouldn't have been able to acknowledge Kofi's wave as he overtook the plane.

But he *did* see it, and suddenly adrenalin pulsed through him.

Kofi was heading for America and, with luck, he'd be there before Jesse landed.

He called for a phone and then headed for the privacy of the toilet.

Dad had to be told.

It was the first time he'd heard his dad's voice in six months and it made his heart lurch.

"How you doing? Good flight so far?" Dad said. "I'll be there when you arrive. Mum's not able to, or she'd be there too."

"Dad," Jesse said, and he said it in that enigmatic way that suggested news Dad wouldn't want to hear. "It's about Kofi," he said. "And I think you'd better sit down for this. He's got this awesome Imam's prayer mat – and … you're not going to believe it, Dad, but … well, with the talisman, he can fly it – and he can cloak it from detection … that's how we got out of Sikaman country."

His dad didn't speak for a few seconds, then he said, "That sounds great, son." Then Jesse grinned, because he knew what had been done couldn't be undone.

"Well, Dad, I think Kofi's slipped the net back in Sabon Zongo. He's on his prayer mat, and he's heading for the States. I've just seen him go past the plane. He's cloaked now so I don't know where he is – but he's on his way, and it's my guess he'll be there before I am."

There was a pause – longer this time, then – "You sure you didn't dream this up, son?" his dad said.

"No Dad, I saw him He's on his way. You can check with the embassy in Sabon Zongo if you like – and you've got to sort it so he can stay – because he's going to be there when I arrive, no kidding."

There was an explosion of dismay at the other end of the line – but then ... "You didn't plan all this before you left, did you?"

"No Dad – honest," Jesse said. "I was as surprised as you are – but I've got to be straight with you. I'm dead glad, because that ambassador back at the embassy wasn't safe. No way was he safe."

"Not to worry then, son," Dad said. "I'll do my best. See you soon." And the line went dead.

Jesse took the phone back to the cabin attendant and he felt easier than he had in ages. He knew Dad would sort it. There would be no problems for Kofi when he got to America, and, then, tomorrow, they could start work on the new computer.

*

Everett didn't have much time for thinking. He'd got about eight hours to arrange things.

He told Ursula, and then he called up immigration. He went straight to the top – Eddie Stanhope, chief secretary at the state department. He and Eddie were good mates and Everett couldn't think of a better guy to pull strings, if strings had to be pulled.

"The kids half way here and he's got no documentation," he said.

"What's he done – stowed away in the luggage, or what?" said Eddie.

But what could he say? That he was flying in on a prayer mat?

"Search me," he said. "All I know is the kid's going to be in the country, and I need to make it legal – like, yesterday."

"Where's his paperwork? Back in Africa?" Eddie said. "Couldn't we just hold him until we've picked it up?"

"He hasn't got any paperwork, Eddie. Not judging by what Jesse told me. There's no birth certificate – nothing."

"It happens," Eddie said. "Kids born out in the sticks – but ... he's got family back in Africa?"

"No," Everett said. "The kid's a foundling – brought up by an Imam. He's got no blood relatives whatever."

There was a pause, and Eddie's voice became more tentative, "Sorry, but I've got to ask. What's your interest in all this, Everett?"

"The kid's been kind of adopted by Jesse, and – I don't know – there's something special about him. There's a bounty on his head, I know that – and Mamba's after him. He's genuine, Eddie. Mamba's people are searching for him everywhere. He's got the strongest grounds for asylum."

There was another pause. "Asylum's a slow process. – How old did you say he was?"

"About Jesse's age – twelve," Everett said.

"It'll be high profile – a twelve year old, wanted by Mamba. The press will love it."

"The press mustn't know. No publicity. There's people in this country that are as interested in the boy as Mamba is."

"Why?" said Eddie.

"I can't tell you that. You meet us at the airport and you'll understand – but, Eddie, it's got to be kept under wraps – big time."

Everett heard a long sigh from the other end. "It's not going to be easy, Everett, and, asylum ... it could take months – years even, and the kid would have to be held in a centre somewhere. That's not a good thing for a young kid."

Everett heard the office door click and he knew Ursula was there. There was something brewing in his head too. He turned and, straight away, he knew. She'd read his mind and ... he didn't need to say a word. She smiled and nodded.

"Say we wanted to adopt him, Eddie?" Everett said.

There was a long silence then, before: "For you, Everett, I may just be able to swing that, but ... are you certain ... you know ... with Ursula's condition and everything?"

"Ursula's absolutely with me," Everett said. "We need this kid, here in the States. He's a good kid. Jesse thinks the world of him."

"You got any details – birthdays and the like?" Eddie said. "I mean, the kid might not have a birth certificate ... but ... some sort of a date would be a start."

150

"He's about Jesse's age, that's all I know," Everett said.

"We'll have to interview the guy. Does he speak English?"

"I reckon he could match Jesse in any argument," Everett said, and Eddie laughed.

"The guy's English is better than mine then. Okay. I'll be at immigration – and don't worry, we'll keep it under wraps. And Everett … no promises. I'll do my best. That's all I can say."

Everett put down the receiver and turned to Ursula.

"It'll be the best thing that's happened to us in ages," she said. "And it'll be great for Jesse. They're so close already. They could be joined at the hip."

She set about preparing a room, and Everett worked on the legal side. His lawyers needed to draw up adoption papers, and they'd have to be at the airport along with Eddie.

He thought this might come as one hell of a shock for Jesse, but he knew his kid. He was certain he would be over the moon at the idea.

*

For a boy whose only experience had been the basics of village life and five years living with apes Kofi was doing all right. He'd landed close to the airfield, he'd hitched a ride on a lorry – and he'd found his way to the *arrivals Hall*. In fact, from what Jesse could see he was loving every minute of it.

There were serious things to sort with Dad though. Jesse knew Dad wasn't the kind to play fast and loose with the law and Kofi was in the country illegally. They'd have to put that right before they did anything.

As they sat, looking out of the window in the VIP lounge they watched the planes crawl across the tarmac, and the whole place was buzzing. It excited Jesse. He was back in the world of commerce and machines … and soon he would be with Mum again.

"We've got people to see," Dad said. "Back down in immigration. My lawyer's in there, and Eddie Stanhope."

Jesse looked at Kofi and grinned. "Eddie Stanhope's top guy in the State Department – a bit like Mamba back in Sikaman country."

"I hope not," Dad laughed, but then his face fell serious. "We've got to talk though, before we go down there. There's something big I've got to tell you. Kofi, am I right in thinking you haven't got any family back in Africa?"

Kofi nodded. "I have my Imam," he said. "My baba ... but he's the only one."

"Well ... and I want you both to listen up for this. It's big stuff and we'll only do it if it's what you both want.

"Getting papers sorted for Kofi is going to be a problem. It'll involve him having to stay in a detention centre. It's the only way we can get him in as an asylum-seeker and it's going to take for ever, even with Eddie Stanhope on the case ... and ... well ... to be honest, that's not what your mother and I really want, Jesse. I mean, Kofi's a good kid ... and ... we've talked it over and – Kofi – Ursula and me ... if you and Jesse are agreeable ... well ... we'd like to adopt you – make you our son."

There were occasions when Jesse would have wanted to ask questions. Was it just convenience, to speed up the paperwork – was it some big sacrifice Mum and Dad were making – with Mum so ill? – Could you adopt a twelve-year-old kid and love him when you'd never set eyes on him before? Was it okay to have a black guy and a white guy as brothers?

But today, his only thought was: Kofi – to be Mum and Dad's kid – to be his brother. If Dad had offered him the universe he couldn't have been happier. Their faces were wreathed in untrammelled joy, and they threw their arms around each other, and around Dad, generating the biggest three-way bear hug ever.

Everett extricated himself, laughing. "No problem with that then," he said.

*

There was no entourage, and Jesse was surprised, but Everett just chuckled. "If a Dad can't be on his own – drive himself to the airport to meet his son after losing him for the best part of six months, then there's not much point in being a dad, is there?"

Jesse grinned. "I did miss you, Dad. I really did," he said.

The paperwork was complicated and, normally, it would have been tedious, but Kofi's answers had immigration buzzing. Reared by apes? Taken over by an Imam? Made a king so he could civilize a bunch of cannibals? A prayer mat as a main form of transport? The bureaucrats had nothing in their armoury to cope with it, and when Kofi demonstrated his mat, it looked as if the whole thing would degenerate into farce.

But they kept sober for long enough to get the paperwork completed, and, for Jesse and Kofi, the form filling was a pathway to heaven.

They'd always felt like brothers ... and now it was going to be formalised

And there was something else, something neither of them had dreamed of.

When Everett's lawyer said: "I don't suppose you have any idea when you were born?" Kofi grinned.

"I do actually," he said. "My baba Imam saw my mother driven into the forest, and she was in labour when she went. He remembered the date, and when I came back to him – we celebrated my birthday every year. I was born on the twenty-sixth of November."

He looked around, because everyone was staring, and Jess 's eyes were sparkling.

"That's my birthday too," he gasped.

He threw his arms around Kofi, lifting him from the floor. "We're not only brothers. We're twins – real twins, born on the same day."

***

153

Chapter 15

Turning the Key

Kofi was excited, but he was anxious. Things had moved so quickly. In two days he'd been shunted from a forest clearing where nothing moved faster than a frightened chicken, to the siren-screaming pandemonium of Washington, and it dazed him.

But he was with Jesse, and that was all right, because, with Jesse, he'd unravel the chaos … and Jesse's dad and Jesse's mum wanted him to be their son … and Jesse wanted him to be his brother.

There were more surprises to come though.

He'd noted the opulence of the embassy in Sabon Zongo … and he understood that. It was an embassy – the public statement of a super-state. But, when he saw Jesse's house, it rivalled the embassy in every way, and that was something he hadn't anticipated. He gasped.

"It's okay, isn't it?" Jesse said.

"All this, just for you and your mum and dad, Jesse Musungu?" he whispered.

"And the staff," said Jesse. "You wait till you meet Mr Anansi. He's real cool. He's from Sikaman country, like you are." And Mr Anansi was the first person Kofi did meet. He was waiting on the steps with Jesse's mum, and his smiling face eased Kofi's anxiety.

But the sight of Jesse's mum shocked him. He knew she was ill, but … she was in her wheelchair and it seemed a sudden breeze could snuff her out.

He watched Jesse, and he knew Jesse was shaken too. As the car came to a halt at the front entrance, Jesse gulped, and all he said was "Mom?" and there were tears in his eyes.

His mum had changed so much.

It seemed that she was clinging to life by a spider's thread and it frightened him.

He looked at Kofi and immediately Kofi touched his hand.

"The talisman won't let her die," he whispered.

Mr Anansi said a few words to Kofi in Pidgin English and that did wonders for his peace of mind.

After a short discussion it was decided that he and Jesse should share a room. Jesse's mum ordered a second bed to be moved in and Kofi and Jesse looked at each other. There was no point in telling them he would ignore the sprung mattress in favour of a prayer mat.

But they did tell Mr Anansi and Mr Anansi laughed.

He'd had a first day in America – a long time ago, but he still remembered.

When they'd settled, after dinner, they were in the lounge. Mr Anansi was still with them and, for Kofi, that was the essential link between the old and the new. Jesse wanted him there too. He'd shared his dreams with Mr Anansi and Mr Anansi knew about the talisman.

Kofi put the disc on the coffee table and it radiated a soft light. Somehow, it engendered a peace in the room. It lit up Jesse's mum's face and, as the light touched her, all the lines of tension and the wasting seemed to melt, and Jesse saw a serenity that was beyond this world.

"It's beautiful," she said. "But, how do you know it will do all the things you said about?"

"You tell them, Kofi," Jesse said.

There was a faraway look in Kofi's eyes. "I just know," he said. "Its power has grown up with me. You can't hold it without knowing. You can't live with it for twelve years without knowing. Some of the power is already there, but, even before Jesse came to Sikaman country, I knew it had greater powers. I knew Jesse would come – My Imam told me, and, from way back, I knew, because a second person, a second keeper of the talisman, had to unlock the disc." His face was reflecting the rainbow light and his eyes were soft. "It will cure your cancer Mrs Tierfelder. I know about that, and I know it will cure you."

A slow smile crossed Ursula's face. She leaned forward and took Kofi's hand. "Thank you, Kofi," she said. "And ... I know this may be hard for you, but ... it is our dearest hope ... Everett's and mine ... that you are soon to be our son ... like Jesse ... and it would mean so much to me if you could find it in your heart to call me mum – or mother or ..."

Her voice tailed off and Kofi gave Jesse a half guilty glance. But Jesse's face was glowing.

"Go on Kofi Bibini," he said. "You're my brother. You've got to."

"Mum ... Dad," Kofi said. He looked down. And then no one said anything for a while.

Even Everett was moved and Jesse decided that this moment, in this room, with these people would be one of the most precious of his life.

At last Everett leaned towards the talisman. "May I?" he said.

"You'd better be careful, Dad," Jesse said. "It's got a kick like a donkey."

They laughed, and Everett took it while Kofi and Jesse held their breath. But there was no violent reaction. Tonight it just glowed, with colours flowing over its surface in psychedelic waves.

"We'll need to analyse it in the lab," Everett said.

"Well, you won't find what it's made of," said Jesse. "Like I told you. There's nothing on earth like it."

"The light's so amazing," Mr Anansi said. "But, I just wonder, Kofi Musa, where's the power in the thing? All we've seen so far is the glow of a rainbow."

Everett laughed. "I've seen the power Mr Anansi, in the immigration offices at the airport. I've seen it carry Kofi around the room on an Indian prayer mat."

Kofi grinned. "Do you want to see it do something, Mr Anansi?" and Mr Anansi nodded.

"That's exactly what I want, Kofi Musa."

There was a set of patio doors leading onto a paved terrace and along the terrace wall Kofi could see coloured glass bowls. "What are those?" he said.

"They're patio lights," said Everett. "The bowls have candles in them. Sometimes of a night it's quite romantic to sit out with the lights flickering along the wall isn't it Ursula?"

Jesse winced. "Dad, you're going soft," he said but Everett grinned.

"You wait till you're in love, son," he said.

Kofi didn't say anything. He was staring at the candles. Then he nudged Mr Anansi, because two of the bowls were lifting from the wall and floating through the open doors. Ursula started and so did Mr Anansi. Their eyes followed the bowls as they came to rest on the mantelshelf, and Kofi's eyes sparkled. He hadn't played with it like this since way back, when he was at the Imam's house. He'd forgotten how much fun it was. Then he fluttered his eyelashes, and suddenly the bowls burst into flame.

"That's amazing," Mr Anansi gasped.

Kofi looked at Ursula. "And this one is for you, Mrs Tierfelder ... Mum ... and for you sir." He turned to the wall on the raised terrace again and immediately all the bowls were dancing, with lights of every colour.

"That's a real sweet thing you've done there, son." Everett said. "Your mum and me, well ... we're really touched."

In that moment Kofi felt a warmth of belonging that he'd never experienced before and he glanced at Jesse, who was beaming.

"Wonderful, Kofi Musa," Mr Anansi said. "Absolutely wonderful."

But Kofi was on a high. "Have you got any relatives in Sikaman country, Mr Anansi?"

"A brother, yes," said Mr Anansi

"And have you got a cell phone?"

"I carry it with me everywhere."

"Would you like your brother to call you?" Kofi said.

"It'll still be night back in Sikaman country," Mr Anansi said. "He won't be awake."

But there was a glint in Kofi's face. "You just hold my hand, Mr Anansi. Brothers like to talk any time, day or night ... isn't that right, Jesse Musungu?"

"It sure is, Kofi Bibini," said Jesse.

"Now, Mr Anansi, you think hard about your brother ... try and picture him ... and think 'call me'. Do it really hard."

They were all laughing because Mr Anansi's face was screwed up like a six year old trying to figure out Maths. Then, from his pocket, his phone rang. He grabbed it, his eyes wide, and he held it to his ear.

There was a crackle of a voice at the other end and his eyes grew to maximum. His jaw practically dropped to floor, and he grabbed Kofi's arm and hissed, "It's my brother. It's my brother."

His brother said he'd been asleep, and he'd had this dream where he'd seen Mr Anansi with a young Sikaman boy, and something had told him he had to ring – straight away – even though it was still the black of night, and Mr Anansi was out of his scull. "The talisman? It can do all that?" he said.

Everett looked at Jesse. "Is that what happened to us, son? All those times we had visions of you – all those assurances your mum and I got that you were okay?"

Jesse nodded. "Every day I sent you messages, and I could see you and Mum. I could see where you were, what you were doing – everything."

"Absolutely astounding," Mr Anansi said.

"Can I have another look?" said Everett.

Kofi handed him the talisman.

"Shall we take it to the lab?" he said.

There was a fully equipped laboratory at the back of the house, overlooking a secluded part of the garden.

The lab intrigued Kofi. It had scanners and substance analysers. It had banks of computers, microscope desks – and more tools than you'd find in a surgeon's theatre. The room had to be kept clinically dust free. They weren't allowed in until they'd been through a decontamination chamber, and they had to wear special clothes – white overalls and goggles.

The first thing Everett did was put the disc under a scanner. Jesse watched. It took longer than usual to analyse.

"It's like I said, Dad. It's not made of anything you'll find in the periodic table. There's nothing like it on earth."

Everett nodded. "It looks like your right, kid," he said. "Either that or my scanner's bust."

Eventually the screen cleared and a message came up. *No identifiable substance found. Nearest element: carbon. Nearest composite: diamond.*

"That's amazing," said Everett. "And it completely backs the legend – a disc coming from outer space. It's incredible."

"What are we going to do with it now?" Jesse said.

"I guess we've got to read it if we can," said Everett.

There was a computer at the back of the room, bigger than the others. He took the talisman and loaded it. It was still radiating its mellifluent aura and he watched closely. "This should read it if anything will," he said. "It's got the biggest memory and the largest reading capacity of anything I've got."

It didn't take long to scan the disc – not like the analytical scanner had, and, in a way, Jesse half expected that. In a second a message flashed across the screen. *Format not recognised, please remove disc.* Then there was another message. *This computer will scan for viruses and then it will close down.*

Its firewall was working overtime.

"Have we got anything else?" said Jesse.

"Not at the minute. We'll have to build something," Everett said.

"With red and green lasers?"

"That's the most advanced system we know of – a holographic versatile disc reader. We'll get working on it first thing in the morning."

Jesse looked at Kofi and laughed, because there was an expression of total bewilderment on his face. "Are you talking English, Jesse Bibini?" he demanded.

"Yeah," Jesse said. "Me and Dad use it all the time. It's called C.J.S, Computer Jargon Speak. Is that right, Dad?"

Everett punched him playfully in the ribs. "It's good to have you back, son," he said. "And it's great to have you here too, Kofi."

*

The next few weeks were a whirlpool of unfamiliarity. Kofi had to be security processed, with finger print readings, retina scans, voice recognition probes, all of which resulted in a plastic pass with his photo so he could gain access to the factory.

He looked at the photo and chuckled. "I am a handsome guy, Jesse Musungu. You have to agree with that."

Jesse grinned. "You're sure not lacking in the self-admiration department," he said. "Get a bigger ego and you'll need counselling for Narcissism."

"Is that Computer Jargon Speak too?" Kofi said.

"You're not far off, Kofi Bibini – but this one's more like Neurosis Jargon Speak. It's okay, though. All decent Americans have therapists."

"I see," Kofi said … but he didn't, and he didn't 'see' a great deal of what went on over the weeks. The language they used bore no similarity to what he'd been taught by his Imam, and the mechanisms were so intricate – tiny microchips that a speck of dust would throw off course – hard discs – software. He did recognise the compact discs because they were like his talisman.

But there was an air of excitement – and Everett didn't miss a trick. He consulted colleagues and friends. Sometimes there were up to a dozen top brains, congregating around the new machine.

Jesse thrived on it. He was in with the best of them, putting his ideas forward.

But there were other things to occupy them – and they weren't so welcome.

When Kofi and Jesse arrived in America, after they'd been through immigration, Everett had given the press its promised briefing, but it had been short because the boys were tired, and Jesse was keen to get back to his mum. It had been enough to rouse interest in Kofi's arrival though – and it had re-invigorated the curiosity about Jesse's six-month disappearance.

There were rumours from Africa, about Kofi's talisman – and the press weren't slow to add things up. A talisman much like a computer disc – Everett's interest. The curiosity was becoming insatiable.

When they went to the factory, there were reporters at the main gate. People kept phoning. Paparazzi camped out at the entrance to the house.

The story that Everett and Ursula were adopting the African boy was big news too, especially as it was known Ursula was suffering some debilitating disease. Speculation raged, and some of the tabloids didn't pull their punches. Everett was used to it, but he was worried about Ursula and the boys.

Eventually he decided to deal with it head on. He'd call a one-off press conference, with him leading, and with Jesse and Kofi there to answer questions.

He trusted them. He'd always trusted Jesse, and, even in the few weeks he'd known Kofi, he realised how capable he was. As Jesse said, you couldn't control a tribe in the Sikaman forest, re-educate them and ward off the connivances of a Kalabulay without picking up a few hints about how to deal with the press.

The meeting was scheduled for a Friday afternoon and they chose conference rooms at one of Washington's most prestigious hotels. Everett was hoping the facilities would soften things – and he was doing it on a Friday because that would give it the weekend for the story to break, simmer and burn out.

But it was a lively occasion and there were media from all over the world.

"Is this normal, Dad?" Jesse said.

Everett gave a wry smile. "Not exactly, son. Looks like Kofi's talisman has caught on, big time. Do you want me to do the talking?"

They'd discussed it and they knew how they were going to play it. Jesse was still conscious of the dangers of being sidetracked. He'd fallen into that trap with the ambassador in Sabon Zongo and, in Sabon Zongo, the ambassador wasn't even fishing for information. Here there were reporters, hell-bent on getting stuff – and these guys were professionals.

But to Kofi, there was no difference between this and his tribe back in Africa, and if things went wrong, Everett was there to step in. "It doesn't bother me," he said.

They waited, Everett tapping a pen against a water jug, until the press settled. Then he made a brief statement. Jesse had been in Africa, on a fact-finding mission linked to the environment. He'd come across a tribe in Sikaman forest, led by Kofi. He and Kofi had become friends and he discovered Kofi had a talisman that seemed to have curious properties. They decided to bring it back to the States where Everett had the facilities to examine it. That's what they were doing now and, as soon as their research was complete, they'd inform every one of their findings.

Then he asked for questions … and it was like taking the lid off a pressure cooker. He looked for some familiar face – someone he knew and trusted, and he singled out a press officer from *The Washington Post*.

"Mr Everett, sir," the reporter said. "Would it be possible to see the talisman?"

… So it was straight in – Kofi up front without ceremony. But Kofi had no qualms.

Before he spoke, though, Everett explained that the talisman was, for Kofi, a very special heirloom, and Kofi liked to be in complete control of it. Then Kofi stepped forward, took the talisman from around his neck and held it out for all to see.

It glowed, emitting soft rainbow light and a ripple went around the room. Then hands shot up.

The talisman – it looked very much like a computer disc. Was that what interested Mr Tierfelder?

He fended that by pointing out his field was computing, and that he thought the talisman might have properties he could investigate.

The next question came from a 'red top' and it was one that, for a second, made Jesse catch his breath. "Mr Tierfelder," the reporter said. "It's rumoured that you and your wife are in the process of adopting this African kid. What's your motive for doing that?"

Everett didn't hesitate. "Kofi has no living parent," he said. "In the last six months he and Jesse have bonded so powerfully – it seemed the right thing to do. And when we met Kofi, there was no doubt. He's a wonderful kid. We love him and we want him as our son."

"Are you telling us the talisman that came with the boy had nothing to do with your decision?" the reporter said, and Jesse watched his dad's face.

He needed to see the reaction; and what he saw was an expression of steel. He could see a white rage in his father's eyes and Everett said nothing for a good thirty seconds. The atmosphere in the conference hall was thick and when he did speak, his voice would have frozen helium. "That is a question, sir," he said, "to which I will not afford the dignity of a reply."

It was enough, and the hard-nosed conglomerate in the hall clapped.

When the noise died down one of the reporters said: "Could I put a question to Kofi? You say the talisman is enchanted. We can see it has some power. It gives off light, and that's impressive, but … in what way is it enchanted … can you give us some kind of demonstration?"

Kofi glanced at Everett and Everett nodded.

Then Kofi smiled. He was good at this. He knew what it could do, and he held it in front of him, both hands clutching the rim, and he closed his eyes. If it was a demonstration they wanted, a demonstration is what they would get.

There was a buzz as the two wide screen relay systems went blank. Then there was a flurry from camera crews, because all their cameras had blacked out. After that the nervous chatter became pandemonium as mobile phones started ringing all around the place – calls from every television station in the world, informing their reporters that the networks had crashed. Voices rose to shouts as the press struggled to make themselves heard above their colleagues.

Kofi stood there, a broad grin on his face, and Jesse grinned too. He had to hand it to Kofi. When the guy chose to make an impact, he made an impact.

Everett wasn't quite so comfortable. He'd never seen the talisman do anything like this. A few tricks in the living room, some stuff with a flying prayer mat and a cloaking device, yes, but what Kofi had done this time was worldwide. He wasn't certain the demonstration was the most expedient example of the talisman's powers. But it was done and Kofi was in charge. All Everett could do was field the awkward questions.

Kofi held his hand up and the chatter faded. But he couldn't resist one more trick and, as the reporters ripped away their headphones, the bank of people responsible for translating stared. The boy was speaking in their language – in their dialect. Everyone of them understood every last word.

"That is the type of power we already know about," Kofi said. "The type of thing that can be achieved without help, but we know there is more and we believe the talisman needs a computer to release the extra powers."

There was an audible buzz around the room. "I will now restore your televisions," Kofi said. "But … for the rest of the conference you can forget your translators. – They can get a coffee or something. We will maintain the talisman's powers so you can understand everything, no matter what your native language is."

As he said it, the televisions and cameras began flickering again and there was laughter as mobile phones started ringing – television stations phoning their journalists to tell them their networks were back.

It took five minutes for order to be restored, and, while the hubbub went on Everett gave Kofi a knowing smile. "That was pretty impressive, son ... but ... God knows what this lot will do with it. There's going to be some big questions when they've settle."

And there were big questions. To Everett's amazement though, Kofi fielded most of them.

At first the first questions were gentle.

Can the talisman be replicated?

Kofi said, no – they had already tried to analyse the material and there was no such substance anywhere on Earth.

The next question ran – when they could use the talisman to its full potential, what did they hope to achieve?

He just said, "I want my talisman to be used for the benefit of everyone in the world."

That brought a ripple of applause, because, even the press could recognise sincerity when they heard it.

"Do you have any idea what it can do?" one reporter asked.

Kofi looked at Jesse and Everett and said: "That is what my brother and my dad are trying to find out."

After that the questions became fiercer.

Wanting it to be used for the good of mankind was all very well ... but ... say it fell into the wrong hands.

There was a glint in Kofi's eye when he heard that, and Jesse knew exactly what was going to happen next. "The talisman has its own in-built protection," Kofi said. He looked at the questioner and said, "Do you want to give it a try?"

The reporter stepped up to the dais.

"Don't grab hold of it," Kofi warned. "Just touch it lightly and then get clear as quickly as you can."

The reporter laid a finger on the talisman and, in the next second he was hopping around the stage with his hand clutched under his armpit, and he was yelping. The rest of the press laughed, but Kofi had made his point.

"Next question?" he said.

Was it true, one young woman asked, that other people were interested in getting hold of the talisman? All he did in reply to this was turn to the reporter who'd touched the disc. The reporter grinned and said, "I'd like to see someone try."

Then one of the reporters said, "Mr Kofi – when this thing is fully operational, you said you wanted it to be used for the good of the whole world, okay?"

Kofi nodded.

"Well, what I want to know is – what kind of profit do you hope to make out of it – exploiting this thing for the 'benefit of mankind'?"

Kofi frowned, and, for the first time Everett could see bewilderment on his face. "We intend to make no profit whatever, sir," Everett said. "The talisman is here to help people, not to fleece them."

There was a buzz again and the same reporter said. "That's what you say, Mr Tierfelder, but I notice the kid wasn't so keen to answer. Now, why would that be, do you think?"

Things were beginning to turn nasty, but, at the same time, Everett understood something about Kofi that he hadn't understood before. "Kofi didn't answer the question, sir," he said. "Because he couldn't. If you knew Kofi as I do, as Jesse and my wife Ursula do, you would understand exactly why he couldn't answer the question. He is motivated by altruism. This boy is a living saint, sir. He simply did not understand the meaning of the word 'profit'. It is a concept that doesn't exist in his vocabulary, and believe me, gentlemen, neither will it, ever."

Over the hubbub another voice shouted. "Is it true, Mr Tierfelder, that this African kid has a bounty on his head?"

He made a conscious effort to control himself. When things settled he gathered his papers and stood up. "No comment," he said, and then: "Thank you, gentlemen. I think you've had your press conference. I want to express my gratitude to you for coming, and hope you enjoy the remainder of your evening."

Then he led the boys off and, as he went, Kofi bowed and the hall erupted. The massed media actually loved him, and they burst into roars of approbation.

*

But the press conference didn't have the desired effect. There were big stories; most notably Kofi blacking out the entire world's television network, and some of the more sensational papers led with panic headlines – *Shock CD Revelation* – *The world's satellite communication at Risk* – *The Blackout CD* – *The Armageddon Factor.*

Then there were frantic editorials claiming that Everett was working on a computer device that could knock out the United State's spy network.

There was nowhere in the world that hadn't experienced the blackout – and there was hardly a human being who wasn't fascinated by the story.

It was bad news, and, within hours, there were activists outside the Tierfelder factory and more outside the house.

The phone didn't stop. Everett was called up by the FBI and it took all his skill to defuse the panic.

He emphasised that the device was not intended to be disruptive. He reminded people of Kofi's wish that it should be used for the good of the world, and he repeated his mission to explore only the disc's potential to enhance life.

Some pro-Everett papers took up this aspect, but interest in the talisman was at fever pitch, and there was no doubt this would be fuelling the likes of Howard Tyson.

The press tried to get hold of names – people who were helping Everett. His friends were hunted down. No one working on the computer came in by the main entrance any more. Most flew to the factory by helicopter and some were convinced they were being tracked when they left at night.

One evening Kofi and Jesse were fooling around in the pool when the alarm went. As soon as they heard it they dashed for the house. There were CCTV monitors in Dad's study, covering every area of the house and factory, and they could see the intruders – hooded men with lights and cameras. They were in the workshop at the factory. Some were examining the new computer. Others were taking photographs, and there were some groping around walls and corners, looking in drawers and cupboards, trying to decode the wall safe.

"They're after the talisman," Everett said. "They think we've got it locked away. You must be careful, Kofi. It won't take long before they work out you carry it around with you. If that gets out, you'll need protection."

"What're you going to do about it, Dad?" Jesse said.

"I've already done it," said Everett. "I've activated a lock-in. They may have managed to break into the lab, but they sure as hell won't be getting out that easy. And the cops are already on their way."

"Say they discover they're locked in and start trashing the place?" Jesse said.

"I've got to get down there quick, to stop them," said Everett. "I'll go down and let the cops in now."

The lights of the police torches and the spotlights set up in the lab together with a good dousing from the sprinkler system, disorientated the intruders so much they were taken without a single shot being fired.

But there was no joy when the police interrogated them.

None of them would admit who they worked for. Even the combined forces of the CIA and FBI couldn't get a word out of them, and, although they were identified through DNA and fingerprints, no one could trace them to any known organisation.

The CIA gave Everett the names, and he put his own security men onto it. He was convinced the break in was Howard Tyson's work, but even his men couldn't make the links.

Tyson was a formidable enemy. He had a fox's cunning and the stealth of a panther, and he was going to be on their backs whatever, wherever and whenever.

They stepped up the intensity of work. Nothing that was known to mankind was left out.

It was so important to read the talisman quickly. There was so much pressure – pressure from activists – from the unrest that had been created – from the fact that even The President was uneasy – and – for the boys and Everett, most compellingly, because of Ursula's decline.

They worked day and night, testing, adjusting, perfecting, until the most advanced holographic versatile disc reader was complete.

It was the end of a long Saturday. They'd run the final tests and even Everett had to admit this machine was greater than anything he'd built before.

He looked at Kofi. "It's down to you now, son. Put the talisman in the disc drive."

They watched as figures and symbols danced across the screen.

"It's working," Jesse whispered.

Everett was staring at the screen. He put his finger up. "Shshsh," he said.

It was taking a long time.

But then the screen cleared, and, for a moment – hardly more time than it took for an eye to blink, they saw a perfect rainbow arch across the screen, and, behind it, on a background of deepest space, a whole galaxy of stars, an exquisite nebulae, so beautiful they gasped in amazement.

But then, with the dullest of thuds, the screen blanked … and the computer crashed.

***

Chapter 16

Seven Rainbow Colours

Jesse looked at his dad in dismay "Where do we go now?" he said.

"We're on the right track," said Everett. "It's just not enough, that's all. Big breakthroughs don't come that easy, Jess. There's something we're missing. It could be staring us in the face."

Whatever it was though, they needed to find it soon, because, early the following week, Mum took a turn for the worse.

It was the middle of the night. The boys were asleep, and in a half dream, Jesse heard noises, doors opening, voices. He shook Kofi.

"Something's up," he said.

They went to the window and, on the drive below, there was an ambulance. Dad was there with Mr Anansi and a couple of housemaids, and they were wheeling Mum out on a trolley.

They grabbed their clothes and dashed downstairs.

"Mum's in a lot of pain" Dad said. "I didn't want to disturb you. Mr Anansi was going to tell you in the morning."

"We want to be disturbed," said Kofi. "If Mum's bad we want to be with her."

"I'm going with her in the ambulance," Everett said. "If you want to come along, Mr Anansi will bring you. But you won't be able to see her, not yet. They'll have to do tests. Perhaps, when she's settled it'll be okay."

At the hospital they upped her dose of morphine, and, although she was conscious, her speech was inarticulate, and her voice grated. It scared Jesse.

They didn't know what to do.

They wanted to be with her all the time … and yet they needed to be in the lab, working on the only thing that could save her.

They were confused and desperate and it wasn't right for two kids to be like that. Everett could see it. Mr Anansi could see it, and, in her more lucid moments, so could Mum see it.

"Get Carl and Sam over," she said one day. "See if that will take them out of themselves."

"We don't want to be taken out of ourselves," Jesse said.

"I'm not going any place, Jess," she said. "And I'm a fighter. You don't need to worry about me. You get Sam and Carl over tomorrow – spend an afternoon with them. Kofi'll like them."

But the only reason they agreed was because it was what she wanted. She was right though. It was okay.

Kofi took to Carl and Sam straight away and Sam had a friend staying – a girl from school – Tina. All three of them thought Kofi was amazing.

Jesse told them his story and they stared at the talisman.

"Your space suit was fab," Carl said. "But this is something else. You say you flew on a mat using this to propel you, and you got here – all the way from Africa?"

"Yeah, and he flew faster than a jumbo jet," Jesse said. "I saw him pass me half way across the Atlantic."

"Can you show us?" said Sam. "Just around the grounds. You don't have to race a Boeing 747 or anything."

Kofi fetched the mat. "It's my baba's prayer mat," he said. "I've had it ever since he took me from the apes."

"Doesn't it fold on you when you fly?" said Tina.

Kofi chuckled. "No. It stays rigid, but it's soft to sit on. I'll show you."

Carl was after something more than just being a spectator though. "We've already seen a flying demonstration with Jesse's space suite," he said, "Couldn't we go up? Couldn't we fly with you?"

The girls seemed uncertain, and that disappointed Kofi because, it was the girls he wanted to fly with – especially Tina. She had dark hair with a hint of a curl in it, and it fell around her face in a way that was really cute. She was pretty. Her face was small and pale, and she had big, dark eyes – almost black. But it was Carl that wanted the ride.

"I'll take you up one at a time," he said. "You can see how safe it is when I take Carl up – then ..."

But the girls were still reluctant. "See how it goes with Carl," Sam said. "If he falls, it won't matter that much."

"He'll bounce anyway," said Jesse, and Carl dug at his ribs.

"If I do fall," he said. "I'll make good and sure I land on you."

They sat cross-legged facing each other. The mat rose and the girls gasped. Carl wanted stunts but Kofi wouldn't. "Later," he said. "If I loop the loop with you, the girls won't fly with me."

"You want the girls to fly with you then?" Carl said. He gave a half smile and Kofi said:

"I think so."

"Which one – or both?"

Kofi swept the mat across a scree of cypress trees. They could have leaned over and touched the tips. "That's for me to know," he said.

He took Sam up next and Sam was okay, but he knew she was Jesse's friend. They'd known each other for years, and Jesse had been with her in Sikaman country.

They flew around the grounds and it amused him because she gripped the sides so hard he could see her knuckles gleaming.

"I guess it's cool," she said. "But I'd feel safer in a Boeing 747."

"You can't fall," he said. "The talisman won't let you." He stood up, balancing on one leg and she screamed.

Jesse and Carl were laughing, but he could see Tina looked anxious, and when she came to sit on the prayer mat her eyes were shut tight. "I'll make it so smooth you won't even know you're flying," he said.

"I guess I will," she said. "The ground will be hundreds of feet away, down there, and the other kids will look like insects."

"We don't go that high," he laughed. "Twenty – thirty feet, that's all." He touched her hand lightly. "I'll be real careful. You'll be safe, don't worry."

They climbed above the perimeter trees, and a breeze caught Tina's hair. Kofi watched it brush across her cheek. "You like it up here with me?" he said and she laughed.

"It's swell," she said. "Now I'm up here."

She looked over the side and her eyes sparkled. "I feel real safe. I didn't think I would."

Kofi knew his face was burning. "Shall we fly over the house?" he said.

They drifted away across the lawn and the others shouted. He heard Jesse's voice. "Kofi Bibini. You're supposed to be doing a trip

171

around the garden. You're not meant to be eloping."

Tina laughed, but there was a tinge of a blush on her cheeks. "What's 'eloping'?" Kofi said.

"Don't take any notice. It's nothing," she said. She looked down as the rooftops slid past. They crossed the pool with its undisturbed water, and suddenly Kofi's stomach lurched. Normally Ursula would be out there and they'd be fooling around in the water to amuse her. The silence sent a shudder through him.

"You're thinking about Jesse's mum aren't you?" Tina said. "It's empty down there without her."

He nodded. "She's my mum too, now," he said. "And I am thinking about her, yes."

When they went back, Jesse was still laughing. "Why d'you give Tina a longer ride than the rest, Kofi Bibini?" he said. "Sam's dead jealous, you know?"

Kofi smiled, but Jesse could see – there was something beneath the mask – an expression that Carl, Sam and Tina were meant to have dispelled.

"We flew over the pool," Kofi said. "It looked very quiet back there, what with Mum away in hospital."

"Your mum's real bad then?" Carl said.

Jesse nodded. "Some days it's like she's almost dead."

"Can't you do something?" said Sam. "With Kofi's talisman. Surely you can do something."

"When we've opened the program – with the computer," Kofi said. "The talisman will cure her then, but ... we've got to open the program first."

"How come?" said Sam. "Surely it can do something now? It made you fly. It can do all kinds of stuff. Why can't it help your mum?"

Jesse looked at Kofi. "You explain, Kofi Bibini," he said.

Kofi could see the activity of rainbow light in the talisman, viscous, like oil on water, and with Sam's question it seemed the activity increased. "Perhaps it could do something," he said. "It's done amazing things. I don't think it can cure her, but it might help."

"Say we give it a go," said Carl. "We could take it down the hospital now – see what happens."

Tina moved closer. She looked at the talisman and breathed in. "Those patterns are so amazing," she said. "It's like they're healing patterns. It must be able to do something, Kofi."

He stood up. "Let's give it a try. We can get Mr Anansi to drive us down."

Mr Anansi and the girls weren't allowed into the room. Mum was having a bad day and was comatose to the point of inarticulate grunts. Her eyes were heavy and, apart from a squeeze of the hand, there seemed no recognition when the boys came in.

Giving her the talisman was risky. Dad had held it and Kwami, back in Sikaman forest, but no one else – not without a violent reaction – and a shock like that would kill her.

It had always been Kofi's belief, though, that the talisman wouldn't let her die, and he took her hand. "Here, Mum. Hold this," he whispered.

There was a helpless compliance in her eyes, and her fingers closed over the talisman's rim. But as the rainbow light played on her face, it was as if all the tension had distilled into peace. For a moment Kofi thought she was dead.

But her chest was rising and falling, and the death rattle had gone.

"It's doing something," he whispered.

Then her eyes opened, and they were clear – there was no sign of doping, no mists of pain, and she smiled. "Kofi? Jesse?" Even in her whispering, they knew the morphine-induced croak had gone. "The relief," she said. "You have no idea."

Jesse squeezed her arm. "It's okay, Mum. Just keep hold of it."

"Nothing the doctors have ever done has given me anything like this," she said. She looked at Kofi. "It's the most wonderful thing. The most amazing thing."

"It isn't curing you, Mum," Kofi said. "The power locked up inside is the only thing that will do that. But it will help, until we've unlocked it."

"Are you certain it isn't curing her, Kofi Bibini?" Jesse said. "Are you sure this isn't a cure?"

It was hard for Kofi, because he *was* sure. – He could understand Jesse's impatience, especially as Mum's improvement was so dramatic. But the doctors confirmed it. What Ursula was experiencing was a remission. That was all. The cancer was still there.

*

Every day they gave her the talisman, and the remission was strong, although the doctors were still insistent. Nothing it did was reducing the cancer. It was only holding it at bay.

And that meant they needed to develop the computer.

But every time they tried a modification the result was the same – a tantalising glimpse of the rainbow hanging against the backdrop of deep space, and then the computer crashed.

Everett didn't know where to go next. He involved more people. He even consulted his rivals, although very little came of that. Rivalries went deep and his approaches were met with scepticism.

He even tried Howard Tyson; but Tyson's response summed it up.

"Why should I pool my expertise with yours, Everett?" he said. "Send me the disc and I'll work on it myself, develop my own computer – but – give you the benefit of my expertise – in a spirit of so-called bonhomie and brotherhood? That's all crap, pal. What you'll do is milk my brain and take the credit – and the profits, I shouldn't wonder."

It meant he was left with mainly his most trusted allies, and they worked around the clock.

Kofi was totally befuddled. He branded it all as 'Computer Jargon Speak' and gave up any attempt to get his head around it.

But, in the meantime, he was taking lessons in the American life. Jesse, Carl, Sam and Tina were his tutors.

They went to the movies and ball games; they took in shows, they indulged in a good few American gastronomic predilections. Kofi's favourites involved beef burgers and a great deal of his formative hours was spent at McDonalds. It made Everett and Ursula laugh.

"If that kid carries on stuffing beef burgers and fries at this rate," Everett said. "He's going to be fatter than the turkey come Thanksgiving."

They decided to try and re-adjust his penchant for buns, and whatever was crammed between them.

174

In Sikaman forest, his main diet would have been rice and chicken, so they thought some kind of food involving that would be a suitable hint that there were other tasty feasts available to the all-American pallet.

They chose a Chinese restaurant in town.

They were going to take Carl and the two girls as well – as the boys seemed to have gelled with them so well.

But Chinese restaurants were as foreign to Kofi as computer speak

He looked at his chopsticks in amazement.

"Do we have to knit something?" he said.

When they served the food they gave him a fork. He'd required training to master that. In Africa they used fingers to whip up the rice.

Everett and Ursula chose a variety of courses, and he coped all right. But, seeing the girls, and Carl and Jesse so proficient at wielding chopsticks, he insisted on having a go. He finished up chasing chicken balls all over the restaurant floor.

There were drinks as well, coke, orange, fruit juices, and, for Everett and Ursula, bowls of green tea. In the centre of the table was another bowl – steaming, and giving off a pungent smell of lemon. Kofi fancied that more than the other drinks and he picked it up while Jesse's eyes widened.

"Kofi Bibini, what are you doing?" he said.

"This lemon dish – I like that better than the coke," Kofi said.

He took a deep swig and his eyes were sparkling. He was really enjoying this, … but the girls were falling about laughing and so were Carl and his mum and dad.

"It's a finger bowl, you dope," Jesse said. "You're supposed to wash your hands in it, not drink it."

No one had told him, but he was a fast learner, and when the sweet course appeared – banana fritters with syrup, he saw a fresh bowl, and this time he wasn't going to be fooled. Straight off he washed his hands in it, and Jesse leapt out of his chair.

"Kofi Bibini, what are you doing now?"

"Another finger bowl?" Kofi said. "It's okay. I'm just washing my hands."

He'd never seen his mum laugh so much. Whatever he'd done, it was worth it to see the tears rolling down her face.

"No?" he said.

Carl was shaking. "Right!" he said. "You got to dip your fritters in that when you put the syrup on. It's to set the syrup."

"What jargon speak is this, Jesse Musungu?" he said.

"It's 'Oriental Gastro-jargon Speak,'" Jesse laughed.

But Tina looked at Kofi and said: "I think your doing real great. This is the best Chinese dinner party I've ever been to." And Kofi wasn't fazed. He didn't care that he'd made a fool of himself because he'd made his mum and dad laugh. He'd made Jesse laugh, and he'd made Tina have the best Chinese dinner party ever.

"Waiter," he said, clicking his fingers. "May we have fresh water for the syrup? Some dummy has just washed his hands in this lot."

It was great.

It was, Kofi thought, a taste of things to come, when Ursula would be cured. When the talisman would be at full strength and when the world would be a better place.

But when?

So far every attempt to fine tune the computer had failed and the failures baffled them.

Sometimes they talked about it with the girls.

Tina and Sam were around a lot and occasionally Carl came too, but often it was just the girls.

Carl wasn't much into computer science. A good game of football or baseball he could cope with ... and, besides, he was beginning to feel out of it. "I'm not coming round today," he said to Jesse once and when Jesse asked why he just said, "It's just ... fours company, fives a crowd ... if you get my meaning."

They were by the pool the afternoon after Kofi's Chinese party. They were still laughing – and the events of the feast were getting embellished to mythological proportions; but suddenly Sam said: "How's the computer doing? Any breakthroughs?" She looked at Kofi and her eyes were glinting. "I mean, I thought you might have fed it lemon water or something – or transformed it with a couple of chopsticks."

"That's just about the kind of contribution I would make," Kofi

176

said. "It's all foreign to me."

Tina lay lazily, looking up at Kofi's laughing face. "Me too," she said. But then she turned to Jesse. "One thing I've always wondered though Jess. You say your working on a two colour laser beam?"

Jesse nodded. "Yeah. Red and green," he said.

"I know I'm a bit like Kofi in all this – it's a kind of mystery to me, but ... the talisman – it's got lights of all colours, yes? All the colours of the rainbow ... and ... well – don't you think – to read it you'd need a computer with all those colours – not just two? Don't you think it might be giving you that message?"

It was so obvious, and yet no one had thought of it. Seven laser lights – it was the most logical thing in the word.

"Go on, say I'm crazy," she said.

"No," said Jesse. "You're not crazy. It's like – the solution has been staring at us all this time and nobody ever saw it – not even my dad."

He got up, brushing the dust from his shirt. "Let's go down to the lab now. – See what Dad says."

Kofi rolled over and planted a kiss on Tina's cheek. "You are a genius," he said, and Jesse laughed.

"This is no time for an orgy, Kofi Bibini," he said.

Tina blushed and Kofi kicked at Jesse's ankles.

"Gee, why not Jesse baby?" said Sam and they were laughing as they headed off to find Mr Anansi, but they were excited too.

*

They weren't sure that Everett would think it such a great idea, but he took it very seriously. "It won't be like anything ever tried before," he said. "And it'll revolutionise computer hardware. The trouble is, if it works, there'll be nothing for it to read except Kofi's talisman. We don't have the technology to produce software that needs a whole spectrum of lasers ... and we've got to be prepared. This might not be the answer."

"It's worth a try though, Dad?" Jesse said.

"It's certainly worth a try," Everett said. He was already sketching ideas on a note pad. But he sounded a caution because there was so much expectancy on the boys' faces. "It's just – we mustn't get our hopes up. What ever we do, we've got to be prepared for failure. That's the route of all great discoveries."

It wasn't failure they were aiming for though. They planned and redesigned, and every detail was built and tested to astronomic specifications.

This time, because the idea was so revolutionary, only close aids and friends were involved, and they were sworn to secrecy.

Everett took out intellectual rights, and registered the idea with the patent office, and he copyrighted every new component.

Work went on apace, and, while Kofi watched in bewilderment, Jesse was in his element. He made suggestions with a grasp of cybernetics that made Everett proud.

Every day they gave Ursula the talisman, and it was as if the soothing effects permeated all the cells in her body. She was so vivacious again – almost back to her old self.

But doctors insisted, the cancer was showing no sign of going away.

And all the time, what they hoped would be the answer to everything, was taking shape. Soon they would be able to put the new computer to the test.

"How will it work?" Kofi said.

Everett was supervising the insertion of a tiny component. "If it works like we hope," he said. "With seven lasers, each tuned to a different level of the spectrum, it won't need a screen. It will create a holographic image, right here in the room – in three dimensions. Chances are you might even be able to touch the images. I can't be certain because we've never tried anything like it before, but that's the theory, and, if it reads the talisman, you'll see what's on it as though it was in the room."

It was late one summer's afternoon when they ran the last test and only the three of them were there – Jesse, Kofi and Everett, and Jesse's heart was in his mouth.

The thought of yet another failure – the thought of watching the computer crash again, made his stomach churn.

He didn't share his fears with Kofi though. Kofi was in the realms of magic. It was all CJS to him. He just watched and waited, and, to him, the outcome was inevitable. Jesse had been pre-ordained to read the talisman, and that is what would happen.

They'd blacked out the lab and Everett looked at Kofi.

"Kofi, son. You do the honours again," he said, and they watched as images flashed in front of the machine – figures, phrases that were there and then gone – an ephemera in space.

"It's reading," Jesse whispered … and then … the rainbow and the galaxies filled the darkened room – ethereal – as if space had invaded them. It was as if they were away from the earth – away from the solar system – away from their own galaxy, and they were standing in a distant cosmos, watching white stars, with a rainbow that was tangible, arching across the sky, and it seemed to fill every corner of the universe. This time though, it stayed, for second after second, and their eyes widened with wonder.

Then it faded … and Jesse was swept up with feelings, because it wasn't a crash; the computer was running smoothly, reading deeper into the disc, silent, perfect, and the mysteries of space were unfolding before their eyes.

As the last ray of rainbow light faded, a frieze filled the room, and the stone-like figures in the frieze were walking. They were passing in front of them, raising their hands, nodding, and the boys were hardly able to believe what they were seeing.

Then, hovering in front of the frieze were the words – in English – *"Interstellar computerised program"*, and a small three-dimensional rainbow appeared, with the words *"Touch to gain access"*.

Jesse's pupils almost hurt with the expansion. "Touch it, Kofi Bibini," he whispered. He could barely focus on the icon. But Kofi stepped forward, and there was a shiver across the frieze as the words faded and the creatures turned back to stone. Then a new message scrolled across the room.

"Access denied. Please apply benison."

The words didn't fade, nor did the frozen figures. The computer didn't crash; but they'd hit a wall.

"What does it mean?" Jesse whispered. He was more frustrated than disappointed. It seemed, if they could get this 'benison', whatever it was, they would be in. And everything the computer had

179

revealed backed up their belief. There was so much more hidden in the disc, and their seven-laser computer had the means to read it.

Everett switched the computer off. "I guess there'd have to be a code," he said. "You wouldn't be able to gain access to something as stupendous as this without.... But, to be honest, boys, I haven't come across this word, 'benison' before. Whatever it is, we're going to need it, but that's not such a big deal. At least we've got a machine that'll do the job. Cracking the code – well – if we can make the computer – then we can crack the code."

All the same, there was a nagging anxiety.

How would they crack the code? And more to the point, if they did, would it be in time for Mum? Because, Mum wasn't getting any better, and the power that was keeping her alive wouldn't go on forever.

***

Chapter 17

Code Cracking

But it baffled Jesse. "You and me – we've talked all around this, Kofi Bibini," he said. "And there doesn't seem to be any way forward."

Kofi was thoughtful "My Imam, when I had a problem with the Nam-Nams," he said at last. "He told me I should share it – talk it through. I used to go to the elders, and sometimes they'd see something I hadn't."

"What are you saying?" Jesse laughed. "Have we got to take up religion – go off to some Episcopal church somewhere and find a load of elders?"

"We haven't got to go any further than McDonalds," said Kofi. "Meet up with the girls. Talk it through with them."

Jesse had no quarrel with that. "But they're not exactly 'elders'," he said.

"It's heads that count, not age," said Kofi. "Call them now. I'm hungry."

There was a McDonalds not far down the road from home. Jesse got Kofi his fries and a double cheeseburger, and then they told the girls about loading the talisman.

"*Please apply* b*enison*. That's what the computer said."

"Might that mean some sort of sacrifice?" said Sam. "A misprint or something. Say it's telling you to kill a deer or something and sacrifice it like in the Bible – because, if it is, that's gross."

"Benison – venison." Jesse said. He ran the words over, but he couldn't believe it.

"You'd think, if there was a password – some code to key in – and it really wanted you to get in – it would give you a clue," said Tina.

"And I don't think it's into sacrifices," Kofi said. "Sacrifice means death. The talisman is all for regeneration."

"And there's the wallpaper," Jesse said. "That didn't make sense either. It was like a Babylonian frieze – grey figures walking around the room. – What were they for?"

"Couldn't we load the talisman again?" said Kofi. "Let the girls see for themselves? Will it let us do it twice?"

"We can do it as often as we like," said Jesse. "It'll just deny us access again, that's all."

Kofi glanced at the half-eaten sandwich and stood up. "Let's go," he said.

The girls had to be processed, and then there was the decontamination.

But the awesomeness of the preparation was nothing to the amazement as they watched the computer probe the outer layers of the talisman – the signature page, the frieze, with its marble figures.

"They look like they're real," Sam whispered. "I could touch them."

"And what are they doing with their hands?" Tina said. "They're like priests in church. I've seen our priest do that."

"They look as old as the world," Sam said. "Do you think they're the people that made the disc?"

But suddenly Tina breathed sharply. "No! They're not," she said. "Look at that one. It's the Pope."

"It is," Sam whispered. "I've seen him in Rome, and when he greets the people that's exactly what he does. He raises his hands just like that guy's doing."

"And there." Tina said. "I know that one too. That's the Dalai Lama. I've seen him on TV."

"And that guy's wearing Rabbi's clothes," said Jesse. "They're not people from way back. They're people who are alive today."

"Touch the icon, Kofi Bibini. Now we know who these people are perhaps that's the code. Think Pope, Imam, Rabbi – all that stuff – see if it'll let us in."

But all that came up, shivering across the frozen figures again, were the words: *"Access denied. Please apply benison."*

"Have you looked up *'benison'* in the dictionary?" said Tina.

Jesse looked at Kofi and they didn't speak. It was so obvious. Google it, or look it up in a good old-fashioned Chambers. "Dad must have a dictionary here somewhere," he said.

They burst into Everett's office and Everett could see they'd made some sort of a breakthrough. They googled the word, and then Jesse shouted in his excitement. "*Benison* it's here. It's an archaic word, meaning ... 'blessing' – 'benediction'. 'Please apply blessing', that's what the computer's saying."

"And all those people in the frieze," Tina said. "The Pope, the Dalai Lama, all those religious people, they were all gesturing like they were giving a blessing. Is that what will break the code? Getting one of them to bless the talisman?"

"It makes sense," Jesse said. "It's like, the wallpaper screen was telling us what to do."

"It makes very good sense," said Everett. "A leader of one of the big religions. I'd go for the Muslims – as Kofi was brought up with a Muslim Imam – but – they don't have a leader – not like the Pope or the Anglican's Archbishop of Canterbury."

"What about the leading Rabbi in Jerusalem?" Sam said. "Jerusalem's a sort of centre for a lot of religions."

"Jerusalem could pose problems," said Everett. "But that makes a lot of sense too. I've got good friends in Jerusalem. I could set that up. But, girls, until this code is cracked, you must keep everything under wraps. There are people out there very keen to get their hands on this stuff, and some of them don't have the best of motives. Best if no one is told. The less people knowing, the less chance there is for something to leak out – by mistake."

*

There were big preparations to be made. Officials in America had to be consulted, visas had to be arranged and flights booked, and Everett was always aware of Howard Tyson's shadow. There was every possibility he, or someone like him, could get to know about this and get into Israel themselves.

If something went wrong the boys needed an escape route.

He also had to square it with the US government.

Since the scare with Kofi blacking out the world's television networks, the President had been very concerned about developments, and, for all this to run smoothly they needed his backing as well.

Everett arranged a meeting, and they went to the Whitehouse, with tea on the lawn – soft drinks for the boys, and sandwiches and cakes. Sam and Tina were out of their heads with envy. Even Carl got to hear about it.

"You got to meet the President?" he said.

"Yeah," Jesse said." He seemed okay, but it was no big deal. After all, the guy's only got the same number of arms and legs as us. He's only got one nose and one mouth – and he didn't do any miracles – not while we were there."

Sam laughed. "Where's all this cynicism come from Jesse Tierfelder?" she said.

Kofi grinned. "He wasn't sort of majestic. Dad said we should have seen Colonel Mamba in his palace. He was imposing, big time – but then, I guess when you're as powerful as the President of the United States you don't have to put on an act."

There were other preparations to be made.

If the boys were to take the talisman to Israel, they'd need a computer to verify the Rabbi's blessing, and there was only one computer that would read the talisman and that was the prototype in Everett's lab … It was way too big to take to Israel, so Everett devised a laptop that would link to the main computer. They could use it anywhere – like an extension of the prototype.

But somehow news got out.

There had been renewed interest ever since Everett and the boys went to the Whitehouse, and Everett had to hold another press conference.

This time he didn't take the boys because some of the rumours flying around were very near the truth and there would be awkward questions.

The conference didn't satisfy the press though. Next day the papers were full of speculation and the FBI and Mossad weren't happy.

In the meantime life went on for Kofi and Jesse. They often met up with the girls. Tina tried to put restraints on Kofi's eating habits. "You're a good looking guy," she said. "But you start putting the pounds on and you just might not be so good looking any more."

He was limited to a weekly visit to McDonalds, and they swam a lot in the pool at home. They didn't spend much time sitting around and Kofi was convinced he was maintaining his magnificent physique.

Every day they gave Ursula the talisman and she stayed well, so much so that her nurses were able to reduce the drugs. But she was still weak, and every time Jesse looked at her, the urgency of the mission impinged on him.

And it all seemed to be going well – until Everett got a phone call.

His suspicions weren't aroused immediately.

The caller claimed to be a reporter and gave the name of a prominent newspaper. He said he was interested in doing a feature on the boys, and a lot of the early questions were just re-establishing what was already known – about Kofi – where he came from – how he came to be in possession of the talisman – how he met Jesse – how he came to be in the States. The reporter slipped in a couple of background questions and they seemed to support the 'feature' idea – how did Jesse and Kofi get along – did they have close friends in America – were there any pre-pubescent romances?

Everett gave the stock answers. He said the talisman was an heirloom, passed down through Kofi's family. He told the reporter half truths about how Jesse and Kofi met, and generally kept the answers as low key as he could. Yes, there were hints of prepubescent friendships – the type of interaction that goes on with most kids – but – he wouldn't give names. Kids of that age deserved their privacy.

Then the reporter moved to another tack.

"Mr Tierfelder," he said. "It's rumoured that the boys are going on some kind of world tour. Is that right?"

"Sure," Everett said. "We dealt with that at the press conference."

"Just confirmation, Mr Tierfelder. We wouldn't want to get our facts wrong, would we? The tour is related to the international status you've afforded to the talisman – is that right?"

"Yes," said Everett.

"Will the boys be taking the talisman with them? Will they be giving countries the sort of demonstration Kofi did at your first press conference?"

He hedged. "The whereabouts of the talisman at any given time has to be confidential," he said. "Too many people are interested in it for the wrong reasons and any information of that kind could put the boys in danger."

There was something cold in the reporter's next question. "But, Mr Tierfelder, sir," he said. "Isn't it true that the boy, Kofi, wears it like a lucky charm, around his neck – all the time – and it goes everywhere with him?"

"That was the case," Everett said. "Before he came to the States and we realised its international importance." He began to be wary of this guy. "What did you say your name was?"

"Dan Nolan," the reporter said. "I'm with the *New York Times*."

Then another question came crackling down the phone.

"Let's get this right. You inferred just now that divulging the talisman's whereabouts could put the boys' lives at risk. I'm concluding from that sir, that the talisman does still go with Kofi. I mean, if it was locked away in some vaults in Washington, there'd be no danger, would there?"

Everett suddenly felt the need to bring this interview to an end. The so-called feature was beginning to look more like and expose. "You can conclude what you like, Mr Nolan," he said. "But, print any speculation that puts my boys at risk and I'll sue your paper to within an inch of extinction. Do I make myself clear?"

The voice came back, level and now there was a hint of malevolence. "Perfectly, Mr Tierfelder. And where's their first port of call? Israel, is it? Are they going to see the Chief Rabbi in Jerusalem?"

"Who are you, sir?" Everett said.

"Like I said, I'm Dan Nolan from the *New York Times*. Is it Israel, Mr Tierfelder – with the talisman – to see the Chief Rabbi?"

"The boys' itinerary is not in the public domain. As I said, print one word of supposition – or any piece of information that has not been verified, and I'll bring your paper to its knees. And I've no further comment to make to you, sir, so, good day."

He was in the process of putting the phone down when he heard Nolan laugh. "That's just fine, Mr Tierfelder," he heard. "You've

186

told me all I need to know – so, have a great day!"

He swore under his breath, and then he dialled the *New York Times* to verify Nolan's authenticity.

But, when he gave them the name, they told him they didn't have, nor had they ever had, a journalist by that name on their books.

He was no more a journalist than Everett. He was one of Howard Tyson's men. Security for the trip would have to be notched up to the highest level. The boys weren't going to be remotely safe if Tyson's men knew this much.

***

Chapter 18

In Search of Benison

The first thing Everett did was contact Mossad. The boys would need protection at the first whiff of trouble – and they needed an escape route that was so slick, the most ardent espionage agent wouldn't crack it. He contacted London too. He had a friend in MI5. If things went wrong they'd need to be ready for an unscheduled flight to the UK.

The boys had been out with the girls when Everett received the phone call. When they got back he called them into the lounge.

"I've heard from one of Tyson's men," he said. "They know much more than we thought they did. We're going to have to rethink the Israel trip."

"Not go, you mean?" Jesse said.

"Nothing's going to stop you going," said Everett. "But we've got to set up a lot more protection. I'm thinking we'll need someone with you from the ambassadorial staff in Israel, and – like you had in Africa – you'll need bodyguards."

Jesse laughed. "Fat lot of good they were. They lost me within two days."

But Everett was firm. "You're going to need protection, Jesse. No-one messes with Tyson's men."

Logic told Jesse Dad was right, but … "I don't want a load of strangers around," he said

"I'd come myself," said Everett. "But I can't leave your mum – not the way things are."

"Besides," Ursula said. "You're going to need professionals – who know about security, and people who know their way around Jerusalem."

"No we don't," said Kofi. "We don't need any of this."

He hadn't spoken before, but his face was set with assurance. "Jesse and me – we're the keepers of the talisman. We have to find the way into its programs – it's our destiny … and we've got to do it on our own – no diplomats – no bodyguards – just us and the talisman. The talisman will look after us around Jerusalem."

As soon as Kofi had said it Jesse knew. He'd verbalised his exact thoughts. "Yeah," he said. "That's right. That's what was in my head. I just couldn't get it out."

"You've got to have back up," Everett said "– People in the wings. It's okay for you to be alone while you're on your mission – but we've set up an escape route – and, if things go pear-shaped you'll need the back up for that – and you'll need the know-how and muscle of Mossad and the British MI5. But don't worry."

"I don't mind that," Jesse said. "As long as there's no-one with us while we're getting the benison."

"You'll have to be smart and on your toes," Everett said. "For all kinds of stuff. If you're being tailed for a start, – people asking questions. Anyone coming up and flashing a press card at you – ten to one it won't be the press at all. It'll be one of Tyson's men. If that happens, alert your contacts straight away."

"But we've got to do the benison on our own. It's personal. We can't have guys hanging around while the Rabbi's blessing the talisman."

Everett nodded. "That's fine," he said. "As long as you're prepared to contact your minders at the first sign of trouble. And – when you're off in Israel, I want you to keep in touch with me. We'll be linked to the computer and you must tell us – about everything – all the time – twenty-four - seven. Contact me through the private network."

*

The journey out of Washington was very different from the trip Jesse had made to Africa. It was night, and, although Dad took them to the airport, there was a security guard in the car – someone from the FBI. The president had insisted, and there would be links with the president all the time they were away. After he'd met them and seen the talisman he told Everett he wanted to be involved at every turn. He'd been totally enamoured with Kofi and Jesse. "There couldn't be two finer ambassadors for the United States," he'd said and Dad had said, "There couldn't be two finer ambassadors for the Human Race,

Mr President."

They headed for a military airport, and they were flying in a specially chartered jet.

The bodyguard from the CIA went with them, but he promised it would be discreet. There'd be people monitoring them, but that was all.

They didn't sleep much on the flight. It was too big an operation and there were so many international agencies involved.

They talked in bursts – about Mum – about Dad and all the stuff he'd done. They talked about being brothers; about Sam and Tina. They speculated about life when the Rainbow Talisman had become a force in the world.

"It's like we won't be kids anymore," Jesse said.

"It's only since I met you that I've really known what it is to be a kid anyway, Jesse Musungu," Kofi said. "Before that I was with the apes, then with my baba and that wasn't like being a kid really. After that I was king of the Nam Nams and fighting off Kalabulay – and no way was that like being a kid."

They watched dawn break over the Atlantic and the plane flew north, skirting the southern shores of Europe.

It was mid morning when they landed.

There was no processing, no immigration procedures, none of the rigorous probing that ordinary visitors were subjected to. Instead they were met by four officials, and, although the officials were dressed casually, Kofi noticed gun holsters strapped to their waists.

After a quick look at their passports Kofi and Jesse were ushered to a black limousine.

The Mossad men spoke excellent English, and they weren't bad company. They pointed out places of interest and the towns and cities they passed were not much different from those in the States.

Jesse watched with curiosity. "There aren't such big cultural differences here as there were in Africa," he said. "Not from America. In Sikaman country there were big differences – women carrying stuff on their heads – those amazing Mami-wagons – and, somehow, life seemed kind of more laid back out there."

The guards laughed. "Israel's a new state," they said. "Although we go back thousands of years, we've only been established here in the last hundred years. A lot of our families came from Europe and America."

Jerusalem itself was different. The old city seemed to be a place where the cultures of the world met, and history was fathoms deep.

They went to a hotel where a suite had been booked.

"We'll leave you to your own devices," the guards said. "But we won't be far away."

They were given a telephone number. "Call us if you sense trouble. But, don't worry, you'll be fine. You just get out there and enjoy our wonderful city for the rest of the day."

As soon as they'd left, Kofi began to laugh. His bed had been made with meticulously folded sheets and bedspread. He jumped onto it and ruffled it. Then unrolled his prayer mat and gave a sigh of satisfaction. "That'll do me," he said. "If only Dad would accept I don't do beds, we could save him a fortune in hotel fees."

After brunch they went out to explore Jerusalem.

But there was something odd about the afternoon. They were both heavy with jet lag … and it might have been the fog of dysfunction, or it might have been their Israeli bodyguards, but Kofi had an uneasy feeling.

"I picked it up from the apes," he said. "In the forest you had to know when something was tailing you. It's like a second sight, and I've got it now. Someone's stalking us."

Jesse looked at the crowds. He couldn't see any sign of furtive movements. "It could be Mossad," he said.

Kofi shook his head. "You get a feeling – that there's badness about – a predatory feeling. I wouldn't get that from bodyguards – and, look." He took the talisman out, shielding it from general view, and the activity was different. There were agitated movements, shapes like fractured glass.

"It's sensing something," he said. "It's like, warning us. Some guy's tailing us, you can be sure of that, and it's not Mossad."

They tried ignoring it, pressing on; exploring the old city's streets, but even Jesse could sense it now.

When they were back at the hotel, they mentioned it to the guards, but the guards were dismissive. "We'd have noticed if there was anyone following you," they said. "We kept you in our sights all the time. More likely it was us you could sense."

At breakfast next morning they made a careful recce of the other diners. "If there is someone tailing us," Jesse said. "Then we've got to recognise the face. If one of these guys is Tyson's man we must be able to suss him when we're out."

Kofi scanned the dining room with the talisman. "It'll note the faces," he said. "And it'll match them. If there's someone out in the street later, it'll identify him."

"Have you done this before?" said Jesse.

"Sometimes I know what it can do," Kofi said. "If there's some guy here, and he's a threat, the talisman will show us."

After breakfast they set out for the old city in the Mossad car. Mossad had clearance that other vehicles didn't have, so they were confident no one would be able to follow while they were getting the benison.

There was only one guard, and they headed for the Jewish quarter. Jesse had hoped they'd do this at the Temple Mount, but that wasn't possible.

The main place of worship for Jews was somewhere called Hurva Square. There'd been a synagogue there once, and, although it was a ruined shell now, there were plans to rebuild it, and it was still an important place for worship. The Rabbi had suggested it and when the boys saw it they knew. The honey coloured stonework had a breath of the past about it and there was a huge arch spanning the stonework.

"It's like a rainbow," Kofi whispered. "This has to be the place, Jesse Musungu."

Jesse had his laptop. They wanted to test the benison straight away. They knew Dad would be at the lab watching on the main computer, even though it was the middle of the night back there. If Mum was well enough, she'd be there too. They would see what happened just as soon as the boys did.

The Rabbi was waiting. "Right, boys," he said. "The guard is going to make himself scarce." He looked at talisman and added. "That's such an amazing thing. Your dad has already told me something about it."

"It has big powers," said Jesse. "But – if we can unlock its programs, it could do miracles."

"Would you like to see what it can do already?" Kofi said; but the Rabbi shook his head.

"I've thought about it a lot," he said. "... And ... well – you two are doing all this because you believe in the talisman. As you said, you believe it will do miracles. You haven't seen it cure a dying person, but you believe it will. I don't want to go plunging into theology or anything, but, what you're doing is showing faith, and faith is the root of all blessings – an act of belief without evidence. I think I want to do this in the same spirit. That's how the talisman would like it."

There was a room in the tower by the arch. It was furnished with religious artefacts – a small seven-branched candlestick, a carved Star of David, other tokens of the Rabbi's religion, and the serenity of the room seemed, somehow, appropriate.

"May I touch it?" the Rabbi said.

"I think you should," said Kofi.

"But you've got to know this first, sir," Jesse said. "Normally, the talisman will kick against any guy who touches it. As it wants you to bless it, you should be okay, but you've got to be prepared."

"Forewarned is forearmed, is that it, Jesse Tierfelder?" the Rabbi said.

"It's just so you know," said Jesse.

The Rabbi put his hands on the disc and he said a few words in Hebrew – and, immediately, they knew. This was benison. This was the key to unlocking the programs. The flow of rainbow light on the talisman increased, and it seemed to plunge deeper into the disc, dropping down to depths and dimensions that didn't even exist, and there was a euphonious feel to the light, a kaleidoscope of colour, and it caught at their breath.

The Rabbi was overwhelmed by what he'd done. "When I touched it I felt the vision of the cosmos," he said. "Never have I known such a feeling – such thoughts. You have something here that is greater than the sum of the world's wisdom."

"And it's all locked up in that disc," Jesse said. "What we need to do now is see if it's given us access."

"I do so hope it has," said the Rabbi. "Can we see it here, now?"

"My laptop is linked with the master computer back in Washington. We can try it straight away, if you'll let us."

"Let you, boys!" the Rabbi said. "It would take a thousand horses to make me stop you. Do it now. I can hardly contain myself."

All the usual figures danced on the screen. Back in Washington it would be filling the laboratory. Then the stars came, and the rainbow, and, even on the screen, the stars looked as deep as infinity. Kofi touched the icon. There was the procession of holy men – only this time there was a faint hint of colour on them.

But then ... they froze and words scrolled across the screen *Benison confirmed* – and that was followed by ... *insufficient benison. Access denied.*

"It's not enough," Kofi whispered.

Jesse's eyes were riveted to the screen. "What do we do now?" he said

"You're doing the right thing boys," the Rabbi said. "It's what the disc wants ... but ... sad as I am to admit it, ... my blessing on its own is not enough. It needs more benedictions. People of other faiths ... but you will do it. You have the belief and the faith, and you have the determination."

But Jesse was disappointed and he found it hard to pick himself up.

"I wonder sometimes," he said. "It's like the talisman doesn't really want us to get into it."

"But it does, Jess," Kofi said. "You can't think it's come through billions of light years just to screw up two kids. I don't know why it's so hard. – Leastways, like the Rabbi said, we're doing the right thing. It's got benison now, and we know how to get more."

"But ... all the religious leaders in the world, Kofi Bibini, and Mum dying, for want of a cure."

"It won't let Mum die," said Kofi.

They were back in the main city now, heading for the hotel.

They needed to talk to Dad and they wanted to get the laptop locked away. There was a heavy duty safe in the hotel suite. Out here any laptop was a target, and it needn't be someone from Tyson's mob either. Any petty thief could make a grab.

They knew Mossad was watching ... but they still felt vulnerable,

194

and then Kofi's senses started playing up again.

He stopped. "There's someone trailing us," he said.

"Not Mossad?" said Jesse.

He shook his head. "No way, Mossad. There's someone after us."

They moved into a shop entrance and looked back down the street; but it was just a sea of faces – hundreds of Arabs and Israelis going about their business, mingling with the tourists. Some invited suspicion – those that were staring at shop windows ... but, who could tell? Every street in every city in the world had window shoppers.

Kofi lifted the talisman. The light was angular, agitated.

"If there's someone here from the hotel ..." Jesse said.

They scanned, watching the disc's surface, and then the rainbow light morphed, pulling itself into the shape of a face – It was dark and swarthy with Mediterranean skin. They'd seen a guy like that at breakfast. He'd been sitting a couple of tables away. He'd spent most of his time with his head in a newspaper, and, now they came to think of it, it was an American paper. They peered down the street, and they saw him. He was looking with half an eye at some suits in a shop window – but he was shifty. Every now and again he glanced at where they were standing.

"What shall we do?" Kofi whispered. "Should we call Mossad?"

"I'd rather get back to the hotel," said Jesse. "Call them from there. If we get a taxi, it'll take the guy off guard. It'll give us a head start."

"But it'll take Mossad off guard too," Kofi said. "Say this guy's got accomplices back at the hotel?"

"There'll be Mossad people back there as well. I want to get out of here." Jesse said. He stepped into the street, raising a hand, hailing a cab and they sped back to the hotel.

But, when they got to their suite Kofi froze He looked around and whispered: "Someone's been here."

"Chamber maids," Jesse said. "They do the rooms every day – they make the beds and check the soap and stuff."

"No – not that. Someone's been going through our stuff. Our bags, they've been moved."

Jesse glanced around nervously. "Lock the door," he whispered.

He could see his clothes. They'd been folded neatly in the drawer, but now they were rummaged into untidy heaps, and the cases – someone had been going through everything.

"We've got to tell Dad," he said.

"Call Mossad first," said Kofi. "They'll know what to do."

He keyed in the contact number. "We're back in the hotel," he said. "We took a taxi because some guy's been following us. We saw him a couple of blocks away and he was at a table right by us at breakfast. Someone's been into our suite too. They've been through our stuff."

There was a pause. Then their contact said: "Kids, I don't want you to move. Lock the door and don't let anyone in till we get there. Give us a password – something no one else would know, and if anyone tries to get in – get the password from them. If they don't know it, call us again like, yesterday."

"They want a password," Jesse said, looking at Kofi. "Something only we know about."

"Tell them 'Mariam'," said Kofi. "That was my mother's name. No-one else knows that."

They opened the laptop. The links between the computers meant there was a permanent connection to Washington, and suddenly, seeing Dad's face made Jesse feel he wanted him there. This stuff was menacing.

"I see you got benison from the Rabbi," Dad said.

"Yeah, but Dad," said Jesse. "… That's not what we need to talk about. We're being followed. Howard Tyson's lot or something, and, while we were out someone's done our suite over."

"Have you told Mossad?" Dad said.

"Yeah, it's the first thing we did."

"What did they say?"

"They said to lock ourselves in till they got here. We gave them a kind of password."

"That's fine then," Dad said. "I'll contact their chief and MI5. You're going to have to get out of there, boys. Once Mossad's with you you'll be okay. They'll get you to London tonight."

"What'll we do in London?" said Jesse.

"You have to grab the opportunity when it presents itself," Dad said. "I'll fix it for you to meet up with the Archbishop of Canterbury. You'll be okay in London. MI5 run a tight ship – and this escape plan is dead secret. You won't have Tyson's men breathing down your throat in London."

Kofi leaned across and looked into the screen. "How's Mum?" he said.

"She's okay," said Dad. "She's real excited about the benison. We watched it when you loaded the disc."

"Is she there now?" Jesse said.

"No, she's in bed. It's still early here remember."

Suddenly Kofi sat up. He looked at Jesse and his face was tense. "I heard something," he whispered. "There's someone outside the door."

They listened and they both heard it, a slight movement, rasping, as if someone's clothes were brushing against the wooden panels.

"Dad," Jesse said. He lowered his voice. "We've got to quit talking. There's some guy outside. He may be listening."

"Okay son," Dad said. "I'll get on to Mossad, and you stay put. Don't open the door to anyone and take care. Make sure of that. Love you – both of you."

Jesse closed the laptop and locked it in the safe. There wasn't any sound for a moment, but then someone knocked and they heard a voice. "You guys gonna let me in?" The voice had an American accent, with a hint of Hispanic – someone from the south. Jesse fingered the keypad of his phone and neither of them spoke.

"You wanna open the door?" the voice said again.

"You got a word you want to say to us?" Jesse said.

There was a pause and then a half embarrassed laugh. "Please?" the voice said.

"Not that word."

"Some password?" the voice said.

"If you don't know," said Jesse, and all the time he was texting Mossad. He didn't want to be heard speaking, but he had to alert them. *We've got an intruder outside the door,* he wrote.

"Okay. How about 'Rainbow Talisman'?" the voice said.

"Yeah?" Jesse said. "That's the word is it?"

"I guess so," the voice said. "You gonna let me in now – because

197

I'd be happy to break down the door if you don't."

They felt their blood freeze, but they didn't respond. They just gripped their fists into tight knots and waited.

Then there was another noise – raised voices and a scuffle. A window smashed further down the corridor and they ran to the balcony. A few yards away they saw the man who'd been trailing them. He was legging it down the fire escape. There was gunfire, but he was at the bottom of the stairway by then and he was losing himself in the crowds. And then ...someone was pounding on the door again. "Kofi, Jesse. Are you okay?" they heard.

"We're all right," Kofi said. But they were scared now. How did they know that this wasn't some kind of double bluff?

"You got something to say to us?" Jesse said.

"Good kid," the man outside said, and then: "You'll be wanting to hear me say 'Mariam'?"

They opened the door and four Mossad agents pushed through.

"It's okay," the men said. "Your Dad's been in touch. We're going to get you to London. We'll take you to a Mossad safe house. You'll be guarded by the military and. tonight a British Air force plane will fly you out. And don't worry. That guy who's been tailing you won't trouble you anymore. You'll be safe in London."

***

Chapter 19

A World Trawl

The Royal Air Force jet arrived at about nine, and they were flying for four hours.

It was a relief to be out of Tyson's grip. The fact that his mob had got so close frightened them.

They didn't talk much on the flight. The day had been packed and they were drained. For the most they just stared out of the window, watching fragments of Europe roll past. Eventually there was a gap in the rash of city lights and it was just small skeins, like glow-worms, dotted randomly. "That's the English channel," said one of the escorts. "We'll be over the South of England soon."

Because Dad had said England was safe, that cheered them and they started peering more eagerly, anxious to catch the first glimpse of the English coast.

Over London, they followed the course of the Thames and everything was lit up. The dockland development and Canary Warf, Tower Bridge and the ancient keep of the Tower of London, Buckingham Palace, the Houses of Parliament and Big Ben. "It's like fairy land," Kofi said.

"It's like the Peter Pan ride at Disney," laughed Jesse. "Dad and Mum took me to Orlando when I was a kid."

They were scheduled to land at Northolt where there was a car waiting.

"It's a bit out of our league, your hotel," one of the guards said. "It's *The Ritz*. We couldn't even afford a coffee there."

A top-hatted concierge met them at the hotel and, in the foyer, there were a couple of minders. Their clipped English fascinated Kofi. "It's like English all done up in cut glass," he whispered, and Jesse nudged him to be quiet.

"We'll keep a low profile," the guards said. "We've been briefed. I'll give you an emergency number, but you shouldn't need it."

They had their luggage carried for them, up to a suite of rooms overlooking a park.

"Come down when you like for breakfast," their minder said. "Or you can have it brought up for you. But there'll be a car waiting at ten, to take you to Lambeth Palace. They say you're going to see the Archbishop of Canterbury."

It took a few minutes to persuade Kofi that, just because they were going to a palace, it did *not* mean they were seeing the Queen.

"Archbishops live in palaces too," the guard said.

The suite meant Kofi could sleep on his payer mat without drawing attention to himself. The two bedrooms led off a lounge. He ruffled his bed, and then they luxuriated in a deep sofa, watching television until they were too tired to stay awake, and, next morning they were whisked away to Lambeth Palace to meet the Archbishop.

He was waiting for them in the garden, and he was a jolly, rotund man. He had a dog collar and purple shirt, and a heavy cross that he sported very much as Kofi did his talisman. He listened, fascinated, to the story of the disc.

"And when you load it into the computer it wants 'benison'," he said. "That's an archaic word – Old English, you know?" He sat back in his garden chair, and he seemed pleased. "Amazing, to think that someone from outer space should use an ancient English word. It's eminently appropriate. And you want me to bless the talisman?"

"It would be great if you could, sir," Jesse said.

"It will be a privilege. The disc seems to be some kind of modern miracle, and so wonderfully inclusive – almost demanding that the world's faiths unite. It has to be an instrument for peace."

He placed his hand on it and pronounced a blessing in English, and the boys thrilled, because it inflamed again just as it had with the Rabbi. Deep pulses of rainbow light plunged into it, and the light seemed to probe into a dimension that was not of this world – deep into impenetrable space.

The Archbishop didn't say anything for a while. He didn't move his hands, and his mouth formed words that neither of the boys could hear, but his face seemed to soften.

When he opened his eyes they could see he'd had a big experience.

He took his hands away and shook his head, and it was quite

moving because he couldn't talk, and when he did, there was an embarrassed laugh, as if he'd been caught doing something wrong. "My English reserve," he said. "I don't know what to say."

"It's something else, isn't it – this talisman?" Kofi said. "It puts you into places you've never been before."

"I thought, for all my life, I'd had religious experiences," the Archbishop said. "But, this – these last few minutes, they've been more powerful than any meditation or prayer. I feel I've had an 'out of body' experience. Your talisman is a truly spiritual thing."

This time they took it back to the hotel to see what had happened. Somehow they weren't expecting a breakthrough, and they were right. The colours in the frieze were deeper, but the frieze was still stone-like, and it still shivered to stillness. *Additional benison confirmed* was the message, and that was followed by: *Insufficient benison. Access denied.*

Dad was watching in Washington.

He came up on screen as soon as they closed the program, and he was smiling. "I guessed that would happen," he said. "It looks like you guys will be doing a world tour. It needs more religions – possibly every religion in the world."

"That's going to take a long time, Dad," Jesse said. "D'you think we've got that sort of time?"

Dad didn't answer, and he had to ask again. "Well, have we?"

"Mum's not so good, son," Dad said. "I guess she's missing the benefit of the talisman."

"Then we've got to move fast," said Jesse.

"I've got you booked on a plane tonight. You've got an audience with the Pope tomorrow afternoon."

That made Jesse catch his breath. An audience with the Pope? That was an awesome thing

"Who is this Pope?" said Kofi.

"He's only the chief man in the Holy Catholic Church," Jesse said. "I know Tina's met him, but – I never figured I would."

That evening they flew out, and, even at night, Kofi was overawed by Rome. They were passing the floodlit Trajan Forum. "It makes London look modern," he whispered

They were taken on a tour next morning, – the Pantheon, the

201

Coliseum, the Forum with its triumphal arches and stone-paved avenues.

"It's like being in a time capsule, Jesse Musungu," Kofi said. His eyes were on stalks. "How old is this stuff?"

"Two thousand years," said Jesse. "Some of it's older than that."

They were driven to the Vatican City for three o'clock and their minders handed them over to the Swiss Guards. Then they were taken to a room in the Pope's palace where official audiences were held. The Pope wasn't there, and they were made comfortable by his secretary, but waiting made them nervous.

When the Pope arrived though, he was so gentle. He didn't laugh or joke with them, but he was really interested in the talisman.

He blessed it, with words from some Latin text, and the disc glowed again, soaking up the benediction. He didn't say a lot afterwards. It was as if his experiences were too private to share. He did put his hands on their heads though, to bless them. And he blessed their mission.

Then they went back to St Peter's Basilica.

They'd arranged to meet their minders at four o'clock. Jesse was keen to show Kofi the Sistine Chapel, although, after the caves in the Gemstone Mountains, he was doubtful he would be impressed.

This was the third wave of benison, and by now they knew the form. There was no urgency to get back to load the disc. They were in Rome, in the Vatican City, and they were hungry to see things.

But, as they waited, Kofi became uneasy.

"What's up?" Jesse said.

"We're being watched again," he said. He took the talisman and they saw the angular stabs of light. Then they looked around, but the Basilica was overflowing with tourists. There were two Swiss guards standing on the steps, and they had their eyes firmly on the boys.

"Is it them?" Jesse said. "Do you think the talisman sees them as hostile?"

"There's someone else," said Kofi. "And they know about the talisman. They're a threat. I can sense it, and so can the disc."

They looked up the steps again, and there, by the entrance to the Duomo were two men, in dark suits and shirts. They had white ties, and they wore dark glasses. "It's the Mafia," Jesse whispered. He looked towards the Swiss guards, and the two men stepped out, pushing through the crowds.

Immediately the talisman went into overdrive, spearing, parrying towards the men.

In a second, one had Jesse gripped by the arms. The other made a grab at the talisman. "You boys wanna come with us?" the man who'd grabbed Jesse hissed. "You not wanna make no fuss?"

Kofi let the grasping hands of the other man touch the talisman. He knew what would happen. The next second the man was reeling down the steps, grasping his hands and dancing like a bear on hot coals.

"I said, you not wanna make no fuss," the one holding Jesse hissed again.

He made a grab for a belt around his waist, but straight away Kofi pushed the talisman against his arm and he folded to a crumpled heap.

By this time the Swiss Guard had swooped. In one move they had the two Mafia men in locks, and in the same instance they'd relieved them of their guns, ripping the holsters from their waists, and, as if from nowhere, two other guards descended, grabbing Jesse and Kofi.

The Mafia men struggled, but they were seriously disabled. Already, without their belts, their trousers were around their ankles and, in spite of the adrenaline that was ripping through the boys, they couldn't help laughing.

As soon as the Mafia had been taken off, the Swiss Guard escorted Kofi and Jesse up the steps to the Duomo.

They led them down the central aisle where there was a large structure entombed in a wooden frame, and beside it, steps leading to the vaults.

"You'll be safe down here," the guards said. "We'll stay with you. We've contacted your minders. They're on their way."

There were questions reeling around their heads now, but, with the guards watching, they couldn't talk.

Were the Mafia after the talisman too, or were they part of Howard Tyson's mob? They knew Tyson was working with Colonel Mamba. If he had links with the Mafia as well, then where would it end? Would he be in league with other underground organisations?

Was there going to be no place they'd be safe?

When they got back to the hotel, they talked to Dad, but he didn't offer much comfort. "Tyson will be in with every corrupt organisation there is," he said. "You must be on your guard all the time, boys."

That night they left for Mecca. They were to meet an Imam, another of Dad's contacts.

The Imam performed the kind of blessing that Kofi understood, and there was the deep glow of benison, and the colours in the frieze had a stronger tincture, but still the message was the same: *Insufficient benison. Access denied.*

It was going to be a slow process, and, when they talked to Dad, the news about Mum was bad.

They didn't know what to do – go back to America so she could hold the disc, or press on with their quest.

But Dad's line was unequivocal.

"You have to keep on, boys. You were born for this, – it's your destiny. That's why the talisman got passed to you. If Mum gets really bad I'll call you home, don't fret."

Next they went to a place in India called Dharamsala – Little Lhasa, to meet the Dalai Lama, but still there was no access to the talisman and they spent the next weeks traversing the world. They had to make the travel random because they were dodging Howard Tyson. If any pattern emerged, Tyson would be on to them.

It depressed Jesse. He stared out of the plane as they flew towards New Guinea. "I can't see how this is doing much good, Kofi Bibini," he said. "We must be fouling the sky with more pollutants than any other kids in the world."

"It's not good, Jesse Musungu," Kofi said. "But it's not our fault. It's down to Howard Tyson, and it'll be put right when we get access to the talisman."

They'd been to every corner of the world. They'd met every religious leader. The amount of benison was phenomenal, and the frieze had metamorphosed from stone to flesh. It was almost there.

Japan was to be their last hope, but, because the frieze seemed to be coming to life, it *was* a hope, and it made their arrival special. They had a *joie de vivre* and suddenly they wanted to immerse themselves in Japan's culture – the bullet train, the ancient traditions, geisha girls, Sushi, Noh plays. "I'd like to stay a month," Jesse said. "I'd really like to see this place."

At their hotel they met a Shinto priest.

"When you go into the shrine with the disc," the priest said. "It will be in the presence of *Kami*. Everything in Japan depends on *Kami*."

"Is that what the talisman calls benison?" said Jesse.

"The acquisition of benison makes complete sense to us," the priest said. "The gaining of blessing through *Kami* – or 'spiritual essence' – is the most natural thing. I suppose benison must be *Kami*."

"Where are we going to get this *Kami* then?" Kofi said.

The priest smiled. "It seems the talisman wants the highest authority. So, tomorrow, we will go to the Ise Grand Shrine in Kugaradan. You have to go through certain rituals before going inside. That's why I'm here, so you'll know what to do."

The boys liked that.

Up until now they'd handed the talisman over to the priest and let him do the work. Here they were going to be involved, and because they were hoping this would be the last benison, that seemed right.

They were taken to the Shrine at Ise early next morning. It was the oldest Shinto shrine in Japan, and the whole place seemed to generate *Kami* – as if the ancient building with its sweeping oriental roofs and woodcarvings, and the door at its entrance, the whole structure, was in tune with benison.

They were more in awe here than they'd ever been, and yet the aura of spirituality made them calm. Even the talisman seemed at peace, and its light melted into the ambience.

They had to take off their shoes, and they performed washing rituals. Kofi was used to that. He'd done it with his Imam, but, in any case, their priest was there to guide them. "It's called 'Misogi Harai'," he said. "You wash your hands and your mouth in pure running water."

"What about our feet?" said Kofi. "Lots of religions have feet-washing. Don't we get to do that?"

"You may, Kofi. It isn't essential – but it will add to your purification and sincerity."

"We're sincere all right," Jesse said. The whole place made him sense the weight of what they were doing.

The senior priest of the Grand Shrine was waiting for them, and they went through a ritual of bowing. Their priest had rehearsed them in that too. And this time, when the senior priest took the talisman, it was magic.

The lights in the disc created a depth that seemed to plummet to the very core of the earth, and it filled the shrine with melting rainbow colours, and they seemed to dissolve into the very fabric of the building.

The priest went so deeply into trance that, for a moment, they thought he'd stopped breathing. Their own priest held his hands together and he bowed his head in the most profound silence. Then, as the light grew, the Shinto bells began to ring around the temple.

When the priest handed the talisman back, he did it with such a deep bow, it was almost as if Kofi and Jesse were the priests. He didn't say anything, he just gave that deep gesture of obeisance, and then he walked slowly back towards the shrine.

Kofi and Jesse didn't move straight away, but, when they did, they walked without turning. It would have been sacrilege to turn their back on such a holy place.

Outside they looked at each other and their priest was wreathed in smiles. "Boys, you are indeed blessed," he said. "You have enriched our shrine with such *Kami*. Did you see how it filled the temple? – And such beautiful light."

Jesse didn't know what to say, but Kofi smiled and said, "I've always known it. The talisman will be the greatest dispenser of *Kami* ever. It will fill the world with healing and peace."

When they got back it was late afternoon.

They'd already arranged a time to load the disc. Since Mum had been so ill Dad was spending a lot of time with her and it was hard for him. He wasn't up to sitting around all night waiting in his lab – and it wasn't necessary. With the benison gained, the boys were happy to wait. They had no need to go straight back to the hotel.

It was probably a reaction after the intensity of the shrine, but, back in Tokyo, they were more like kids, throwing off all semblance of the morning's serenity.

They exploded onto the city like a couple of hyper-active tourists – going off into shopping malls, nosing around the streets, searching out places of interest and generally dispensing with all caution. It fascinated them, because the Japanese culture seemed to be light-years away from America and yet it wanted to reach out to it, making the boys feel out of their comfort zone, and in it at the same time.

"There's a McDonalds," Kofi said. "Just like in Washington."

"I reckon we'd have to leave the planet not to come across a McDonalds," Jesse said.

"Yeah – but … a McDonalds Jesse Musungu." Kofi's eyes were sparkling.

"You know what Tina and Sam said about you and McDonalds," said Jesse.

"But it's been ages. Come on. I could kill for a double cheeseburger and fries, … and … a coke. Imagine it – a McDonalds' Coke."

There was no point in arguing. They had to order Kofi's 'fix', and then they came out to one of the walkway tables, and it was fun. It was without constraints. Their guard was down.

If Kofi had taken the trouble to listen to his inner instincts he would have sensed something. If he'd glanced for one moment at the talisman he would have seen it, rampant with agitation. But, Kofi was only listening to his stomach, and they weren't ready.

The traffic was flowing freely. Occasionally a taxi would pull up and drop its passengers. Sometimes a passing delivery van would draw in – trams and buses snarled by. It was just one of the world's myriad cosmopolitan centres.

And then a black limousine pulled up, windows smoked, obliterating the insides. It had an American number plate. Suddenly a man in a dark suit and shades leapt from the back. He grabbed Jesse and, with a roar, the limousine was gone. And Kofi gasped, because, so was Jesse, and he panicked.

He hadn't got the phone to contact the security guards, and the way the man from the limo had grabbed him, there was no way Jesse would be able to contact anyone.

He leapt from his chair, grabbing the talisman, and he stared.

The limousine had already disappeared and he had no idea where it had gone.

He was alone in a strange city, and, over the months he'd lost the ability to cope with that. Jesse had been his constant companion, and now Jesse had gone. Not only that, but the very worst had happened. Howard Tyson had struck. His mob hadn't got the talisman and they hadn't got the laptop. That was in the hotel, in a safe. But ... they'd got Jesse and they were a bunch of desperadoes.

Street sounds imploded on him. It was a labyrinth of surreal madness, and then, hovering on the edge of his consciousness he saw Kalabulay's face ... and he knew. – He could deal with this.

He took the talisman and willed it. Images of the captors hovered on its surface, and Jesse was there, in the back of the car, pinned down, struggling

Immediately he turned, scanning the street, and in seconds he'd located his guards. Then he sent them a telepathic message, drawing then towards him, and it was only a matter of minutes before they were there.

"They've got Jesse," he told them. "Howard Tyson and his mob. They grabbed him off the street – right here."

As he was talking he made for the car.

"We've got to get to these guys," the driver said. "Did you get a number or anything? Can you tell us what direction they went in?"

"No number. They went straight off down the road," said Kofi.

"We'll need something to locate them," the guard said. "What kind of car was it?"

"A limo."

"That's not a lot to go on. We'll have to get back to headquarters – get surveillance helicopters up."

"But that'll take too long," Kofi said. "Can't we try and catch them ourselves?"

"They could be anywhere. Did Jesse have any sort of tracking device?"

Suddenly Kofi gripped at the talisman. "No," he said. "Well – he might have – but we don't need it. I can locate him, no problem."

He held the talisman out and stared at the quivering surface. He saw Tokyo's central station. – There was an abandoned limo – and four men bustling Jesse towards the trains. "They're going for a bullet train," he said.

The guard looked at his mate. "We've got to put out a general alert. We'll take a helicopter and try to intercept them." He turned to Kofi. "Were these men armed? Did you see any guns?"

Kofi looked at the talisman again. "They're well armed," he said. "They've got guns trained on Jesse."

"You can tell all that from this little disc?" the guard said

"I can do more than that. And don't bother with helicopters. Just take me back to the hotel."

The guards looked at him, puzzled. "We've got to put out an alert. We've got to put up helicopters. It's our job," one of them said.

"You can put up what you like," Kofi said. "But you don't need it. Just get me back to the hotel."

They radioed headquarters, and, at the same time, swung the car around towards the hotel. "If that's what you want," the guard said. "There's not much we can do until the helicopters are up anyway."

But when Kofi turned up with the prayer mat under his arm, the guards gasped.

"What in hell's name are you going to do with that?" the driver said.

He laid it on the floor. "It's my baba Imam's," he said. "Just get on it quickly."

"This isn't the time for games," one of the guards snapped. "Your friend's in big trouble. You've got to take it seriously."

Kofi looked at him and his eyes burned with frustration. "Just get on. Trust me. I know what I'm doing."

They didn't ask any questions after that. They just shuffled onto the carpet.

"You can't fall off," Kofi said. "– But don't do anything stupid. – Just hold tight."

As he spoke, the carpet rose and the security guards held on to each other like limpets. One of them swore in Japanese.

"Are you ready for an adventure?" Kofi said. His adrenaline was flowing now and the talisman was flashing messages. He could see a route. He knew exactly where he had to go.

They rose above the city and the guards just clung on. None of them said a word until, at Kofi's instigation, the mat shot off towards the railway station. Then they half screamed and muttered something in Japanese. But Kofi didn't care. He was in control and it was all coming back to him.

He knew where the train was going. He knew which bullet train it was.

He located the line and headed out of the city.

The guards were fighting against their animal fear – because – not only were they grouped precariously on an Indian prayer mat, but they were flying above the rail track faster than the bullet trains.

"We'll be alongside soon," Kofi said. "I'll bring us in line with a door and we'll get on board."

"All the doors will be locked," one of the guards shouted. He was gritting his teeth.

"It's okay," Kofi said. "You're not in any danger. Look." And he lifted one leg and began dancing a kind of jig. The guards breathed sharply and grabbed him. "See – no danger," Kofi said. "And when we come alongside, the talisman will open the door."

He could see a train snaking between the rolling fields. "That's the one," he said, and swooped down, running alongside. He could see Jesse in one of the carriages with his captors. Two were on a seat facing him, and the other two were sandwiching him, with guns trained on his back. For the captors Kofi cloaked, but Jesse saw him. He didn't show any response, but Kofi knew his heart would be thumping with relief.

"You can take these guys, even though they're armed," he said. "I'll freeze them with the talisman."

He brought the carpet parallel to the first set of doors in the next sector of the train and directed the talisman. The doors clicked open.

"Now – jump," he said.

He held the prayer mat steady, running at the train's speed and he saw the four guards glance at each other.

"Just step over onto the train," Kofi said. "It's okay. You won't fall. It's like stepping from one boat to another. Now ... go!"

The first one stepped onto the running board and shuffled away from the door. Then the others followed.

"Stay there," Kofi said. "Don't move."

He leant down and held the corner of the mat, stepping onto the bullet train at the same time, pulling the mat in after him. Then he directed the talisman, bringing the doors back together.

One of the guards spoke to the passengers, waving identity cards. Then Kofi moved them into a corner where they couldn't be seen from further down the train.

He could see Howard Tyson's men, half way down the next carriage. They'd heard the disturbances and Kofi could see one of them twitching, with his arm hovering by his gun holster.

Then they saw Kofi.

The one with the twitching arm made a move to stand and immediately Kofi aimed the talisman.

"Now," he said, looking back over his shoulder, and, before anyone else could move, the guards were down the aisle, grabbing and disarming Tyson's men. They threw their guns to the floor and held the men clamped. Jesse took the guns and relief flooded his face.

"I thought I'd had it, Kofi Bibini," he said later.

The guards had taken Tyson's men to the back of the train to be held in a secure unit. "They had guns trained on me. They're definitely Howard Tyson's men. They didn't think there was any way I could escape – and that kind of loosened their tongues. I didn't think there was any escape either. I've never been so scared."

"But you knew I'd get to you. The talisman – it wasn't going to let Tyson's men take you."

"How did you trace me?" said Jesse, and Kofi held out the disc.

"I didn't think," Jesse said. "When you get a couple of gun barrels pressing into your thighs it doesn't half cramp your thinking style."

The train stopped at the next main road junction and a posse of police took Tyson's men away.

At the next station, Jesse and Kofi were transferred to a train back to Tokyo and, when they arrived, they headed straight for the hotel. They needed to contact Dad and load the talisman.

Dad would be in the laboratory and they were convinced that, this time, the benison would open the programs. It had to. The Shinto rituals were so in tune with the talisman.

But there was no Dad. Instead, at the top of the screen, was a text icon.

"Something's not right," Jesse said. "There's a message.
He activated the icon and the message appeared, bleak and bare.

"Jesse, Kofi," it said.
"Heard about the episode with Tyson's men. Thank God you're safe.
"This can't go on, boys. It's too dangerous. In any case, I have to tell you, you're needed back here. Your mum is worse.
"You've got to come home. I've booked a flight for you tonight.
"Sorry to pull the plug – but your mum needs you. Besides, I can't let you take risks with your lives anymore. There'll be an escort at the airport in Washington. I'll see you at the hospital.
"Take care. Thinking of you always,
"Dad."

When Jesse could find his voice it was choked.
"Is it too late, Kofi Bibini?" he whispered. "Have we lost Mum? You said the talisman wouldn't let her die."
"I've always believed it wouldn't," Kofi said. "… But …say I was wrong?" His words caught in his throat and they turned, empty in their hearts, and began packing.

***

Chapter 20

Towards the Rainbow's End

Mr Anansi was waiting for them in the hospital foyer.

"You look older – more travelled," he said.

"We are, Mr Anansi. I reckon, in miles, we've journeyed halfway to the moon and back," said Jesse.

"And Jesse was kidnapped," Kofi said.

"I know. We were worried," said Mr Anansi. "And your poor mum ..."

"Yeah. How is Mum?" Jesse said, but the expression on Mr Anansi's face frightened him. "She is ... she is still here ... isn't she?" he added.

"She's very poorly Mr Jesse. Very poorly. Your Dad has hardly left her for the last few days."

It was grim, and they weren't ready for it.

Mum wasn't propped on pillows like she had been before. She was lying staring into space. There was a morphine drip strapped to her wrist, and she'd wasted completely.

Jesse couldn't move. He half saw his dad coming to greet him from the side of the room, but he couldn't turn. How could anything – any malfunction of the body – do that to a person?

Dad pulled the boys towards him. He didn't speak, but words would have been fatuous.

Then Jesse broke loose.

"Mom," he said. He ran to her and held her bony hand, staring into her face.

Kofi was there too, and he was holding the talisman. There was desperation in his voice.

"Mum," he said. "If you can hear me, listen. I'm going to put the talisman into your hand – and ..." He pressed it against her. Then he looked at Jesse and Everett, and at Mr Anansi, and he said: " And I'm going to pray, Mum, to Allah, and Jehovah, and to just about every name of God there is, and I'm going to call down *Kami*, and ...

213

Mum, just stay holding the talisman."

There was no flashing light, but the disc glowed deeply, finding its fourth dimension, and still Jesse gripped his mum's hand.

Then, he noticed her grip tighten. Her eyes opened and she looked, first at Kofi, then at Jesse, and she smiled.

"Hold on," Kofi whispered, and his mouth formed silent words. Jesse watched – and still the talisman glowed, and it seemed its light was filling her body.

Then she let go of his hand and signalled she wanted to sit up. Mr Anansi and Everett lifted her, plumping the pillows.

She was still weak, but there was a respite.

Gently, Kofi took the talisman away and she put her arms out.

"We were so worried, boys," she said. She looked them up and down and her face warmed. "But you look so well."

What the talisman had done was only a respite though, and they were almost afraid to leave her, but they had to test the benison.

On the way to the lab, Jesse was feeling low. There were doubts creeping into his head.

"If we get into the talisman," he said. "We still don't know for certain it'll make Mum better. It's only what we believe. It's only … like the Rabbi said … a thing of faith. It could be programmed to do something completely different."

"I've always believed it would cure people, Jesse Musungu," Kofi said. "Ever since I understood what it was."

"Yeah, but who told you?" said Jesse.

"No one. It's just what I've always believed."

"I guess Jesse's right," Dad said. "We've got to be realistic. I'm certain the talisman has some great power, or some universal knowledge – but – until we get access, we won't know which. It might not do anything for Mum. We've got to be ready for that."

Jesse had hoped Dad would give him some kind of reassurance, and even Kofi was shaken.

Seeing Mum like this had shocked him. She'd been so near the edge.

"I'm not sure any more either, Jesse Musungu. You may be right. We don't know what's locked in there," he said.

And they still didn't when they'd loaded the disc into the computer, because, in spite of their confidence, the program remained closed.

This time even Dad was at a loss.

"I'm running out of ideas," he said. "I don't know of any other source of benison – unless we try every religious leader in every town and village in the world – and that's not feasible."

"Perhaps it doesn't want us to open it at all," Kofi said suddenly. "Whatever we do – it seems to block us." And to hear Kofi say that sounded obscene to Jesse – it was like hearing the Pope say he didn't believe in God.

"Don't say it, Kofi Bibini," he said. "You've got to believe in it. If you don't – who's going to?"

But nothing looked right.

They went to sit with Mum after they'd been home to unpack – and Mum could tell. "It hasn't worked, has it?" she said.

"Nope," Jesse said. He couldn't say any more, because he was so low.

He was sitting beside his mother, and she was dying. And, for the first time he was facing a void. Their conviction that the talisman would save her had plummeted. The fact was: She could die. She *would* die. Every attempt they'd made to save her had failed.

She smiled and squeezed his hand. "You're tired," she said. "Both of you. You've been chasing all over the world – you've been sleeping in different time zones practically every night, and this time you're out of kilter by half the world's circumference – and now you're stuck here in this dreary hospital. You're bound to feel fed up."

Kofi held out the talisman. "Hold it again, Mum," he said. "At least it can lift you out of your sickness."

She looked at their shattered faces. "It does help," she said. "It helps so very much, and I haven't given up. Miracles do happen; but this afternoon, I want you to do something for me."

"Yes?" Jesse said. "Anything you want, Mum."

She laughed. "I want you to call up the girls. I want you to go off to Kofi's favourite eatery. Then, go home and have a good sleep. Things will look better in the morning, I promise you."

They didn't feel much like doing it, but seeing Sam and Tina wouldn't be the worst thing in the world, and, for Kofi, McDonalds could never lose its allure.

Even with the girls, though, they couldn't keep off the subject of Mum and their failure. Having told them about Israel, London, Rome and Tokyo – and just about everywhere in between, Jesse put down his coke and stared. "And we still can't get into the program," he said.

Sam touched his hand. "You've got to have missed something," she said.

"Yeah, sure we've missed something. We'd have got into the program if we hadn't missed something."

"You say those stone figures have changed," Tina said.

"Yes," said Kofi. "They've taken on a flesh colour. It's like they're coming to life."

"Do they look completely real?" said Tina.

"Sure. When we saw them in the lab this morning it was like having all the religious leaders in the world walking around your room, and you couldn't tell between the real people and the hologram," Jesse said.

"All of them?" said Tina.

"Yeah, I reckon so, don't you, Kofi?"

But Kofi didn't answer. He hadn't thought about that before. He searched his memory for what he'd seen this morning, and then he said: "I don't know. I did think there were flashes of grey sometimes – but that could have been a holy man's habit. They were so real – it was like, I wanted to talk to them."

"Can we see?" Sam said.

"I don't see why not," said Jesse. "But it'll be just like we said."

Kofi downed his double cheeseburger, and he decided that a double cheeseburger tasted better in their home McDonalds than anywhere else in the world.

"Let's do it, Jesse Musungu," he said.

But it was just as they had described, a rainbow, the breathless sight of space stretching into infinity, the procession of holy men.

But there was a flash of grey. They hadn't noticed it before, and it was as if something was hiding behind the figures – some intangible spirit that they couldn't quite make out.

Then the procession froze and the words came up, *insufficient benison. Access denied* – although it wasn't the words they were looking at this time. It was the frieze.

"What's that?" Tina said. Her voice was tense. "Way back there – look – behind the Dalai Lama?"

Kofi followed her pointing finger, and then he breathed sharply.

There was just a hint of one more figure. It must have been there all the time, passing unnoticed, and it still had its grey lustre. It was like one of those group photos when someone is reluctant, hiding behind the others.

"I know him," he said. "That's my baba Imam."

The others were speechless. They looked at the figures of the holy men, but then the frieze faded, leaving the message hovering in the blackened laboratory.

"That makes so much sense," Jesse said.

"It's always you that sees these things," Kofi said, looking at Tina. He planted a kiss on her cheek. Then they went back to the house.

If Mum and Dad agreed they would go to the Nam-Nams in Sikaman country. That's where they'd left the Imam.

"We'll go on the prayer mat," Kofi said. "That way Howard Tyson won't have a clue what's going on."

There was still a hint of doubt in Jesse though. The disappointments and knocks had told on his confidence. "We still don't know the talisman will cure Mum," he said. "Even if we do get access."

"It will cure her," Sam said.

"You can say that," Jesse said. "But – well, me and Kofi, we've had a lot of disappointments over the weeks."

"But we've had successes, Jesse Musungu," said Kofi. "We've had really big successes – and you've got to remember them as well."

*

Even before they landed in Sikaman country, they knew something was wrong.

They'd flown out early in the evening.

The prayer mat had taken them way above the stratosphere, so

217

they looked down on the earth like men in space. The talisman had created its own eco system – pressure, oxygen, warmth – they were entirely protected from the ravages of space and they were over Africa in a flash.

It was morning there and they were hoping to find the Nam-Nam village much as they'd left it, but it wasn't. There were animals straying, unpenned, and the cultivated areas were running wild. They could see activity around the mouth of the Gemstone caves, and it bothered them.

Kofi cloaked, and they lowered themselves – and what they saw filled them with dismay.

None of the men were tending flocks or working the land. They were carrying spears, and some of them were painted, ready for hunting. One man set out after loose cattle, his spear poised. None of the women were preparing food or milling grain. The children were running naked and there was no sign of a school.

But what horrified them most was the activity around the caves. There were men there, armed, moving in and out of the Gemstone Mountains and Kofi recognised them.

"They're Mamba's men," he whispered.

They could see others going into the caves with pick-axes and shovels. Some were carrying dynamite.

And then they saw him, emerging from his Baobab tree in full ceremonial dress. It was Okomfo Kalabulay. He shouted across to the armed men by the caves and then swore.

"Where's your baba Imam?" Jesse said. "Where's Kwami?"

Kofi's face was grim. There was a look of an African prince usurped.

"Do you think they're dead?" Jesse said.

"I know my baba's alive," said Kofi. "I know from the talisman – because he was on the frieze – and, if he's alive, then so is Kwami. They'll have escaped somewhere." He swung the prayer mat away from the settlement. "My baba will have gone back to his people. He probably went before Mamba's men came. He must have thought Kwami was okay. None of this would have happened if my baba had been there. Kalabulay must have overcome Kwami."

"But where is Kwami?" said Jesse.

They uncloaked and flew across the forest, following the river's path, turning, moving towards a scree of rocks.

"You think he's with the apes?" Jesse said.

Kofi's didn't speak. He lowered the prayer mat towards the settlement and immediately the apes came clamouring, beating their breasts and dancing. He responded, signing to them, and they began a ritual dance, dragging him towards the outcrop where the guard stood. The guard began banging his chest too, and gnashing with his mouth, and then, from the forest came another group of apes, and, with them, carrying foraged fruit, was Kwami.

He was wearing a loincloth, and his arms were scarred with scratches where branches had caught him.

When he saw Kofi he dropped the fruit, and ran. They threw their arms around each other and spoke for a few minutes in the Nam-Nam dialect. Then they came across to Jesse.

It was as Kofi had surmised. Things had gone well with the tribe and the Imam was growing restless. He was concerned about his followers back in the village. He was confident Kwami had the authority to rule, and he could see no danger in going back to his own village, so he'd left Kwami. This had been fine except for Kalabulay. Kwami had noticed Kalabulay going off alone into the forest. It didn't bother him. He thought the old man was resentful and wanted to get away.

But one morning he'd come back with a whole band of Mamba's men, and the village had been routed.

They'd captured Kwami and imprisoned him.

Kalabulay had taken over, destroying all traces of what Kofi had done. He insisted the tribe go back to their old ways.

He made a pact with Mamba and Tyson. Mamba's army needed money, and there was an infinite source in the Gemstone Mountains.

Kwami's family had helped him escape, and he'd headed for the apes.

As Kofi listened, his face hardened. The apes brought him fruit and tried to groom him, but he hardly noticed.

When Kwami had finished, he stood up. "I should have thrown that foul piece of rubbish out when I caught him roasting you, Jesse

Musungu," he said. "I should have put him into the forest then and I should have left him to rot in hell. But … this time … no chances. Right? We've got to sort him once and for all."

He held out his hand to Kwami. "You're coming with us, Kwami," he said. "There are wrongs in the Nam-Nam camp, and they need to be put right."

*

When they landed Kofi stepped off the mat. The people stared and Mamba's men turned with their rifles trained. But before one of them could line up his sites, Kofi had the talisman paralysing them, and their guns were numbed to their fingers.

There was a stifled cheer from some of the younger men, but the women grabbed their children; their faces twisted with apprehension.

Kofi didn't say a word.

He moved to the centre of the clearing, gesturing for Kwami and Jesse to follow and he still didn't speak. He was using his eyes, sweeping the faces, leaving no one in doubt as to the depth of his fury.

It was only when he'd drawn them completely into his circle that he spoke.

Then he said, "Kalabulay?"

There were a group of elders hovering by the Baobab tree. "Where is he?" he said.

"He is in the Baobab tree," said one of the elders.

"Come out Okomfo Kalabulay," Kofi said. His voice was clear, brittle with authority and Jesse could sense fear rippling through the crowd.

There was a piping from the Baobab tree, but Kalabulay didn't appear.

"What's he saying?" Kofi snapped.

An elder stepped forward. It was one of Kalabulay's henchmen, and there was a hint of defiance in his voice. "He said he is the rightful leader of this tribe," the elder said. "He said he is leader by the authority of the forest spirits, and he's not coming out just because some pup who doesn't even bear the marks of a man yet tells him to."

"Then drag him out," Kofi said.

There was the usual scuffle – howls of protests, fighting and kicking, but, with Kofi back, most men were very happy to bring the reprobate to book.

"What have you done, Okomfo Kalabulay?" Kofi said.

Kalabulay began gumming. He was chewing kola nuts, and every now and again he squirted the black juice from his mouth.

"Strip him," Kofi said. "We'll burn his fancy dress all over again."

The men paused, uncertain for a moment, but then they ripped the robes and headdress away while Kalabulay fought, and immediately the talisman sent flames across the ground igniting the pile of clothes. This time the fire burned so close to Kalabulay that he was singed before he could leap away.

Then Kofi turned to the villagers. "Nam-Nams," he said. "My people. Where are your animals? Where are your fields? Where is the food that made you healthy and put flesh on your children? Where are the boats – the good fish – the traders – the machines that tilled your ground? Where are your chickens – your cattle? Where is the comfort and civilization we bought you? Where is the school and the learning that made your children wise?"

The crowd was stupefied.

"Did the shrivelled hulk from the Baobab tree make you give all these things up?" Kofi said. "And would you rather have that putrid carcass with his vile ways, than Kwami?"

It didn't take long for the mutterings of Kwami's name to swell, and Kofi held up his hand. Then he turned to Kalabulay again.

"So, it's the forest spirits is it, Mister Kalabulay? That's what gives you your authority? Well – to the forest spirits you will go, and understand this, old man. You will never come back to this people or this village again. If you do, there are animals out there – my brothers and my sisters – who will tear you asunder and feed you to the worms."

The old man glared, crouching in his foetal position, his tiny eyes glinting. But then Kofi lifted the talisman and Jesse caught his breath, because suddenly, Kalabulay, still crouching and muttering, still spitting kola juice, shot into the air. It was like watching a human cannon ball, and he was spinning like a formation diver, only, in Kalabulay's case, the trajectory was up. He shot away over the trees, rocketing into the distance, until he was nothing but a speck and Kofi looked at Jesse and grinned.

"It won't kill him, Jesse Musungu," he said. "He'll land safely – a bit dizzy – but no harm done. But he'll be in the depths of the forest – miles from here. The animals know. I spoke to the apes about him. They'll see he's all right. It's just, they won't let him back – not to the Nam-Nams or to the Gemstones Mountains."

Then he turned to the crowd again. "With Kalabulay's help," he said. "Colonel Mamba and his men have raped your sacred caves. They've looted your treasures, robbed you of your gems and gold, and that must never happen again."

There was a group of young men – boys that he knew and trusted – hovering by the gunmen. He looked at them. "Make sure there's no one inside that cave," he said. "Because, until Mamba is no longer a threat, we must make the treasures secure."

The boys shouted into the mouth of the cave, but most of the men working there had come out. There were a few stragglers, and when the caves were empty, he turned to the boys again. "Disarm Mamba's people," he said. "Put their guns in the cave."

When they were certain the soldiers were completely disarmed they nodded and Kofi told them to stand clear.

Then he swivelled Mamba's men around so they were facing the cave. "Now – watch and take note," he said. "– And tell the Colonel when you see him that the treasures of the Gemstone Mountains are beyond his reach."

There was a sudden flash. It struck the rocks above the cave, and the ground shook. Boulders fell into the cave mouth, and the cliffs started pushing together until they'd closed. And the people crouched in terror.

Then, without ceremony, Kofi began shooting the mercenaries off into the sky, much as he'd done with Kalabulay, only this time there were dozens of them, hurtling off like fireworks, spinning in different directions. And it was so funny the people started laughing and so did Jesse and Kwami. The sight of outraged surprise on the soldiers' faces was irresistible as, one by one, they lifted off, following their various trajectories into the forest.

Kofi was working the talisman like the trigger of a *game-boy*, punching his targets into the air. "They'll find their way back to Mamba all right," he said. "They're used to guerrilla warfare. They could find their way out of anything. But you can bet your life none of them will be in a hurry to come back here any time soon."

They spent the rest of the day re-instating Kwami, setting up plans for the repair of the village. They sent men off to reclaim their fishing boats and they searched out the farm machinery.

Kwami wanted Kofi and Jesse to stay but their mission was elsewhere, and, towards evening something amazing happened.

From nowhere – arching into the darkening sky – a rainbow materialised. It hovered over the earth just like it had when Kofi and his Imam came to the village nearly two years ago.

It was the clearest of signs – a summons from beyond space. "We must go," Kofi said. "It's our call. You'll be okay." He looked at Kwami. "The people are on your side. Kalabulay won't bother you – and we'll be back before you know it. It's just that ... well ... we've got an urgent mission to complete."

"What have you got to do?" Kwami said, and Jesse grinned.

"We've got to open doors onto the universe," he said.

*

The path of the rainbow took them directly to the Imam's courtyard. He was waiting for them, his face bathed in smiles.

He led them into the room adjacent to the courtyard, and Kofi couldn't help looking around, feeling for his past. But this time it seemed less part of him. He still had a deep tenderness for the memories, and he loved the Imam, but he knew – he'd moved on. He'd changed. He was brother to Jesse Tierfelder, and son of Ursula and Everett. He'd become accustomed to American ways, to air travel and hotels. Somehow this lovely old place didn't fit him so much anymore, and he felt a slight sadness.

But the Imam wanted to know everything – about the collecting of benison, the journeys around the world. He was horrified to hear of Kalabulay's coup, but he loved the tale of his ejection into the forest.

"He won't die out there," Kofi said.

"He certainly won't, Kofi Musa. That man's a survivor. His life has been the life of a wild animal. He's suited for the forest."

"It wasn't just to tell you our stories that we came though, Baba," Kofi said. "We had to come. That rainbow – we didn't set that up. It was put there by the talisman."

"That's exactly right, my little novice," said the Imam. "And it's only right and proper that the talisman needs my blessing. I was the one who saw it, through your dear mother Mariam, and I led you through your childhood with it. I've seen you grow with it. I've seen its power evolve."

"You knew about the blessing?" Jesse said. "You knew we'd come?"

"I had dreams, Jesse – dreams about the rainbow – dreams about you and your prayer mat. I dreamt of holding the talisman, and I dreamt of the wisdom of the universe."

There was a depth of light coming from the talisman now and it was already plunging into its fourth dimension.

Then the Imam took it, and there was such a power in the room. It had a sanctity that was breathless – more than any church or mosque or synagogue – more even than the temple at Ise, and the old man closed his eyes. He was mouthing words – blessings that defied speech, and it wasn't the talisman that Kofi and Jesse were looking at – not at first. It was the Imam's beautiful face. He looked like an angel, radiating soft light, and all the lines of age melted into something so wonderful. They just stared, hardly able to breathe.

Then they saw the light in the talisman, and it was deeper than anything they'd ever seen. They could almost feel it. The room was alive with it and there was the most amazing music – wordless voices, voices that came from beyond the world, vibrant, nebulous, like the music of the spheres.

The Imam lowered his hands and he was trembling.

"I've seen it, boys," he whispered. "I have seen the power and the wisdom. I have been party to the power of life."

"What can the talisman do, Baba?" Kofi said. He was holding the disc watching the serene pulses.

"I haven't the words my little prophet. I don't have the language … and besides, it's better you don't know – not yet."

Jesse put the laptop on the table. He hardly dared breathe.

"Kofi," he said and Kofi placed the disc into the drive. And already, something amazing was happening.

The screen that, until now, had displayed the image from the main computer had become its own projector and the image was filling the room.

They were in space, eons from the earth. The room itself had become part of space. There were no walls, no floor, no ceiling, just a vast emptiness punctuated by a myriad stars – and, as the image faded to the procession of holy men, they gasped, because each of the men had an aura around him, pulsing with rainbow colours. There were no flashes of grey, just people walking, glowing, dispensing benison, immersed in their own *Kami,* and, again, the room filled with that strange, heavenly music.

Then the rainbow icon emerged.

"Touch it, Kofi Bibini," Jesse whispered.

With one finger, Kofi touched the icon and, this time, the procession of holy men did not freeze. They just faded into a backdrop of rainbow light – rainbow piled on rainbow, filling space and across the rainbows hovered the title: *The Omega Program for the Third Planet.*

Below it was the word:

Menu

"Again, Kofi – touch the *menu* icon." Jesse hissed.

This time there was a list of options: *Animal, Mineral, Vegetable. Other.*

"Touch *Animal,*" whispered Jesse.

Then: *Mammals, Birds, Fish, Insects, Invertebrates.*

Then a variety of species, pages long

"Find *Human,*" Jesse said, but he was so impatient he touched the icon himself.

And the words, *Regeneration, Detoxification, Genetic Correction* came up, and Kofi looked at him. "Which one?" he whispered.

Jesse touched *Genetic Correction* and they were so tense they could hardly feel their own limbs.

Hovering in front of the rainbow wallpaper now was the phrase: *Name of Subject.*

Jesse's fingers trembled. "I'm going to type in Mum's name," he said.

The words *Ursula Mary Tierfelder* appeared, hanging in space in front of them. He had to put in other details, date of birth, place of birth, and, underneath he saw a new icon, in the shape of a heart, and, beneath it was the word

Activate

He touched the heart and suddenly the rainbows shivered into a million shards, breaking into ever-smaller particles until it appeared like a primordial soup. Then it re-assembled and there were other words.

Genetic correction complete.

They watched as the rainbow faded and the stars of distant space filled the room again.

"Is that it?" Jesse whispered.

Kofi stared. "How can we tell?"

But the Imam had tears in his eyes. "You've opened the door into the future, boys," he said. "You've always known the talisman's power. You've seen it do great things. Now you have to believe. You have to hold on to that thing we call faith. Faith and patience. Your Dad will be calling you very soon. I am certain of that."

***

Epilogue

Everett was with Ursula all the time now. He couldn't take time to go to the lab, even though he hoped this would be the final benison.

Since the boys had given her the talisman she seemed to have shied back from the abyss. She was conscious. Sometimes she talked – and they were able to decrease the morphine doses because the pain had eased.

"Do you think she's turned the corner?" he said. He was with Jed Herman, the consultant – but he knew he was clutching at the wind.

"It's not likely," Jed said. "If anyone this sick ever turned the corner it would make medical history. It would be a miracle."

They were standing away from the bed. They hoped Ursula couldn't hear, but she did, and her voice was strong. "I believe in miracles," she said.

Everett sighed. "I wish I did." He lowered his voice. "Can't we do just one more scan?"

But Jed shook his head. "It's a big upheaval, Everett. Best let her be, don't you think? Besides, she's been exposed to enough radiation already."

"I want you to do a scan," Ursula said. "I have to know. All this new strength, is it an illusion, or is it real?"

Jed still looked doubtful, but Everett was an important man, and what was happening to Ursula was no way normal. "Okay," he said at last. "Just to be sure – But, Ursula, you have to be prepared for disappointment. It's never happened before."

They were going to do a complete body scan, and, as the images appeared on the screen, Jed sighed. "See?" he said. "It's all over. In every organ, and I've got to tell you, Everett – there's no sign of it receding. It's going to kill her. In fact, it should have killed her already but …"

He tailed off, because, while he was speaking, something was happening and it snatched the words away from him.

Ursula's body was clearing, and, within seconds there was nothing but perfectly healthy organs.

"Good God, man. Is there something wrong with that scanner?" he said.

The technician began pushing buttons, focusing on individual organs, but there was no sign of cancer, and there was no sign the scanner was malfunctioning. All the organs were functioning and the scanner was reading them. It was just that every trace of cancer had gone.

"There's something wrong here, Everett," Jed said. "Don't hold up hope. This sort of thing doesn't happen. We'll try another scanner."

But Everett's voice was verging on choking. "There's nothing wrong with the scanner, Jed," he said. "The scanner's fine. What we've just seen is that miracle you were talking about."

Jed stared at the screen. "But, how?" he said.

"It's a long story," said Everett. "– And – this miracle – it's not happening here. It's happening away in the wilds of Sikaman country – in Africa. And it's the first of many. This is Kofi's talisman – the one the boys give her to hold when they're here – the one that's made me infamous over the past weeks. They've got access – and, what we've seen is its first act of healing."

There were tears in his eyes as he headed for the door, and, looking back at the dumbfounded staff, he just said: "Now, if you'll excuse us, Ursula and me – we've got a long distance phone call to make."

*

Night had fallen.

Kofi, Jesse and the Imam were sitting outside, looking across the plain.

They'd put the laptop away and the talisman was around Kofi's neck again.

But the boys felt uneasy. Faith was an uncomfortable bed-mate.

Overhead the sky probed domes of infinity, blue, tingeing towards black, and the stars glistened. The stillness was breathless.

Then Jesse's cell phone rang and he jumped, even though he'd hoped. Even though he'd expected it to ring.

"Is it Dad?" Kofi whispered.

Jesse held up a finger and put the phone to his ear.

"Yeah?" he said. Then "Yeah," again. Then "That's great, Dad," and after that he couldn't speak.

He held the phone to his ear for a full minute, and only whispered into the mouthpiece once to say: "Sorry Mom … but … I can't speak. I'm just so full at the moment."

Kofi was beside himself. "What's happening? What's she saying?" he whispered.

But Jesse just closed the phone and gazed across the plain.

For ages he seemed lost, and then he said. "It was Dad. Mum's cancer's gone." And after that … he couldn't say any thing.

House lights glimmered. There was an occasional flicker as someone lit a fire. Voices drifted over the scrubland – laughter – children playing – men and women taking their ease after the day's work. Someone shouted to a neighbour. There was a reply followed by another peal of laughter.

A plume of smoke drifted up catching the first rays of the moon and behind them, in the trees, cicada began chirping, crickets of the night.

"This is a beautiful place," Kofi said.

"Tonight," said Jesse, "it's a wonderful place." Then he said: "I wonder if the people over there know a miracle's happened here tonight."

Kofi didn't answer. Instead he went across to his baba. He threw his arms around him and said: "It was you, Baba. It was your blessing that did it. I love you my baba Imam."

But it was time.

Jesse clambered to his feet. He was reluctant, and yet he was eager. "I guess we should be leaving," he said.

"Do you mind?" Kofi said, looking at the Imam. "We'll come back, I promise."

The Imam smiled. "If Jesse hadn't suggested you go now, Kofi Musa, I would have insisted," he said. "Your place is with your mum and dad, and it's out there in the world working with the talisman. I know you'll come back. It will be part of your mission to come back."

Kofi held the disc. The talisman was glowing – a deep glow, and occasionally it sent flashes westward into the sky. He could see the words burnt onto the leather thong, 'His name is Kofi', and he felt, somehow, his first mum was with them tonight. Suddenly he turned to Jesse, grinning.

"Come on then Jesse Musungu," he said. "We've got a miracle to see, and a sick world to sort out."

They laid the prayer mat on the ground and sat, facing west and, as they did so, a rainbow leapt into the sky, climbing into space, following the retreating sun.

Then they waved to the Imam and Kofi held the talisman, allowing its rays to melt into the bow, and gently they lifted into the air, and, in a split second, they were gone, shooting across the skies towards Washington ... and towards the rest of their lives.

***

George Acquah-Hayford was born in Ghana, where he taught in primary school. He came to Britain in the early seventies. He has been planning this book, the first in a trilogy, for many years.

Website- www.georgeacquahhayford.com

John Kitchen was, for many years, a teacher and he retired from teaching in 2002 to write children's books. His first novel 'Nicolas Ghost' won the Writers Digest prize for 'Best young adult novel' in 2011.

Website- http://johnkitchenauthor.com.